BUSTING THROUGH

VANESSA M. KNIGHT

Busting Through

Published by Inked Publishing

Cover Design by Najla Qamber Designs

Edited by Nancy Canu & Tera Cuskaden

Busting Through is a work of fiction. All names, characters, places and events are the product of the author's imagination or are used fictitiously, and any resemblance to actual persons, living or dead, or to actual events or locales is entirely coincidental.

978-1-7344206-0-9

To Jen. For talking me off the ledge again and again.

ONE

"WE'VE BEEN BREACHED!"

Marek Skala's phone was going off like Saturday night fireworks, so this wasn't news. "Breached." Somehow saying it out loud made it real.

One of the software developers—Steve—stood in the doorway to Marek's office. His black hair was as wild as his eyes. Normally the kid looked calm. "Someone accessed the servers. All of our data is compromised."

Obrona Security—his company, dammit—secured people's data. It was all they did. It was in the damn name. If the data wasn't secure, they were screwed. "All?" Marek could apparently only say one-word sentences.

Steve waved a hand. "I'm still running the diagnostics. I can tell the Green server was hacked, but I'm still working on the others."

The Green server. The server where anybody who wanted extra security sent their documents, pictures, or whatever. Not ideal, but not worst-case scenario. He couldn't get arrested for losing family recipes.

On the other hand... His breath wavered. "What about the Dragon server?"

"It's been compromised. It's just a matter of how bad."

The Dragon server was for top-secret, military-grade information. Most of their own employees didn't even have access to the Dragon server. Panic balled in Marek's chest.

"Did you take the servers offline?" he asked.

"They're all down. I need to roll back and restore, but I was waiting for Jalen."

Jalen Boon was the real computer genius behind the company. And he was the only one Marek trusted to fix this. "Why isn't Jalen here already?" Yeah, it was six fifteen in the morning, which was why no one but Steve— who preferred working nights—was here yet. But Jalen lived two blocks away. He should be here.

Steve shrugged. "He's on his way, but I wasn't sure what backup to use."

Marek ran a hand through his long brown hair. He needed a haircut. One more thing he wasn't going to have time for. Not until the servers were locked down or Obrona went dark. No one had thought he could handle a company this large on his own. Maybe they were right. He was a computer geek, not a Harvard-bred CEO. What did he know about running a company?

He wouldn't go down without a fight, though. Marek woke his computer. His fingers flew over the keyboard. He might not be a computer genius like Jalen, but he could do this. "Don't wait for Jalen. I'll let you know which backup to use."

Steve gave a jerky nod and ran out of the office.

If the Dragon was compromised... *Shit.* He pinged the

server just to make sure. Down. Thank God Steve knew to pull them all down. Now they just had to analyze the damage.

Marek looked around the office. No sound. Nothing. The sun was barely peeking over the horizon, just starting to glint off the high-rise buildings in Chicago. It was way too early to be dealing with this crap. Steve was the only one here—except for Marek. And he'd just come in to grab his running shoes.

The walls didn't look any different. Nothing had changed—yet everything had changed.

Somehow, Marek felt there should be more chaos—people screaming, crying babies—mass pandemonium. There should be some type of noise when you found out your company was destroyed.

MAREK LEANED back in his chair. Eleven hours. Nonstop. They were trying to stop the hemorrhaging. And they were hemorrhaging—data, customers, and money. Everyone was leaving their platform, taking their data and running. At this rate, they'd be without clients by the end of the week.

Not that he could blame them. The mass chaos Marek anticipated this morning had descended on the office. Everyone ran around like pinballs. The sky was falling, and they were trying their damnedest to keep a few stars hovering overhead.

His secretary poked her head in the room. "Check channel five. Dave's addressing the press. Also, Jill called. Wants to see how you're doing."

"Tell her fine." He appreciated his ex-wife reaching out. Right now, his focus was on Obrona and the press.

The press was probably skewering poor Dave Nelson, who took care of running the business while Marek focused on new projects. Eight years ago, when Marek had talked about creating a data security company, his college buddy Dave had encouraged him, even offered seed money to help get it off the ground.

Marek clicked on the TV remote, and Dave's face filled the television screen above the couch on the other side of the room. The announcer sounded gleeful, or maybe that was just Marek's imagination.

"If you're one of the thousands of people who use the Cumulous app to store pictures and documents, your private life just might be splashed all over the internet today. Just ask box office smash, Calgary Bennet. Earlier this morning, the parent company for Cumulous, Obrona Security, identified multiple unauthorized entries into their servers. According to Dave Nelson, president of Obrona, they are currently analyzing the extent of the breach. So far, at least 167,000 files have been accessed."

The picture changed to a live shot of Dave. *"We have secured all of our servers,"* he said, *"and are working closely with German security firm, MetalWolke, to scrub all the stolen data from the internet while we determine how this breach happened and who is responsible. Questions?"'*

Marek shook his head. "Don't open it for questions." Throughout the day, Marek and Dave had sat down and talked strategy. He'd thought they'd decided to make the statement and get out. Why was Dave doing this?

"Does this have anything to do with Marek Skala's continued donations to the hacktivist group Free for All?"

That was the reason they didn't want to open it up for questions. Marek wasn't an advocate of using computers for civil disobedience, he was more interested in honesty and truth. He advocated the use of technology to help the little guy, which was why he supported Free for All and their belief in open-source applications.

Dave put on a serious face. *"Mr. Skala's personal donations and any links to today's unfortunate events are being investigated. No stone will be left unturned."*

Personal donations? Links to today's events? It was like the meeting this morning never happened. Marek turned off the television in disgust.

"Status?" Dave waltzed into Marek's office ten minutes later, his face stuck in his phone.

"We're working on it," Marek bit out. Dave didn't look up from the buzzing annoyance in his hand, so Marek asked, "So... Are we going to talk about what just happened?"

Now Dave looked up from his phone. "Don't tell me we have more data loss."

"No. Your interview."

Dave shrugged, his attention immediately back on the screen. "The interview went fine."

"Can you take your eyes off that damn phone for one minute?" Marek's blood pressure spiked. He wanted to throw Dave's phone out the window, but the windows didn't open.

Dave slid his phone into the pocket of his button-down shirt. "Okay. It's away. Are you happy? What do you want?"

Happy? Marek was so far from happy, he'd need new developments in space travel to get there. "My personal donations are linked to today's events?"

"I didn't say they were. I said we're researching it."

"It? You mean me. Why?"

"You've gotten all cozy with those hacktivists. And now look, we've been hacked. Calgary Bennet's privates were splattered all over the internet on our watch."

Our watch? It was his watch—Marek's watch. And the press was going to have a field day. Calgary Bennet was Hollywood royalty and hugely popular since his starring role guarding the galaxy in his latest action movie. To say Bennet's people were upset about explicit pictures circulating the web was an understatement. His legal team was making it known just how unhappy they were—to anyone that would listen.

That didn't mean that Dave should go off script.

Marek took a deep breath. "But that wasn't the plan."

"MetalWolke and I sat down and talked about it. We felt—"

"We felt?" Marek couldn't sit any longer. His skin felt too small for his body and his head pulsed. "Since when are you and MetalWolke a *we*? I thought we were a *we*. You and I own this company. We decide how things are handled."

"Calm down, Marek. It's not that big of a deal. It's not like we'll find anything. We're just throwing it out there to help instill confidence."

There was that "we" again.

Although Marek didn't want to admit it, the plan made sense. He only wished he'd thought of it. Guess that was why he put Dave in charge of the business side of the house.

Dave's phone rematerialized in his hand. "Any word on the Dragon?" He was never like this. Just showed how crazy everyone was while cleaning up this mess.

"Dragon was compromised, but we're not sure about the damage. It's looking minimal. Whoever hacked us didn't know they needed my iris scan and fingerprints to get into the secured area."

"Shouldn't we have redundancy built in? Who's your backup?" Dave's fingers flew over the face of his cell phone.

"I have it under control."

Dave stared at his phone, frowning. He always did like to worry.

"Don't sweat it, man. We'll get this back on track." Marek sighed. "Any lawsuits filed yet?"

"We've had five clients threaten to sue. It's down to three now, but I'm working on that." Dave shook his head and walked out the door.

Too bad Calgary Bennet lived in LA now. They'd hit a few clubs together over the years, back when Calgary was still in Chicago, so maybe Marek could talk him out of siccing his kettle of lawyers on Obrona. He picked up his phone and found Calgary's number. He dialed. He had a few more hours of groveling before this day would even be close to over.

TWO HOURS LATER, and Marek was caffeinated and exhausted at the same time. Most of the office staff had gone home. They'd managed to roll back the server and wipe away the traces of the leaked pictures and documents they could find, bribing quite a few site owners to relinquish the smut. Problem was, every time they pulled down the naked pictures of Calgary Bennet, someone else put them up.

Luckily, one of the developers put together a program

to identify the pictures. Now all Marek needed was a program to inform all the sites that had illegally posted the pictures to take them down. Now *that* program would make him millions if he could get it to work.

There wasn't anything else he could do, for now. Marek slipped his laptop into his gym bag. Maybe after something to eat, or after a nap, he'd get back to work. He hiked his gym bag onto his shoulder and headed for the back stairs to the parking garage in the basement. It was dark in the stairwell, the whole building a tomb. The calm after the storm. He couldn't wait to grab a pizza and fall into bed.

Hell, he might even skip the pizza. He didn't get his run in today. Maybe he should avoid the carbs.

Inside the parking garage, everything was still dark, still quiet. His Porsche chirped as he hit the remote. One of the perks of being the first to the office was a prime parking spot next to the stairwell door.

A loud thud and squealing tires echoed off the walls. Teens drag racing in the parking garage again. When Dave and Marek were scouting for someplace to house their company—their legacy—they really should have chosen a building without condos. But teenagers playing chicken in the garage had never even been a thought. Fantastic.

The squealing got louder. A car whipped around the corner, headed toward him. One car. A man dressed all in black jumped out of the car and barreled toward Marek before the wheels even slowed to a stop. He wasn't a big guy. Marek could take him. Then the handle of a gun tucked in the front of the guy's jeans glinted in the overhead fluorescent lights. Time stopped. Marek's heart stopped.

"Stop where you are." The man pulled out the gun.

Shit, he was being carjacked. Marek pulled out his wallet and tossed a wad of cash onto the ground. "Take it."

"I don't want your fucking money. Stay still."

The gun barrel pointed at Marek's chest. The guy kept coming. He was only feet away. Marek needed to make a move.

The car door opened again. Another man in black. Another person with a gun. At least this guy put the car in park first.

They didn't want money, so what *did* they want? "You can have my bag. This computer is worth a lot." And with the security on the laptop, as soon as they attempted to log in with the wrong credentials, the hard drive would wipe clean.

"I don't want your fucking computer." The first guy waved his gun. "You're coming with us."

Going with them didn't sound like a good idea. Marek inched toward the exit door for the garage. He wouldn't be able to overpower them both. He had to run. He was good at running. He just needed a distraction.

He threw his computer bag at Goon One, aiming for the gun, and bolted for the exit door.

Ear-splitting crack.

Marek's shoes slapped the concrete as a bullet lodged in the garage wall. He yanked the door open and dove through the opening practically on all fours, his face almost colliding with the concrete stairs.

Swearing. More gunshots.

Marek clawed to his feet, shoes sliding on the yellow paint lining the edge of the treads. His foot planted and launched him up the stairs as he tripped toward the door leading to the outside. The doorknob in his hand creaked as something clicked behind him.

He flew through the main door and into the alley behind his building.

The warm evening air ripped at his face as he ran around the building to State Street. The summer night was holding in the heat. Which was good. That meant the Chicago streets would be crawling with people looking to get their drink or appetizers on. Especially with all the restaurants on State.

Witnesses.

That's what he needed. He melded with the crowds of people lining the sidewalk just as a taxi pulled up to a group of men standing by the curb.

Taxi.

That's what he really needed. He ran over and slid into the front seat.

"What are you doing?" The cabbie looked at him, wide-eyed. The guys in the back were too busy talking to notice Marek.

"I need a ride." He needed to get far away from whatever the hell just happened. He had no idea how he'd made it out alive. He needed to regroup with vodka, and then he needed to find some answers.

The cabbie shook his head. "I'm taking these guys first."

Marek pulled out his wallet, yanked out the cash that was left. Which wasn't much. Most of his money was sprawled on the garage floor. "Just let me tag along."

"Sure thing, pal." The cabbie nodded and pulled away from the curb as the guys in back asked to be taken to Willis Tower. Not exactly where Marek needed to go. But where *did* he need to go?

The men from the garage appeared on the sidewalk. Marek ducked. He needed a plan. He needed help.

Who would help him? Who *could* help him? Besides the police.

Danni Stein.

Red hair, beautiful eyes, and a sweet smile—he could almost see her. The one that got away. She was running a private investigation firm, and he needed a PI. He needed someone to help him figure out what the hell was going on —someone he could trust. And he could trust her.

He had to.

TWO

DANIELLE STEIN WALKED through the back door of Busted Detective Agency. Late. Danni was never late. But after spending yesterday afternoon and most of the night running a brute force attack on a bank server and the bank president's laptop, she was exhausted.

The client who'd hired them to prove that her husband was cheating was in for a rude awakening. It was one thing to think your husband was a cheater; it was a whole other thing to find out he was a pedophile, too. There had been enough child porn on his laptop to make Danni's stomach heave.

And her dad wondered why she refused to get married. Her job gave her a front-row seat to marriage implosions on a daily basis. Not that matrimony brought out the warm and fuzzy feelings it gave most women. Her mom and dad couldn't be in the same room without bakery goods being thrown. If that was what marriage was, no thanks.

Aside from the whole marriage-sucks part, sometimes she hated her job. Cheating spouses and significant others were the norm. She expected that. But what she uncovered last night? The pictures and the emails he'd sent to other creepo friends? She'd sent the evidence to her partner, Maggie Lane. Maggie was the PI, it was her job to deal with what Danni uncovered. Then Danni turned off her phone and slid into bed, hoping the images wouldn't haunt her. Hoping apparently didn't work, because she'd slept like crap. That was five hours ago. *Ugh.*

She should probably just quit and only do consultant work. Writing code for nameless, faceless entities was so much easier. She'd finished a project last week—no inappropriate pictures, no bad guys—just code. And then she got paid. Simple. None of this aftermath. No dealing with nightmare results.

Danni's sneakers didn't make a sound as she walked past the bathroom at the back of the office and headed for the stairs that led to her space. All she could hear was squealing. She toed off her shoes and slid on her work slippers.

Yes. She wore slippers at work. The main benefit of joining her best friends in building their own private investigation firm was wearing Ren and Stimpy on her feet. Sue her.

"Oh my God, look at his ass." Jessi Xu's voice carried through the wall separating the reception area from the offices.

"Does he have an ass? I'm too busy looking at his..." Leticia Ramirez—the other partner, the money girl, and the girliest of them all—sighed loud enough for Danni to hear. "...family assets."

"You can barely see it from this angle," Jessi yelled.

Danni walked into the main office area and stopped to one side of Leti's desk. The woman was staring, oblivious to everything but whatever was on her screen. Maggie's desk was empty.

"Did you know Calgary Bennet had a tattoo on his hip?" Jessi's disembodied voice called out.

"I don't think I've gotten that far." Leti's finger poked at the mouse like it cheated on her. "I can't find it."

"What the hell are you doing?" Danni checked the screen, and there was the famous heartthrob and overall sex god Calgary Bennet. It was a grainy pic. Not professional, very X-rated, and probably private.

Not probably. Definitely.

Leti jumped—actually jumped—in her seat, and tried to click the X at the top of the browser. Like Danni had caught her with her hand in Calgary Bennett's cookie jar. "I'm..."

Danni almost laughed. This was so far outside Leti's normal behavior. She didn't look at nudie pics. She wouldn't have known how to find them if someone paid her. "Where did you find these?"

"They're everywhere." Leti flushed.

"Define everywhere."

"Internet?"

Danni nagged them daily about clicking unknown links and the threat of viruses. Turns out she was wasting her breath.

Although the lure of a naked Calgary Bennet would make anybody click a link. Not that she'd tell Leti that —especially if Danni's server had a virus because of this.

Leti glared at her. "Why are you looking at me like that?"

Really? Danni's expression must have said it all, because Leti huffed. "I didn't click anything," she protested. "Isn't it your job to know what crap is going on in the zeroes and ones of cyberspace?"

"You remembered." Danni's heart swelled. She'd sat the women down for a crash course in Computer 101. She was surprised they'd listened.

"I remember zero and one, but don't ask me to explain what they mean."

Leti was a whiz with numbers, but if she could do her job without a computer, she'd be one happy number-cruncher. Maggie and Jessi were more or less computer illiterate, too, but Danni would have to just keep trying to enlighten them. Danni did the computer work. She dug and scrounged until she found data, and then Leti translated it into something useful. Which meant Danni could never leave.

"All I know is this appeared in my feed this morning." Leti scrolled to another picture, mesmerized by the naked man in front of her.

"Those are probably stolen or leaked."

Leti turned to Danni, horror written in her rounded eyes. "You think? I thought it was a publicity stunt or something."

"Move over." Danni bumped Leti's shoulder till she vacated the chair. Once Danni sat, she took a look at the source code for the page. Something was off. She clicked on another page and scanned the code. Obrona Security. Obrona, with text art of a happy member of the male anatomy at the top of the page. Whoever did this wanted everyone to know where this data came from.

Obrona. Marek. The man who walked away and broke her heart. The man she'd loved but couldn't love her back. The man... She had to get her mind off the man and back onto things that didn't suck.

How had someone gotten into Obrona's servers? He hired the best. Hell, he'd tried to hire her. If she'd thought they could work together and not end up in bed, she would've jumped at a chance to work with him. But the man was married, and she didn't do married guys.

"Are you done yet?" Leti's stiletto heel tippy-tapped against the concrete floor. The sound made the hairs on the back of Danni's neck stand up. Her shoulders tightened as a headache began to brew.

"Don't make me give your computer a virus." Danni shook off the distraction and sifted through the pages of code. No indication of who did this. There was too much data. She needed to do this from her own computer.

"You wouldn't ruin your precious network with a virus." Leti's arrogant tone made Danni want to prove her wrong.

But Danni would never do it. Her server setup and Busted's computer network was a thing of beauty. She wasn't letting anyone or anything near it.

But Leti needed to be knocked down a peg or two. Perhaps Danni should add a nice screen recorder to Leti's PC so Danni could watch every move she made. Or, even better, hijack her web browser.

"Who said anything about ruining my network? I could make it so every time you open your internet browser, porn pops up."

Talk about a thing of beauty—the terror written across Leti's face was priceless. "You wouldn't dare."

"The question is, what kind of porn." Danni leaned back in the chair and pretended to consider her options. "I'm thinking furry."

"What the hell is furry porn?" Leti's foot stopped tapping, and her face turned an eerie shade of ash.

"Don't make me show you." Danni found out about furries while searching for a teen runaway. Thank god Maggie was the one who told the parents their son was a squirrel in woodland porn movies. The pictures were... weird at best.

Danni scrolled, and found another picture of a naked Calgary Bennet. She could admit the man looked good. Not that she was looking at him and his...family assets. She was, but for research purposes only. She took a look at the source code. More of the same. Obrona. Penises. She scrolled further. Something about this looked familiar, but she couldn't put her finger on it.

Wait. Her finger *was* all over this. This was her code. She remembered writing this. Well, not writing, exactly.

Holy shit. The consultant work last week.

Did she mention shit? It was her and Marek's polymorphic code, from a project they'd done together back in college. She scrolled down further. This part wasn't hers, though.

Her code—no, Marek's code—was the linchpin used to lynch Marek's company. And she'd probably given it to the people who did it. She'd had a deadline and been in a rush. And it's not like nobody reused code from time to time. Why reinvent the wheel when you can build on it? So, she'd taken the easy way and sold some code she had no right selling.

If Marek found out... double shit. With her luck, his lawyers would have her in prison so fast her laptop would spin. Her stomach rumbled as tears balled and lodged in her throat.

"Um... Danni? Are you okay?" Leti's foot stopped tippy-tapping.

Danni was so not okay. "I'm fine." She emailed herself

the link for the new pictures. Maybe she was wrong. Maybe it just looked like her code. Yeah. She wasn't buying that.

She wasn't a bad person. She wouldn't break into someone's computer and post whatever she found to the web. She wouldn't be party to something like that. She worked for the common good, not anarchy. And she had to prove it, because she could never hurt Marek like that. Not on purpose.

And if Marek didn't know about the code yet, he would soon. Last she'd heard, Jalen was at the helm over there. Jalen was a badass. He was the guy Mr. Robot warned you about. If he was on the case, he'd figure out it was Danni.

And Marek would hate her.

"It's all yours." Danni tried to keep her voice even as she stood up.

She had to fix this before everyone found out. She looked good in orange, but that didn't mean she wanted to wear it every day.

SIX HOURS and two Venti coffees later, Danni sat upstairs at Busted, in her lair, surrounded by screens. Two laptops ran search scripts on the dark web while she tried to find the person who'd bought her code using her main computer. She checked the name on the payment, but either a deceased grandma from Omaha sent her the money or someone used an alias.

She was going with alias, and so far her scavenger hunt hadn't come up with a damn thing. She felt dumb for not checking the client out ahead of time, but they'd sounded legit. She didn't even want to think about what Maggie would say.

She needed to get into Obrona's servers, but was having a hell of a time. They must have upped their security, because none of her usual tricks worked.

The television sitting on a stack of old computer towers showed the news. When an old picture of Marek popped up in the corner, she grabbed the remote, hit rewind until she found the beginning of the story, and turned up the volume.

"...in other news, the FBI has begun their own investigation into the Obrona Security server breach that leaked hundreds of thousands of private photos and documents. Marek Skala, CEO of Obrona Security is wanted for questioning in connection with this latest development. No one from Obrona Security was available for comment."

Danni turned down the volume. None of this seemed right. No one could actually think he'd had anything to do with this...unless they found her code and thought it was his. She had known Marek since college. They'd been close. Dated for six months, so yeah, their bodies had gotten real close—until they weren't. But even back then, Marek was a stand-up guy. It was why he'd had to leave her.

She took a sip of her coffee. Cold. Tasteless. Time for a refill. She grabbed her keys and tossed the cup before walking down the creaking stairs.

At the bottom, she stopped. More giggling. Giggling normally meant nothing. Today it probably meant they were ogling some other naked celebrity on the computer.

Maggie had come and gone, and her and Leti's desks were empty now. Danni still had tons of work to do. And it sounded like Jessi was still manning the front desk. Oh, and giggling.

Danni tripped over her sneakers, nearly losing her slippers, as she slid around the doorway and into the front of the office.

Jessi sat at her desk, staring at what appeared to be her screen saver as Panic! At the Disco sang "Amen". The office phone rang, and Jessi tucked the handset between her ear and her shoulder. "Busted Detective Agency... Maggie left for the day, but I can transfer you to her voice-mail... Thanks." Jessi pressed a few buttons and the light next to the caller went dark. "Shit."

Danni eyed the phone. "Isn't that light supposed to stay on?"

Jessi glared. "Aren't we supposed to have a new phone system? It's dropping more calls than we get."

"That's mathematically impossible. How can it drop calls we don't receive?"

"If any phone could do that, it would be this one."

Danni sighed. "That's why I'm looking into a new system." Well, supposed to be looking into a new system. She hadn't gotten that far between all the cases they were juggling.

Danni slid in behind her and looked over Jessi's shoulder. Calgary's pecs popped as his arms rested on his head. "Nice screensaver."

"I know, right?"

"You know those pictures were personal and stolen from his phone. How would you like it if someone went through your personal information?" Danni waggled her fingers at Jessi's phone. "I'll just tap into your phone and go through your selfies and texts. Maybe post a few on the internet."

Jessi's eyes popped to cartoon proportions. "You wouldn't do that."

Considering there were currently some questions as to who the father of Jessi's son was, Danni would just bet Jessi wouldn't like that at all.

People who lived in glass houses shouldn't revel when others threw stones. If Obrona's data could be compromised, anyone's data could be next.

Danni shook her head. "No. I wouldn't go through your personal information." It was one thing to do it for the job, but she refused to do that to her friends. If she did, she'd never have any friends left.

Jessi changed her screensaver to a picture of Matty covered in sand at the Chicago Children's Museum. The little guy was adorable.

"I think he's getting cuter," Danni told her.

Jessi smiled. Her face glowed. "Isn't he? He gets more and more like his fa...mily."

Like his father. A few months ago, Danni and Maggie found out that Matty's father might be someone they knew, but Jessi refused to talk about it and they were afraid to ask.

Jessi grabbed her phone and turned her back. This was the point where people deleted incriminating evidence.

Danni sighed. "Don't bother deleting something you want to keep. It'll still be in your history. It'll stay on the cloud. I'd find it. If you want it, keep it."

Jessi's mouth hung open as her eyes went from the phone to Danni. "You're scary."

"I wouldn't do that to you. Know that. Anyway, I'm only scary to people who have something to hide. But you don't have anything to hide, do you?"

"Nope." Jessi didn't look all that convinced.

"Everyone has something to hide," a man said, from over by the door. Danni hadn't even heard the front door open. This was why she wasn't a PI like Maggie. Honestly, if it wasn't on a computer screen, everything and everyone got by her.

And then she saw him. Dark eyes. Dark hair. Taller than her, and lean and...and symmetrical. He'd always been the hottest guy at the nerd table. Check that. Marek was the hottest guy at *any* table. Although, according to Cherise Horton, her best friend in college, Jalen Boon had been the world's sexiest nerd. Many debates had occurred over Boone's farm on that topic.

"Marek? What are you doing here?" He knew. Why else would he be standing here? She hadn't seen him in years. Now, bam. He was looking at her like he wanted her to spill her secrets.

Dammit. She thought she had time to find out who'd used her code before anyone at Obrona figured it out.

He stepped over to her and wrapped his arm around her. A bit too tight. A bit too long. It took a bit out of her heart. He didn't know about the code. He couldn't know, not if he was talking to her. Touching her.

She hadn't felt his arms in years, but it still felt like home. Her head rested on his chest, and she took a deep breath. He smelled like spicy citrus and edible. And the feel of his arms around her body made her melt into him.

He pulled back. "I need to hire you."

Nope. He didn't know. She wanted to say no, so why "Hire me for what?" came out of her mouth, she had no idea. Okay, maybe she did. He looked good. His dark brown hair was longer, down to his shoulders, and curled at the ends. The cleft in his chin was barely viewable through the five o'clock shadow covering the lower half of his face. Most guys couldn't pull off the peach fuzz, but his high cheekbones just made Marek rugged and delicious. All she wanted to do was wrap her arms around him and climb him like Kong climbed Skull Island. But his wife wouldn't appreciate that.

Which was just one of the reasons why *hiring* her would never work out. That, and the fact he'd be looking over her shoulder and she'd have a harder time fixing what she'd done without him finding out. Then he'd just hate her.

Down the block, a garage door closed with a bang. Marek turned and stared into the blackness outside the door. He looked like a cat during a thunderstorm. She hadn't noticed when he first walked in, but she could see it now. Fear. And not "my company is under attack" fear. There was something more.

"Someone tried to grab me," Marek said.

"What? Like, a woman?" She couldn't really blame a girl for wanting to grab him. He was so grabbable. Not that grabbing someone without their approval was okay. No did mean no. But why would that freak him out?

"Not a woman. Two men with guns."

Danni blinked at him. "Why would men with guns want to grab you?"

"That's why I need to hire you and your agency. I don't know."

Since no wounds were visible, Danni figured it was time to ask, "Are you okay?"

"I think you need the cops, not a detective agency." Jessi's voice had an edge. Probably because she didn't want to be held at gunpoint—again. The girl had a gift for attracting bad guys.

Danni could admit neither of those options sounded fun. But this was Marek. And Danni owed him. He might not know it now, but he would. Unless she could fix it before he found out. "We can't call the cops."

Marek's eyebrows arched. "Why?" He didn't know.

"Why can't we..." Jessi looked so innocent—and annoyed. Either look, Danni needed some time alone with Marek.

"Jessi, why don't you head home?"

"Why? Tonight's the night I stay late."

"Because I've asked nicely." Danni hoped her smile said *give me a break and get the fuck out.*

"Fine. But the phones are your problem."

Danni watched Marek. He looked so confused. He must not have heard the latest updates. Which meant she got to be the bearer of the crappy news. She nodded to Jessi. "I got the phones."

Jessi headed for the back, purse over her shoulder. Naturally, the phone started to ring as soon as the door slammed shut behind her.

Danni lifted the receiver. "Sorry, we're closed. Call back tomorrow." She hung up and turned on the answering machine. Maggie would string her up by her toenails if she found out, but that had to be a perk of being a co-owner, right? Danni had bigger issues. "You probably shouldn't go to the police. You're wanted in conjunction with the stolen data. They're saying it was an inside job."

"I didn't do it. You know that, right?" He ran a hand along the back of his neck. The stress just pulsed from him in waves.

He wasn't the type of man to screw the people who paid his bills. She knew that. It didn't even make sense; he always did the noble thing. What would he have to gain? "Do you know who did?"

"That's what I need to find out. I need you to find out who broke into my company. My employees. My customers. They trusted me."

See? Noble. He didn't care about who sold him out or that someone shot at him. It was about his customers and employees. "I've done some research online," Danni admitted. "MetalWolke has put up one hell of a firewall. It's impossible to get in. And if they did their job, they've probably started encrypting the data."

"They couldn't do that. I wasn't there to approve it."

"Well, you might not have been there, but the firewall is up."

"You already tried to access my server?" His brows arched again.

"After I heard what happened. I wanted to see whose signature was on the code. See if I could help." So she could make them pay for what they did. They'd used her to hurt Marek. She might not be so noble.

"And?"

"I couldn't get in. It's Fort Knox."

The look on his face was heartbreaking. "So you can't help me."

"I didn't say that. I just need to be behind the firewall. Do you have a laptop or something that's behind the firewall? A remote desktop or anything?"

"I did." He shook his head. "It had to be sacrificed for the cause."

"The cause?"

"Operation Don't Get Marek." He dragged out one of the chairs in front of Jessi's desk and sat.

"So far, it seems to be successful."

"I'd like to keep it that way."

Her too. "Okay. I just need to grab a couple things and we can go." She turned and jogged through the back and up the stairs to her office. After saving the software she needed to a flash drive, she locked her computers.

Her keys jingled as she slid them in her jeans pocket along with the drive. Running down the stairs and into the front, she found Marek holding his head. Danni took a deep breath. "Ready?"

He raised his head, hands flopping on his knees, eyes bleak. Then a smirk landed on his lips. "Nice slippers. Still watching Ren and Stimpy?"

She was still wearing her slippers. Of course she was. Because when the ex-love-of-your-life walks in the door, of course you're wearing slippers. A grown woman with cartoon characters on her feet and a Tardis on her shirt. At least she wasn't in pajama pants. Thank goodness for small favors.

She'd seen him in interviews. He might not wear suits, but he wore dress shirts and slacks. She didn't own slacks. The word was just dumb. Slacks. *Slacks.* If you said it enough, it didn't even sound like a real word. Either way, he was a grownup.

She held up her index finger. "One second." Up to her office at the speed of light. First things first. Slippers off, gym shoes on. Grab the drive. Down the stairs. Who needed to go to the gym with all this cardio?

"Better?" She couldn't quite meet his eyes as she came around the wall. "Let's roll." And get this over with. Because if he found out what she'd done...? She couldn't even think about that right now.

THREE

MAREK'S HEAD thudded against the ceiling of Danni's SUV. "Did you always drive like this?" His knuckles whitened as he held onto the armrest.

"Awesomely? Yes." Headlights came at them as she swerved...and still managed to hit a gaping hole in the asphalt. The car bounced and shook, taking Marek with it.

"Are you trying to hit those?"

She cut left. Marek's body molded to the door and snapped back when she straightened the wheel. "I'm so tired of people saying that. There's nothing wrong with my driving. It's these crappy Chicago roads."

Yes, the roads were crap, but even the one elderly taxi driver who'd texted during the entire drive to O'Hare a few years back gave a smoother ride. Not that he'd mention that. Apparently, it was a sensitive subject.

The car jerked and lurched down the streets of Humboldt Park, toward the Loop. After fifteen minutes— that felt more like fifteen hours—the familiar rumble of the elevated train overhead told him they were close.

He loved having his company in the Loop. It might be named after the L train overhead, but it was where everything happened. It was where foodies roamed, and entertainment surrounded you. It was where businesses thrived. It was where his business thrived. Had thrived.

Danni pulled past the building and angled into the alley for the closest garage.

"No. We can't park there."

"Why?" Danni stopped the car midturn. Traffic sat behind her. Waiting.

"Those guys might still be here."

"I thought they chased you." Danni flipped off the car behind them when the driver honked their horn.

"They lost me, so they might still be here."

"Fine." Danni continued down the street, letting traffic move again. She turned left into a self-park and drove up the narrow ramp, passing sign after sign indicating the levels were full.

He generally didn't park in this garage; he stuck to the one under his building. But he'd parked here once or twice. He never noticed how tight the climb up the ramp was, until now. Each time getting closer and closer to kissing the concrete walls. Hell. Marek was close enough to ping the wall with his knuckles.

Not that he was going to do that. At this speed, the grooved surface would probably remove the skin.

He liked his skin.

The car slammed right when a sign showed open parking. Thank God. Danni streaked down the aisle of cars, throwing the car into the nearest free space.

He got out of the car and nearly kissed the ground in appreciation. He didn't realize how much he liked living until he almost died. Twice. In the same day. If the guns didn't get him, apparently Danni's driving would.

The guns. Being with Danni almost made him forget about the damn guns pointed at his head. Almost. Thank goodness she was a private investigator. Otherwise he'd feel pretty damn bad getting her involved in this whole mess.

"Did you bring a gun?" he asked.

Danni's scowled as she opened her trunk. "No. Why?"

"For the people trying to kill me." The whole reason they were there.

"Um. If they're waiting, they're probably in the garage in your building."

"But they could be here." He looked toward a darkened corner where he swore something just moved.

She dug deeper in her trunk. "They can't stake out every parking garage in the city."

"But..." He looked around. He had no idea, but he didn't think they'd just disappear.

"We just have to get to the building." She sighed as she pulled herself out of the bowels of the trunk. Her hands full. "You have security. No one can get past your security team in the lobby, right? That's probably why they hit you in the garage."

"But how do we get to the building without a gun? That's why I came to you."

"For a gun? When have you known me ever to carry a gun?"

"We haven't seen each other in a while." His eyes aimed at the ground. "You're a PI now."

"I'm not a PI. I'm computer forensics." She slammed the trunk and shook out something red and shiny before handing it to him. "Just because a person works for a PI firm doesn't mean they're Magnum." She pointed at the red shiny thing. "Put that on. We'll get to the building by hiding in plain sight."

"What is this?"

"Your camouflage."

"Why am I putting this on?" Even as he asked the question, his arms slid into the jacket, like he didn't need an answer. He was ready to do whatever the great Danni Stein told him to do. She always did have that effect on him.

"Quick, before someone sees you." She produced a pair of pink-framed sunglasses and slid them on him.

"Sees me with the stuff on, or see me without it and recognizes me?" He honestly couldn't say which was worse.

"No one will recognize you." She helped him pull the jacket closed. "You blend."

He turned toward the car window and checked his reflection. The large pink frames covered his face, and the bright red jacket had the arm length of a toddler. It barely covered his elbows. This, mixed with the workout gear he was still wearing from the morning, made him look like a Project Runway reject.

Not that he'd ever seen the show, but he saw commercials. He didn't see any blending. It looked like him in drag.

"Come on. You look adorable." Danni laughed. The overhead lights washed over her face, highlighting her brown eyes with their flecks of gold. He'd missed those eyes.

"Every man's dream, to look adorable." He'd look adorable any day of the week to see that sparkle.

He'd forgotten how beautiful she was. How the light in her eyes danced. He'd forgotten that red hair flowing down her back. He'd forgotten that body. And from what he could see, she hadn't changed all that much over the last four years. She was still breathtaking.

Although that was never why she was so dangerous to him.

"Adorable is good. So is alive." She grabbed his hand and led him toward the elevator. "Keep your eyes down and keep moving once we get outside."

Danni hit the button and the elevator doors opened. Once they were inside, she pressed the ground level and looked up at him intently. "Are you ready?"

The concern in that one look warmed his chest. Was he ready to get ganked by the bad guys? Not really. But he needed answers. And he wasn't going to get them standing in an elevator wearing a tiny coat and huge sunglasses. "I'm ready."

"I'll get you to the building. Just keep your head down."

As the elevator opened on the street level, he followed her. As usual. He'd like to think he wouldn't just blindly follow anyone. But her? Yeah. He'd follow her to the ends of the earth because she made him feel.

She made his life brighter just by being in the same room. He'd forgotten that. He'd forgotten the pain he'd felt when he'd walked away. And now that he remembered, he'd never be able to let her go. And that was why she was so dangerous to him.

———

DANNI COULDN'T BELIEVE he was wearing the

ridiculous glasses. Between the pink frames and the tiny raincoat, he looked like Elton John's geekier younger brother. Somehow, though, the look always seemed to work on Sir Elton. On Marek? Eh, not so much.

Although it was hilarious.

But Marek had always been hilarious. Freshman year of college, he'd tried to bribe the baker at Dunkin' Donuts to put extra chocolate frosting on her donut, and she'd ended up with chocolate soup and a floating ring of dough. Then, to make up for it, he took her computer apart to upgrade it and left her favorite pen inside. He'd stood there, in his underwear, shaking the tower like a maraca.

When they'd been good together, they'd been really good. He made her laugh, a laugh she felt down to her core. So it wasn't a surprise he could still make her smile.

She led him through a double door and out onto the street. The smell of pizza and beer wafted from next door. The sidewalk was filled with laughter and desperation as girls wearing black elastic bandages around their hips bounced along in their halter tops. Tiny women showing more skin than Danni had on her entire body—she was sure of it—giggled and made googly eyes at all the men bro-ing it out as they stumbled from bar to bar.

Marek and Danni walked across the sidewalk to the curb, and Marek looked both ways before stepping forward. *Bam.* He bumped into a blonde in the required skimpy uniform. "Sorry," he mumbled.

"Hey, baby." The woman ran one hand up the red raincoat on Marek's arm and flipped her curly blonde hair over her shoulder with the other. Blonde multitasking. Her assets stretched her cute little halter top like they wanted to escape. And the way her nipples poked through the material, there was a good chance they might. "Nice jacket."

Marek didn't look. He didn't even seem to see her. How could he not see the light bouncing off all that skin like a homing beacon? How could anyone miss those escaping orbs?

He didn't notice. Not at all. His feet kept moving toward the Obrona Security building across the street. His face was set. His eyes focused. Not even two watermelons held together by gauze made him lose focus.

In college, Marek had always been good at keeping his mind on the task at hand. Unless. Unless a woman with a nice rack shoved her shelf in his face. Then he was like every other coder—every other man—and his eyes would be glued to the mounds like there was a tractor beam involved.

He might have changed, but no man changes that much. She looked at him—really looked—and saw the white knuckles holding the raincoat closed. Her heart skipped. There could be bad guys. Guns aimed at him. People wanting him dead. Shots. Blood.

Her chest pounded at the memory of all the blood during the last big job she'd done with Maggie. She might have only been behind the camera, but she saw it all, and they'd almost lost one of their own in the process.

She didn't want to lose Marek.

Marek stepped up on the curb and looked back. "You coming?"

Of course she was coming. She'd followed him this far. She'd follow him anywhere.

Idiot.

That what his wife was supposed to do. Not her. She was an old friend—barely an acquaintance. Pathetic.

She ran to the revolving door and shoved at the glass. Nothing happened except she hurt her wrist.

"Those doors are locked at night." Marek waved a key fob and opened another door, off to the side, and held it for her. Apparently, he had keys to the building. Which totally made sense if they didn't want to let the riffraff in late at night.

"Thanks." She slid inside the warmth of the spacious atrium. Large plates of glass covered the ceiling, probably letting in the sun during the daytime. Six-foot trees stood off to the right, with a stone half wall running the length of the opposite side, enclosing a lot of shrubs and flowers. In the center, wooden chairs and tables sat among all the green. An outdoor paradise plopped right in the middle of the city.

A tall man walked around a stone countertop at the back of the room. His balding head glistened. "Excuse me—"

"Hey, Enrique. I just need to go to my office for a few minutes." Marek tilted the sunglasses down.

Enrique's eyebrows arched, and his shoulders stiffened. "Mr. Skala. Is that you? Are you in trouble?" His gaze found Danni, and it didn't look all too welcoming. Like she'd forced him to put on pink sunglasses and a red raincoat under duress. Well, there might have been a bit of coercion, but she wasn't the one threatening him.

"I'm fine. I just need to get something from my office."

"Male clothing?" Enrique seemed to be fighting laughter, but then he turned serious. Probably realized it was never smart to laugh at the boss. No matter how ridiculous he looked. "I was told not to let you upstairs."

Marek took out his wallet and removed a keycard. "Why?"

"The cops," Enrique said.

Danni blinked. "Are the cops here?" She should have seen that coming. It made total sense.

Enrique looked left, then right. "There's no cops here now, but Dave told me not to let you up."

Given the look on Marek's face, he was as confused as she was. Why wouldn't Dave want Marek upstairs?

"The police have you down as a suspect. You know how he gets. I'm sorry."

"Look. I get it." Marek must get something she didn't, because back in college he and Dave were like brothers. "Can you do me a favor, man? I just need to go up and get some personal items. It'll only take me a minute."

"I don't know. I don't want to lose my job." Enrique bit his lip, eyes shifting back and forth.

"Enrique, you know me. I'm not here to start any trouble."

"Maybe I should go with you?"

Danni wanted to tell him no, but Marek beat her to it. "You need to watch the door. Look, I'll be right back."

"Ten minutes." Enrique nodded toward a hallway behind him.

"Got it." Marek grabbed Danni's hand and headed down the hall to the elevators.

If they weren't in the middle of the third degree with Barney Fife and running from bad guys with guns—oh, and running from the good guys with guns—she might get excited that he was holding her hand. As it was, she didn't have time because he let go to push the button on the elevator.

Four elevators. Not much action. One door slid open, and they stepped inside. "Take this." Marek handed over the sunglasses and raincoat.

"Don't you want to wear them a bit longer?" She hung the sunglasses on the neck of her T-shirt and folded the jacket over her arm.

"I'm good." He pressed the button for the thirtieth floor, and the doors closed. Mirrors surrounded them. She took a quick look, but all she saw was how gorgeous he looked even though their lives were in danger. His hair was perfect. His face was kissable. His body lick-able.

She, on the other hand, looked like she'd fallen asleep on the couch after a month of binge drinking and had just woken up. Hair in a ponytail, frizzed at the ends. No makeup to hide the dark rings under her eyes. She closed her eyes so she didn't have to look anymore.

Not that it mattered. It didn't matter how she looked. Or how he looked. It didn't matter how he felt against her skin. It didn't matter that she was barely keeping her head above the memories that threatened to drown her. None of that mattered. He was married, and she was not his wife. She needed to remember that. Subject change. She needed a subject change. "So, what the hell is with Dave not letting you up?"

Marek shrugged it off, but his face gave him away. He was hurt. "He wants to keep the bad press away from the company. I understand." He turned his back, but the mirror showed her his frown just fine.

Apparently, this wasn't a subject he wanted to talk about. Not that she blamed him. She'd be devastated if Maggie turned on her. Thank goodness that would never happen.

The chime as the car zipped past the floors was the only sound, and when they stopped, the doors opened to a quiet floor. So much quiet. She followed him through rows of gray cubicles along a huge bay of windows. Inside his office, metal furniture made up the work area—desk, chairs, and shelving. The other side held a white couch and a black table.

"Nice office." She tossed the sunglasses and jacket on the couch, following him around the desk as he sat and logged into the PC on the desk. It was a great office. Warm. Welcoming. And then she saw the pictures. Marek and his wife with Bill Gates. Marek and his wife with the guy from *Mr. Robot*.

The room felt hot, like Danni didn't belong. She inched farther away from the photographs. She needed to get to the bottom of this and then get far away.

"Thanks." Marek stood up. "It's all set."

"Okay." She waited for him to move. She didn't want to accidentally bump him or touch him or even be in the same vicinity. His arm slid against hers. Slowly. Almost lingered. Maybe it was the feeling of security being in the building, or maybe it was the way his arm lingered, but that old attraction zinged through her. Love, lust, swirled through her veins like fine wine.

Too bad wine made her dizzy and nauseous. Not too different than the feeling left in Marek's wake when he dumped her. And he would leave again—go back to his life and his wife.

There was only one thing to do.

Fix what she'd done. Save Marek's company and get far away. And then she could move on.

FOUR

MAREK STOOD behind Danni as she plugged in the jump drive. After a few seconds, a command prompt and a blinking cursor appeared.

"How long will this take?" he asked.

"It depends on how much data it has to sift through."

"We have ten minutes." He watched her type, and then watched the blank screen. Not much was happening. The cursor just blinked.

Danni shrugged. "I know. I know."

This was one part of computer espionage that TV and movies never got right. There were no bright lights and fanfare. No pictures or countdown clocks. Running a program was usually anticlimactic.

Danni turned toward him, and that simple act sent her hair flying, leaving the scent of roses in the air. It took him back. Roses always reminded him of her.

She always did like roses. She called it her one nod to female stereotypes. Normally, she was a slipper-wearing, makeup-scoffing, scrunchy-worshipping tomboy. Everything about her screamed that she'd rather battle online as Kratos than shop at the mall. But then there were the roses.

He breathed in, and the smell went straight to his gut. Sweet and somehow hot. Made him happy. Made him sad. And maybe it made him a teeny-bit horny. But mostly it took him back to a simpler time.

A time when he was madly in love with a girl who loved him back. A time when they'd stayed up all night trying to hack the gas company so they could push back the due date on their gas bill. A time when all they needed was each other, their PlayStation, and Cheetos. Life had been good.

Until it wasn't.

Take paradise, add one ex-girlfriend who'd thought she'd been sick for months after the breakup only to find out she was pregnant, and you get two broken hearts. Paradise was destroyed. And in its place, a marriage built on heartache.

But he didn't want to think about that right now. Right now, he needed to figure out who was coming after him and his company. Although the building was currently quiet. Safe. Right now, he was with Danni.

She leaned away from him. "Are you sniffing me?"

"No." Yes. "You're just very close, so I can smell you. It's not like I was trying to smell you. I can't stop breathing just because I'm next to you." Fantastic, now he was the creepy old friend who sniffed things. He moved from behind her and stood by the side of his desk.

Out of smell-zone, out of mind.

"Dude, settle. I was joking." Her eyes never left the screen. "I have something."

Marek might not want to get too close to Danni—between the scents and the creepy-factor—but none of that mattered. If she found the hacker, he needed to be there. He needed to see.

Long lines of code zipped past as she scrolled. "Here. Look." She jabbed a finger at the screen. "Whoever did this, they didn't want you to know what they were doing."

Marek had to agree. It was like they'd listened to all the experts on how to write code and did it the opposite way. "Whoever did this was either a savant or just lucky it worked."

"It's weird, right? I don't think I've seen anything like this." She shook her head. "I'll make a copy."

The door to Marek's office opened. "How did you get up here?" Dave filled the space, and his squinted eyes said he wasn't happy.

Dave might not be happy to see Marek, but Marek wasn't all that happy to see Dave, either. Which was sad since they'd been friends through so much. "What are you doing here?" Marek asked.

"Jalen called me in. There was another attack, but they didn't get through."

"Why didn't you call me?"

"Danni?" Dave's eyes rounded as he took in Danni behind the computer. He was changing the subject. But that didn't mean the subject was done. Dave didn't trust him anymore. He hadn't called.

"Hi, Dave. Nice to see you too." Danni leaned back in the chair, but her focus never wavered from the screen.

"Oh, hey, Danni. What are you doing here?"

"Baking brownies." Her lip quirked, eyes still on the screen. "Brownies are the world's perfect food group. They fix everything."

Marek couldn't stop the smile on his lips if he wanted to. It was their inside joke. When Danni's father found out he had cancer, Danni and Marek had baked. When Marek found out he'd gotten his ex-girlfriend pregnant, they'd baked. It never really fixed anything, but in the end, they had brownies. It reminded him that life wasn't all that bad.

No. Danni reminded him.

That pregnancy had been the reason he'd left Danni. The reason he'd married his ex. And the reason their marriage ultimately failed.

"I see you haven't changed—bad attitude and all." Dave didn't get the joke. He rarely did.

"I see you haven't changed either. Still immune to a good joke."

"When I hear one, I'll laugh."

That got her attention. Danni lifted her head, tilting it to the side, one eyebrow raised. "Really?"

"Probably not." Dave shook his head and turned to Marek. "What is she doing on your computer?"

"Getting all of my personal stuff off the computer before it's confiscated by the cops." Like Marek needed help getting files off a computer. He was terrible at lying.

Dave narrowed his eyes and pursed his lips. He wasn't buying it. "Why are you here?" Dave's attention switched from Danni to Marek. Which was good, except his eyes were still narrowed. Marek hated that look. Disappointment. Disbelief. Anger. It reminded Marek that his best friend didn't seem to trust him. Fourteen fucking years meant nothing.

Dave shook his head. "You're in a lot of trouble."

"That's what I hear."

"Come on, Marek. This is serious. These cops are coming after you."

"I get that. I'm public enemy number one." He'd seen enough in movies and real life to know that nobody cared about innocence. They cared about scapegoats and blame. And right now, he was the It Boy of bad choices. "But what do you think?"

"I think you need to be smart—"

"No, Dave. Who do you think did this to us?"

"I don't know who did this." Dave didn't come out and say Marek was guilty, but he also didn't say he was innocent, either.

"Dave, I finished the coding—" Jalen burst into the office, stopping when he saw Marek. "Hey, Marek. And Danni. Holy crap, girl. I haven't seen you in years."

Danni jumped up and wrapped her arms around Jalen. "You're looking good." She was being kind. Jalen was not looking good. He wasn't a bad-looking guy if you got past the bags under his brown eyes and the way his hair spiked from his head like he'd been running his hand through it over and over again.

She pulled away and smiled. "Nice shop you've built here."

Marek stared at Danni. He built? Jalen was a big part of the creation and success of Obrona, but it was Marek's idea. So what if Jalen perfected it?

"Nice shop you've both built." Danni smiled at Marek. It was a full smile, and it lit up her face. It was hard to believe she could look more beautiful.

"You know, I had a hand in it too." Dave was on the edge of a whine. "And if Marek doesn't turn himself in, we're going to lose everything we've built here."

Dammit. Marek didn't want to lose anything. But he

also didn't want to turn himself in. He'd never figure out what the hell was going on if he was rotting in a cell. Or worse. What if the guys with guns found him in jail, with nowhere to run, nowhere to hide?

He couldn't be a sitting target. He was going to save his company, stay one step ahead of the guys with guns, and find out who was after him. There was no choice. The other option wasn't even an option. He wasn't ready for his eulogy just yet.

A FEW MINUTES LATER, Danni stared at the screen and waited for the software on the jump drive to finish doing its thing. It didn't matter that the screen wasn't moving or that staring at it wouldn't do a bit of good. She wanted to watch it. She wanted the drive out and safe in her hand before Dave or Jalen figured out what she was really doing. Before they figured out what she'd done.

If they knew whose code was used to hack them, they'd be giving her the look they were giving Marek right now. If they knew the truth, they'd kick them out of the building. At least, Dave might. Something seemed off with him.

Then again, something always felt off with Dave. They'd never gotten along. If there was a kegger, Dave would remind you that you had a test the next day. Dave was where fun went to die.

Marek sighed. "We're not going to lose anything, Dave. Jalen, what's going on with my servers? What have you found?"

Jalen stared at Dave, frozen in place, and Dave glared at Marek. Because of what happened, or was there something else going on? A heartbeat later, Dave's focus moved to Danni. Great. Did he really think she was a threat? He knew her. They might not be besties, but the four of them had run in the same circle for years.

Yet here he was, acting like she was a stranger. His stare was like an ultimatum for a toddler. *Get out.*

Too bad she listened about as well as a toddler. She wasn't leaving Marek. Not unless he told her to go.

"You can talk in front of her." Marek's hand rested on her arm. That was all she needed. She wasn't going anywhere.

Dave shook his head and pinched the bridge of his nose. "It's not her I'm worried about."

"What does that mean?" Marek's voice rose.

Dave looked at Jalen and shook his head again, running his hand up and down the back of his neck.

"So far, we've found..." Jalen looked at the floor. Shrugged. "The code used matches your signature."

Marek stared at him. "Are you saying you think I wrote it?"

"Either that," Jalen said, "or someone wanted it to look like you wrote it."

This was getting worse and worse. Any second Marek would look at her and realize there were only three people on the planet who know how he wrote his code, and she was one of them.

"So, who would gain if they wrote the code to look like mine?" Marek asked, frowning.

"That's what we need to figure out." Dave shook his head. "Unless you have something to tell us?"

"You can't possibly believe that I would do anything to hurt this company. Our company." Marek looked sick.

Wide-eyed. If at any point Danni thought he was guilty, that look would have fixed that. "I fucking couldn't."

His hair might be longer, and his face lost that baby fat he'd had in college, but there were a few things she was sure of. For one, he wouldn't destroy what he'd built. If only Dave—his best friend—could see that.

"I'm trying to figure out how this happened." Jalen looked miserable. "Who."

"Thanks." Marek ran a hand through his hair as silence engulfed the room. The men all stared at each other, no one saying a word. That silence made it hard to breathe.

"Well, I should get back to researching." Jalen gave a weak smile. "Sooner I figure all this out, the sooner we get back to normal." He walked out the door without another word.

Dave's phone buzzed with a text. "I need to head home. Grab your files and call the police. They want to talk to you." He turned and walked out the door. The heaviness in the air lifted once Danni was alone with Marek. The silence did not, until the download completed with a ding—almost making her jump. "I have what we need."

Marek slid behind her and looked over her shoulder. She could feel his breath.

The hairs on her neck stood at attention, reaching out, trying to get closer to him. Traitorous hairs. Her head bobbed to the side, letting his breath slide lower along the curve of her shoulder. Traitorous head. Her eyes closed as soft tingles caressed her and shot straight to her core. Traitorous core.

The heat from his body pulsed along her spine. It took her back to a simpler time—to a time when they were falling in love. And she'd loved him. Not that she'd gotten a chance to tell him that. Things had happened too quickly. One day they were talking about meeting family and moving in together, the next he'd left to start a new life as a husband and father.

"I really can't thank you enough." Marek touched her shoulder, his fingers playing at her collar. Strong fingers rubbed down her neck, stopping when the crook of his thumb hit her shoulder. His fingers arched into her skin, just above her chest. Holy. Crap. He rubbed again. Did he even know what he was doing to her?

Every touch, every breath, reminded her of what they'd had. How he'd stood behind her and massaged her shoulders as she worked. How she'd stop working, and they'd consummate their relationship over and over again, meaning she'd be up all night finishing that homework. She didn't want to feel this way again.

"We should go." She inched away from him. She needed to get far, far away.

Marek stepped back, palms up in surrender. "I'm sorry. Habit." He reached forward. Toward. Her.

Are you kidding? She took another step back until she bumped into the bookshelf. Picture frames shook. The frames with his wife.

"Did I do something?" He kept moving that arm toward her.

"Stop." She pushed his hand away and grabbed one of the frames. "How can you sit there and touch me and be all sniffy with your wife watching?"

"My wife?"

She pointed to the woman in the picture. The size-two supermodel with perfect blonde hair. Danni would love to say the woman had aged poorly, but she'd be lying. "Your wife probably wouldn't appreciate any of this."

He laughed. Actually laughed. He thought this was a joke. She never thought he'd become a cheating bastard. Not just cheating—heartless.

"You mean my ex-wife?"

Wait. "What? When?"

"Two years ago."

"I didn't hear about you divorcing." She sounded like a stalker. Maybe he wouldn't notice.

"Dave wanted me to keep it out of the papers, so we kept it quiet." A smirk curved his lips. "Were you checking up on me?"

"No." Yes. She might have one or two Google alerts set up on his name. No one needed to know that. "But you have her picture plastered all over your office."

"Not her picture." He took another one off the shelf. "That's Steve Jobs. I'm not going to toss a picture with Steve Jobs just because she happens to be in it. Would you toss a picture with Harry Potter if your ex was in it?"

Harry was her absolute favorite. "No."

"Exactly." He set that frame back on the shelf, picked up another one. "These are all things I can't recreate. So, I kept them." He looked at the picture a little too long and slowly put it back.

"Do you miss her?"

"Not really. That's probably a really shitty thing to say, but it's the truth."

"Was the divorce nasty?"

"It wasn't good, but are they ever? It could've been worse. I just gave her everything she wanted. Kept it civil."

The phone on his desk rang. Security flashed on the screen.

Marek lifted the receiver. "Enrique? Yeah... When? We'll leave now. Thank you." He put the phone down and opened the bottom drawer. He grabbed a blue vinyl bag and slammed the drawer shut. "We have to leave. Now. Some detectives are on the way up."

"Isn't it a little late for detectives to be snooping around?" Danni grabbed her phone and the drive and aimed toward the door of his office. "Are there stairs?"

"Down the hall and to your left." He opened another drawer, pulling something out and shoving it in his pocket. "Let's go."

They jogged down the hall. As they passed the elevator the door dinged.

"Run," Marek told her, one hand on Danni's back. They made it to the heavy metal door at the end of the hall just as two men came out of the elevator. Tall. Both wearing jeans and a T-shirt. One had blond hair hitting his collar, but he wasn't looking at her, he was looking the opposite way. The taller guy had a large, angry scar on his right cheek and a tattoo ringing his neck.

"Who the hell are you?" the taller guy barked. Talk about angry—his voice wasn't warm or fuzzy. She'd met a lot of cops when she'd worked at the precinct. Nothing about this guy screamed cop, from the tattoos to the way he talked. He wasn't law enforcement. Which meant the other one probably wasn't either.

She ran through the door after Marek, into the stairwell, her feet tripping as she tried to keep up. "I don't think they're cops," she told him. One flight of stairs. She whipped around the edge and flew down the next flight. Her chest hollowed as the air sliced down her raw throat.

This was why she sat behind a computer. She wasn't cut out for the whole exercise thing. Her legs slowed.

The door flew open two flights up, and she heard heavy boots hit the stairs.

Shit.

She ran faster, legs pumping, matching Marek stride for stride. Her toes stuttered, catching the edge of a tread. She clutched the handrail kept going, the banging behind them getting closer and closer. Maybe if they hit the ground floor, they could get away. She glanced at the wall by the landing as she swung past. Eighteen. They still had eighteen floors until the lobby.

She was going to die. Her thighs burned. Flames flickered down her throat and scorched down to her lungs. Either her heart was going to thump clear out of her chest, or the bad guys were going to shoot her. Either way, this was how it ended.

Marek opened the door on the seventeenth floor and dragged her through it. "There's a freight elevator we can take from this floor," he whispered.

Down another hallway, the plain white drywall and abstract paintings reminding her of a cheap hotel. Around a corner, into yet another hallway. Marek stopped at a large elevator door and jabbed the button.

And they waited.

The halls were empty. It was after hours. There wasn't a sound, because all of the other companies in the building were closed for the night. No doors opening. No boots thudding in pursuit. Thank goodness. Danni eyed the hallway, back the way they'd come. Those guys were pretty damn fast for wannabe cops.

A door slammed open down the hall, and somebody scuffed along the cheap tan carpeting.

Shit. Marek gave her a terrified look, and she was pretty sure she threw him a matching one. She jammed her finger against the down button. Hitting the shiny square wasn't going to make the damn thing come any faster, but she had to do something. Anything. The scuffling was getting closer. She and Marek weren't getting any farther away.

They were so fucked.

FIVE

MAREK WATCHED Danni poke at the elevator button and refused to panic. How the hell were they going to get out of here? The freight elevator was obviously operated by some manual pulley system. Otherwise it would move a hell of a lot faster.

The door dinged and slowly slid open. As soon as there was enough space, Marek wrapped his hand around Danni's wrist and twirled her into the car. Two men came into view. T-shirt. Jeans. Not exactly a police uniform.

A gun raised. Aimed straight at Marek. Again.

He hit the ground floor button and shoved Danni against the side of the elevator car. "Hurry," he muttered. The boots stomped harder, thudding against the carpet. Getting closer.

Marek stood there. One hand hitting the button. The other around Danni. Hoping if they got off one shot, it would hit him and not her. Praying they couldn't get off two shots before the doors closed.

The rubber between the doors finally snapped together, and the cab jerked. Gears whined as it lowered.

Bang. Bang.

The closed doors didn't muffle the sound of gunshots. Danni fell to the floor and screamed. Marek wrapped his body around hers. The only sound was the car rumbling down the elevator shaft. Or maybe not. Danni shook in his arms. Teeth chattering.

He pulled away. "Are you okay?"

She didn't say a word. Tears lined her eyes. A red bump was forming on her temple.

"Shit. Are you okay?" His heart squeezed as he ran a hand along the side of her face. She must have hit the railing when she ducked. *Dammit.*

The door would be opening any minute, and they needed to run, to get as far as they could. He stepped back, and Danni's hand left a red smear on his shirt.

Son of a bitch. He ran a hand over her head. Nothing. No blood. Where was it coming from? His eyes ate up every inch of her body. Images of pooled blood and her lifeless body fogged up his vision. "Danni?"

She touched a small bright red stain across the side of her calf.

"Move your hand," he said, fighting to sound calm. She didn't move. "Danni, sweetheart, I need you to move your hand." He peeled back the bloody digits. Her jeans were sliced. A wound gashed along her leg—a red valley along the skin.

Thank fuck. It was just a graze. There was blood. She needed help, but it could have been so much worse.

He still needed to compress the wound and cover it, but they needed to move first.

"It's not too bad." He rested his hand on her cheek. He needed to feel her warmth, to feel that she was still here. "Can you stand?"

She looked at him, the glaze still shining in her eyes. "Am I shot?"

Relief flooded through him. She was talking. "The bullet just grazed you. The door's about to open, and we need to move."

She looked at her leg and nodded. "Okay." She went to stand and bit out a whimper.

He didn't want to, but he pulled away. "I'm going to lift you. Okay?" He wrapped his arms around her and pulled her onto her feet. She wobbled. Another whimper snuck out as the elevator doors slid open.

"Don't move." He stepped away slowly, making sure she wouldn't fall over. "Ready?" He stepped to her left side and rested a hand on her waist. The area around the freight elevator was clear. "Lean on me." He started forward, supporting her as she limped. "I'm going to get you out of here."

"Okay." She cringed. Right. Left—Nope—Hop. Right. She was trying to keep up, but at this rate, a snail could catch them.

He held her close to his side and started to run, down the hall and out the freight doors to the alley. It was a slow run, but it would have to do. He needed to get her as far away from here as possible, which meant leaving the quiet, dark alley and finding transportation. Their cars would be a bad idea. For all he knew, more bad guys were watching the garage.

Out on the street, Marek tried hailing a taxi. Danni slid down, just an inch. He pulled her closer as a yellow cab rolled up to the curb. Thank fuck. A group of five guys, all wearing black silk shirts with the collars hanging wide, whipped open the taxi door and piled into Marek's cab.

"That was my cab." Shit. There was no way these assholes were going to give Marek back his taxi.

The last guy looked Marek up and down. "Get your own."

Marek's car was still in the garage, but there was no way he'd make it there with a limping Danni and these assholes on his tail. Same with Danni's SUV. Crap. All the taxis he could see were full of drunks and club-hoppers.

"We need to keep moving." Danni pulled to the right on State, toward the Red Line.

"Where are you going?" Marek pulled her to the left.

"I'm going to the train." She nodded down the block to the Red Line entrance.

"But if we go right to Monroe, we can grab the Blue Line and find a hospital." The Blue Line was the same distance, but in a different direction, and led to someone who could look at Danni's leg. They didn't have time for a steering committee on direction. They were still being followed. He dragged her along before she could answer.

"I don't need a doctor." Danni followed him around the corner and down the street. Followed was a strong word. More like he carried her.

She needed a doctor. But that was an argument for later.

The street was busy. The Loop was always busy. Marek pulled Danni close as they navigated the crowd of theatergoers and bar-hoppers.

Exhaust tinged the air as they crossed under the elevated train. Horns honked. People talked and laughed. The city wasn't stopping. Life went on, as it always did, while Marek helped Danni across the street.

Screams erupted behind him. A loud pop sounded.

Danni jumped. Marek ducked, drawing Danni down with him. Her knee buckled, and she hit the ground like an area rug. People ran. Cars swerved.

They were sitting ducks.

The initial shock must have worn off, because she squirmed, avoiding her bad leg until she was almost standing. "We need to move." She hobbled away without him.

"We do this together." Marek hunched, getting one arm around her waist, and squat-walked toward the entrance to the Blue Line. His trainer would be proud.

The gunshots stopped, probably because the people on the street were blocking the bad guys from seeing him. That didn't mean they weren't following, though.

"Are you okay to go faster?" he asked Danni, trying to not crash into the people running in the streets.

"Yes." She wrapped her fingers around his shirt and held on.

Calling on any reserve strength he could find, he busted forward down the block and down the stairs.

"There they are," someone yelled from above them.

He straightened to his full height and ran inside the station. Shit. He didn't have his card, or cash, and using a debit card would leave a trail the cops could follow. He didn't have a choice. He lifted Danni, angling her over the turnstile. He set her on her feet—or foot—on the other side.

His hand found purchase on the metal, and he jumped the turnstile. He'd make it up next time. Desperate times and all. He wasn't letting those guys take another shot at Danni. They'd hit her once. Luckily, she was still alive and mobile. If they hit her again, he might not be that lucky.

They followed the halls, feeling the rumble of the

train. Was it arriving or leaving? *Crap*. What if the next train wasn't arriving until later? They didn't have time for later. He needed a plan B. Running. That was all he had. They'd run out the other side of the station.

The high-pitched wail of the train's brakes told him they didn't have time. He followed Danni as she pushed through the people loitering in the hall listening to a homeless man tap on his drums.

He went to help Danni, but she put up her hand. "I got it." She jog-limped ahead to the edge of the Monroe platform.

The wheels squealed as the brakes engaged. Wind from the moving train blew against him, practically blew right through him. He grabbed Danni's hand and held on; with one good leg, she was like a pendulum in an earthquake.

He held her tight as the cars slowed, her face buried in his shoulder. If they weren't running for their lives, he'd be enjoying the fuck out of having her nuzzle in his neck. Unfortunately, he was too busy watching the platform to enjoy the high of having her this close.

The screeching stopped, and the doors rattled open. Walking her into the car, he helped her find a seat. He had to get her to safety—far away from whatever the hell was going on.

This wasn't her fight. And she was way out of her element. Not that he was in his element, but he didn't have a choice. She did.

DANNI SAT on the hard-plastic seat. The train was bathed in the awful scent of mold and urine—even that couldn't get her mind off her throbbing leg. She looked at the blood covering her jeans and groaned. Moving the leg, bad idea.

She was shot. Fucking shot. She wasn't going to tell anyone the bullet grazed her. She might have a tad more street cred, well, she'd make sure she had more street cred. In her version, there was going to be a brush with death.

If it didn't hurt so damn much, she'd be excited.

A woman across the aisle got up and took a seat on the other side of the train, her wide eyes focused on Marek. Everyone else obviously hadn't noticed Danni's bloody leg, or they just didn't care. The low rumble of conversation and laughter filled the train car.

"How's your leg?" Marek's hand slid down her leg as he looked at the gash. "It's not bleeding anymore. You might need a few stitches but nothing more." He eased her jeans away from the gash.

"Ouch." She tried to pull away, but his hands kept her in place.

"Sorry." He rubbed along the uninjured part of the leg, giving her another sensation to focus on instead of the throbbing and burning.

The train shook as it angled up the ramped track to burst from the tunnel to the above-ground track. Soon after, they hit the Halsted stop.

"A couple stops, and we'll get you fixed up," Marek said.

Fixed up? "Where are we going?"

"I told you already, the hospital."

"I don't need a hospital. I'm fine." She fixed a smile to her face that she didn't really feel. *See. Fine.*

Marek shook his head and laughed. "Your leg begs to differ with you."

"We'll stop at the pharmacy. I'll be fine." She wasn't looking forward to walking when they got off the train, but eventually, they had to get off. Right? Or they could just ride until her leg stopped hurting.

A yawn ripped from her chest. It had been a long night. They'd managed to shake the bad guys, which meant she could finally breathe. And with every breath, she wanted to sleep. "Where do we go now?" *Bed. Please say bed.* And not in a let's-get-freaky way. Although that way would be good too, just later. Now she wanted a warm bed so she could study the back of her eyelids.

"We'll stop at the hospital." The wheels screeched as the train pulled into the Racine stop.

"We're not going to the hospital." That wasn't even an option. He was a wanted man, and hospitals were crawling with cops.

He kept shaking his head like he wasn't hearing a word she said. Maybe if he stopped shaking his big fat head, he could understand the words coming from her mouth. She could admit she might be getting a bit cranky. But between the pain and the slowly diminishing adrenaline from her near-death experience—yep, that story sounded great—she was beaten like a dollar-store piñata.

"You can't force me." She sounded like a belligerent toddler.

Marek laughed. A deep, rumbling laugh. "Thank you," he breathed between rumbles. "I needed that."

"Needed what?" She hated to admit that laugh made her insides all mushy. Especially when he was laughing at her.

"Needed the laugh." The train started to slow down. The Medical Center. "We have to get off here."

"I'm not going to the hospital."

"You are."

"They'll have to call the cops." Her leg might be offering the lion's share of the pain, but the side of her face was throbbing. She probably looked like she'd survived a fight with Laila Ali. "It's barely bleeding."

He reached under her arm, helping her stand. The train wobbled and shook, and her hands attached to his chest so she wouldn't fall over.

The falling-over thing would be bad, but his chest was so hard. And it felt so good beneath her fingers. She moved with him as the train swayed. She inched forward as people shuffled around her.

She'd follow that chest anywhere.

The doors to the train closed. And somehow, she was on the wrong side of them. How the hell did that happen?

Damn chest.

The passengers flowed along the platform and up the ramp. Cold night air nipped at Danni's cheek as they followed up the ramp to the street. She'd like to think she was keeping up with the crowd, but the fact was they were outpacing her five steps to one.

"Do you want me to carry you?"

"No. I'm fine."

He smirked as he slowed his steps to match hers.

"Just because I'm letting you lead me off this platform does not mean I'm going to see a doctor," she whispered as a woman holding a toddler's hand passed them and slid through the barred turnstiles.

That smirk didn't leave as they made it to the sidewalk on Paulina Street. He headed right.

She didn't.

He walked a few feet and turned around. "We need to get you checked out."

"I don't need—"

"Look." He moved in closer—way too close. His breath slid along her cheek before he leaned down. Then —holy crap—then his breath was dancing with hers. He was close enough to lick her lips. Close enough to kiss.

The air balled in her lungs. Waiting. Hoping he would close those inches and put his lips on hers. He closed his eyes. She closed her eyes.

And then...

Nothing. He sighed.

She opened her eyes to find him staring at her—no longer inches from her. He was about a foot away. But with that look of concern on his face, it might as well be a mile. Apparently, the whole kissing thing wasn't going to happen. Despite the throbbing leg, disappointment flooded her system, becoming the focus of her overeager libido.

"What if I had been shot? Where would we be heading right now?"

She knew the answer he wanted because it was what she would have done. Because she would do anything to make sure he was okay. "Fine. I'll go to the hospital, but you can't go with me."

"I'm not leaving you there by yourself."

"I'm an adult."

"You are, but you can barely walk. And I don't want you to go through this alone. We'll be fine." He said the words, but the conviction was lacking. He couldn't know if they'd be fine. But he also didn't appear to be budging on this.

"Fine. The first sign of cops and we run."

"Fine." He wrapped his arm around her and led her toward the lights of the hospital. A block up and they were walking through the sliding glass doors of the emergency room.

Stale antiseptic lingered in the light-soaked atmosphere. After the darkness outside, she practically needed sunglasses. Danni leaned into Marek as she hopped up to the reception desk.

"I have a gash on my leg," Danni told the woman sitting behind the counter. Just a gash, nothing to see here. Maybe, if she was lucky, she could get them to believe that and get out of here without a police escort.

"Name?" The woman glanced up from her computer as she typed.

"Danielle Stein."

The woman printed out a label and stuck it to a piece of paper attached to a clipboard. "Enter the information while you wait."

"How long is the wait?"

The glare she gave told Danni that the question might be obvious, but it was not welcome. "We'll call you."

Don't ask us, we'll call you. Not exactly an answer, but it appeared to be all she was going to get.

Danni sat in the black vinyl chair and looked over the paperwork. Annoying. It was bad enough being in pain, but then they made you do homework, probably so you didn't realize how long it took them to call your number.

"Do you want me to fill that out?" Marek must have seen something in her eyes because he kept going. "Not that I want your personal information or anything..."

"Sure." She handed over the clipboard. This could be interesting. Like a pop quiz. See how well his memory held up.

The cheap pen in his hand hovered over the paperwork. He entered her name and asked for her address. He shouldn't know her current address. If he did, there was some stalkerish shit going on. He entered her allergy to penicillin.

"You remembered that?"

"How could I forget your hands blowing up into balloons?"

When she'd found out she was allergic to penicillin, her whole body had blown up like the Stay Puft Marshmallow Man. But for some reason, her hands were the worst. She couldn't touch anything without pain.

That he'd remembered after all this time—her girly parts were sighing. If only the rest of her wasn't throbbing in pain.

They continued to play the Memory Game as he filled out the form. She almost forgot that her leg hurt. Almost. They waited. And waited.

Maybe if she were in more dire need, they would have taken her to an exam room more quickly. Maybe if she'd told them she was shot, that would get their attention. All kinds of attention.

Then she'd have to spend time hanging with the po-po. Exchange several boring hours on crappy chairs for another few boring hours on crappy chairs.

"Danielle Stein," a deep, almost orgasmic voice called out. Tall, Dark, and Handsome came through the secured back door in bright blue scrubs.

Danni tried to stand, but one leg was throbbing, and the other, well, it had practically hopped a marathon.

Marek stood, and stuffed the clipboard under his arm. He offered his hand, and she took it. She leaned on him again. That seemed to be the theme for the day. Not that it was a bad theme, but Marek felt strong and solid as her hand wrapped around his back.

She'd done this before. It wasn't something she wanted to go through again. She might not know the grown-up Marek, but every time she looked at him, she remembered the Marek who sang her to sleep when she had the flu, the one who loved her.

But this wasn't college. This wasn't like it was before. She needed to focus on something else. Someone else.

TD&H held open the door and gave her a glorious view of his teeth. He had a gorgeous smile. Kind. Beautiful.

She nodded. "Thank you."

He winked. Flirty and hot.

This was what she needed to focus on. Stop remembering the past and focus on the future. She limped down the hall clutching Marek like she was a Capuchin monkey. Maybe she could let go of the past if she wasn't currently hanging onto it. Literally.

Once her leg was patched, she'd be fine. She could help Marek and keep her distance.

SIX

MAREK HELD onto Danni as they walked down the hall and around the corner, following the unreasonably tall male nurse into a cubicle.

"Sir, this might take a while. Perhaps you'd like to wait in the waiting room?" Pretty boy nurse was trying to get rid of him. Like that was going to happen.

"I'm good."

Danni groaned, and her face screwed up. "Don't leave."

Not that Marek had any intention of leaving, but now there was no way in hell. She must be in pain. A female nurse walked in the door as Pretty Boy left. Thank heaven. If Marek had to watch that guy treat his woman, there would be hell to pay.

Not that she was his woman.

Marek helped Danni onto the bed in the center of the stall—a three-walled room with a yellow curtain pushed to one side of the opening. An IV pole stood in the corner, next to some kind of monitor and other technical gear.

The nurse smiled at Danni. "I need to take a few vitals."

"Of course."

"I'm Crista. We'll get you all fixed up." She slid a pulse oximeter on Danni's finger and patted her knee. Producing a pair of bandage shears from somewhere, Crista opened the leg of Danni's jeans until the wound was exposed. "What happened here?" She glared at Marek.

"I didn't hurt her." No, it was just his fault.

Danni didn't miss a beat. "I burned my leg on a piece of metal bracket at the train stop. They were working on the turnstile, and I wasn't paying attention." She was good. Marek almost believed her, and he'd been there.

"Did you hurt your eye on the turnstile too?" Crista obviously wasn't buying any of it. She pulled the oximeter off Danni's finger and moved on to checking blood pressure. The usual doctor's office routine. "Can you lean back?" She pulled a shelf out of the end of the bed.

Danni lowered herself onto her elbows and slowly lifted her legs. There might have been a few groans, but the nurse glared when Marek stood, so he let her help Danni move.

A man with thinning long gray hair walked in, wearing a white coat. "I'm Doctor Dalai. So, what do we have here?"

"Metal bracket jumped out and got me," Danni groaned.

"Bracket?" The doctor put gloves on before folding the cut material of her jeans out of the way. He grabbed a giant swab and doused it in some sort of liquid. Wiping away the blood, he examined the gash. "Are you sure a bracket made this? It's rounded."

His eyes went from her to Marek. Of course, the doctor could tell the difference between a burn from a bracket and a bullet graze. He probably saw this kind of shit all the time. The wound and the lying.

"I didn't see the shape of the bracket, just this metal thing sticking out." Danni dipped her chin and smiled. "I'm sure that sounds stupid."

Dr. Dalai clearly wasn't buying it, but he just nodded. "Not at all. You should see the stupid things I see every day. You don't even make the top thousand."

"Metal pole, bracket. It's all the same." She laughed, but it was an "oh, shit" wannabe laugh. The one saved for when she was caught with her hand in the cookie jar—or taking the last piece of pizza.

Given the looks the doc and the nurse were sharing, they weren't buying any of this. But so far, the doctor wasn't calling bullshit, either.

"It doesn't look too bad." The doc hovered over the leg. "Any pain here?" He poked at the skin around the wound.

"No." Danni cringed, but her voice never faltered.

"Are you sure?" The doctor poked another spot, and she gave the same answer. "You keep wincing."

"Because eventually you're going to poke at something that will hurt."

"How's the pain on a scale from one to ten?" The doctor leaned in to inspect the wound.

"When I walk, twelve. Right now, about an eight."

Dr. Dalai laughed. "We can give you something for that." He nodded, and the nurse left the room. The doctor scooted closer, moving Danni's hair to the side and eyeing the lump on her temple. It was mostly red, with a hint of blue. "How about this bump."

"It would hurt if my leg didn't throb so much."

"Of course." The doctor smiled as Crista came back with a tiny paper cup, a larger cup, and a syringe. "This is Tylenol three for the pain," the doctor said, "and I have an antibiotic for any infection. When was your last tetanus shot?"

"Umm...not sure." Danni took the contents of the tiny cup, and followed it with what Marek figured was water.

The doctor lifted the sleeve of Danni's shirt. "Crista, grab a tetanus shot." He pressed the syringe to her shoulder. After that, he made another pass over the wound on her leg, and checked the rest of her for any other damage.

The nurse came back with another syringe. She sat at a terminal off to the side and clicked it awake, typing as Dr. Dalai called out information—superficial tangential laceration, suspect gunshot graze...

Gunshot graze. This could get ugly.

"I'm thinking four stitches should take care of your leg."

"Four?" Danni sounded so disappointed.

The doctor smiled and picked up a syringe. "This will numb the area so we can close you up. It'll take a few minutes, but we'll be back." He nodded at Danni before looking over at Marek. "Crista, why don't you get what we'll need for that." He headed for the cubicle opening. "I'll be back in a few minutes."

Fifteen minutes later, Crista still hadn't come back. She was, hopefully, battling another emergency and not trying to hunt down some cops. Danni hadn't moved. Her eyes were closed.

"How are you doing?" Marek asked, voice low.

Danni's grimace of pain morphed into a small smile. "This is going better than I thought, but only four stitches.

There's no street cred with four stitches," Danni whispered. She sat up and moved her hand to the blue lump on her face. "Ouch." She ran her hand along her cheek. "Ouch."

"Stop doing that." Marek walked over to the side of the bed and held her hands. Her skin was silk, warm and soft. And as she sat there, bruised and beaten, it took everything inside him to not wrap his arms around her. He wanted to take her home, protect her. Hold her and never let go. But...

"Time for stitches." The doctor was back. "Are we ready?" He snagged a rolling chair and put on another pair of gloves. "I need to flush the wound, then we'll stitch you up." He pressed near the wound. "Am I hurting you?"

Danni stared at the ceiling. "It doesn't hurt."

"Are you sure?" the doctor asked.

"She doesn't like blood." Marek wasn't exactly sure that was the problem, but since she'd nearly passed out in college when he'd cut his hand during a computer rebuild, he had a feeling she hadn't changed enough to be okay with a little bit of gore. Especially her own.

The doctor nodded at Marek. Questions and judgment swirled in his stare. They thought what happened to Danni was done by Marek's hand. He didn't know if he should be disgusted or offended—maybe a little of both.

"So, Danni, are you okay?" Dr. Dalai focused back on her and dabbed at the wound with some gauze.

"Yep." She looked down at her leg, and her eyes bulged before she looked back up at the ceiling. Her face was an interesting combo of pale and green.

The doctor pulled back with a laugh. "There's not really any blood."

"She doesn't like *any* blood." Marek wanted to be

mad that the doctor was practically laughing at Danni and her blood disgust, but it was kind of funny how she couldn't handle blood at all. Well, in video games it was fine, but IRL—nope.

After a few minutes, the doctor sat back. "You can look now."

"Thank you so much," Danni said, still not looking.

"No problem." Dr. Dalai tapped her foot, leaving a tray of extra bandages. "I'll get your instructions so you can get out of here." Then he disappeared.

Danni inched down the table until her legs hung over the side.

"How does it feel?" Marek asked.

"Not bad. The pain isn't there."

He wasn't surprised. Between the local injection and the pain meds, she should be feeling pretty good. When those wore off, she was going to be in a world of hurt. Maybe they'd be willing to give her a prescription for some of that magic medication. Anything to take that edge off.

"Good evening." A Chicago police officer walked in the door. Complete with uniform and notepad. "Danielle Stein?"

"Yes." She smiled, but it was forced. Marek could practically see the freak-out in her eyes. Hopefully, it was just that he knew her so well, and the cop wouldn't see it. They had parts to play if they were going to get out of here together.

"I'm Officer Bing." The cop turned to Marek. With Marek's face plastered all over the television, it wouldn't be long before the guy recognized him and put him behind bars. "And you are?"

"I'm an old college friend. Alex." There, lying wasn't so hard.

"Alex who?" The cop asked.

He needed a last name. Marek looked around the room. Bowl, bed, cabinet. Alex Cabinet? So dumb. They made it look so easy on television. You use the name of the first thing you see. All he could see was stupid shit. The cop stared. Waiting for the last name. All he could think of was Skala, but since that really was his last name and it had been plastered all over the news, using that was ill-advised.

Marek would be a sitting duck in jail. Anybody could get to him. These guys—whoever they were—seemed to be intent on getting to him. He couldn't figure out why or find out who they were from a five-by-five cell.

The nurse walked back in. "Here are the directions for aftercare and your medication. One every six hours for pain." He handed Danni a bottle of pain meds and then a box. "These are the antibiotics."

A scream came from outside the room and another nurse ran in, busting through the yellow curtains. "Officer, we need your help. We have a patient trying to escape."

Funny. That's what they needed to do too.

"I'll be back in a minute. Don't go anywhere." The cop's gaze burrowed into Marek. He knew something wasn't right, and it wouldn't take long for him to figure out what it was.

They had to run now.

The cop followed the nurse out of the room, closing the curtain, and Marek grabbed the medications, extra bandages, and tape sitting on the tray and shoved it in his pocket. "Can you walk?"

She wriggled her butt, sliding closer to the edge of the table. Although the bouncing was cute and he appreciated the way her chest moved as she wiggled forward, they needed to go now.

He held out his hand. "Let's go before they come back."

She slid the rest of the way off the table. A little wobble, but she was on her feet.

She rested her hand on his and slowly put one foot in front of the other. Her leg shook. Marek wrapped an arm around her waist and pulled her close, whispering as he kept her upright, "You can do this."

She took a step. She swayed, gripping his arm as if it were her lifeline. And it probably was. "You're so pretty." She ran a hand down the side of his face.

"You're so hopped up on drugs." He slid closer to her, wrapping an arm across her back and lifting under her arm. He needed to be her crutch. They weren't going to get far with her stumbling, but if they could get outside, they could get a taxi.

He looked outside the curtain. People were moving around, all with purpose. The cop was nowhere to be found. Yet.

He pulled her out into the main hub of the emergency room and headed toward the door with an arrow and EXIT in large red letters, and then down the hall until he saw automatic doors leading to the outside world.

Two county cops stood by the door, talking and drinking coffee. A man in a wheelchair brushed past them as a nurse pushed him out the front doors. A woman stood by an open car door, and waited as the man slowly eased into the passenger seat of the car.

Release procedures. When Marek sprained his ankle

playing basketball a few years ago, the hospital insisted he use a wheelchair. Legal reasons or something. No one else was hobbling out of the ER. The cops would notice him. They'd notice Danni. They'd ask questions.

Marek looked around and saw three wheelchairs right next to the wall. "Sit here," he whispered as he helped Danni into one of them. "Be cool." He pushed the chair down the hall and past the police officers, who were busy discussing some cop marrying some badge-bunny. Busy enough to not even glance at Marek and Danni.

Fifty feet. Twenty feet.

The front door and cool night air hit him upside the head. The few cars that were on the road flew by. A car with an Uber placard sat by the door. Marek knocked on the window. "Are you available?"

The guy was staring at his phone. "You have to go through the app."

"Are you kidding me? We're right here." Marek looked back at the doors to the hospital. The two gossiping cops were talking into the radios on their uniform collars and looking outside. *Shit.*

"And I'm right here. Doesn't matter. App." Mr. Personality kept clicking on his phone. Maybe he was on a break and could only be a decent human being when on the clock.

Marek scrambled for his phone and opened the app. Over twenty drivers were milling about the area. Too bad he was in a hurry and desperate. He found the car sitting right in front of him, in the cul-de-sac in front of the hospital, and hit confirm.

The hum from the hospital's sliding doors opening hit him in the chest. The cop from the ER stood just on the other side of the door.

Mr. Personality popped his head through the car window with a smile. "Are you ready?"

"Yeah." Marek helped—more like shoved—Danni into the back seat before running around to the other side. "Let's go."

The car pulled away from the curb, toward West Congress, and rolled up to the stoplight. The two gossiping cops ran outside, with Officer Bing in the lead. A van stopped behind the Uber, and Marek saw the cops whip out their flashlights and approach the van.

Marek leaned over into the front seat. "Can't we just go? Aren't we turning right?"

"No turn on red." The guy pointed at the sign hanging from the signal.

Dammit. Marek leaned back as the flashlights drew closer, sliding down in his seat and dragging Danni with him.

The light changed from red to green. Marek gripped the edge of the seat as white light illuminated Danni's face. "Go."

Uber guy hit the accelerator before the light reached Marek, and relief flooded through his system.

They were getting away. Getting to where? He had no idea. One thing at a time.

"I TOLD you the hospital was a bad idea," Danni whispered as she nuzzled the car seat. She pressed the side of her face that wasn't a Jackson Pollock painting into the cool fabric. The medication was wearing off. Her head throbbed, and her leg felt like it had been through a blender. But that wasn't why she was whispering. She didn't want the Uber driver to hear.

She didn't want anyone but Marek to hear. She didn't trust anyone. That was not a new development.

Trust wasn't something she had in abundance. Her father left her mother. Her mother left to marry a new guy. Marek left. The fact that she'd trusted him over the past few hours was scary. But she had always had trusted him. Even when it hurt.

"They stitched you up and gave you antibiotics." He reached out and touched her hand. It felt nice. After all the pain. It felt nice to have his hand on her. The concern. The caring. "And we got away."

"Away to where?"

"Well, if they haven't put together that you're with me yet, they will soon." He looked so sad, or maybe tired, probably a bit of both. This whispered conversation wasn't helping with the whole tired thing. She never realized how much energy it took to whisper.

"Exactly." They couldn't go anywhere they'd normally go. They needed somewhere off their beaten path. "Let's go to a hotel."

"A hotel?"

Just the way he said the word made her insides heat. Even half out of it, she could feel the glide of his words on her body. *A hotel.* Thoughts of what she could do with Marek in a hotel bed managed to niggle through the pain. Not that she meant any of that when she said hotel. "Because it's anonymous. You know, so we could sleep...in separate beds. And regroup."

His smile was wary. "But what if someone recognizes me?"

"Why? Because you're a celebrity?" She couldn't help

but smile at his ego. He'd always had a healthy one. He'd had healthy lots of things.

Marek shook his head. "No. Because my picture has been plastered all over the television today. Remember? Wanted."

Oh, yeah. She forgot about that. That felt like a lifetime ago.

"I'll check us in." If she could make it inside the hotel without falling over, that was. But that was a later problem, not a now problem. The new problem was not falling asleep until they were both safe. With every mile, her head felt more and more like Thor's hammer in the hands of Loki. "They won't know who I am yet, or our connection. I have a fake credit card."

"What? Why?" He glared at her. Of all the things she'd said today, why did that merit this much attention?

"I don't like anyone being able to track me."

"So, you use credit cards you don't pay?" Marek looked disgusted.

Danni felt that look to her bones. How could he think she'd do something like that? "I'm not a thief. I pay them. They're just in someone else's name." The car turned onto I-90 North. *Wait.* "Why are we going north?"

"We were in a hurry, so I just used my home address."

"So, he's taking us to your house?" Where the cops, no doubt, were waiting.

"Um...yeah." Marek leaned forward toward the front seat. "Can we change the destination?"

"In the app." The driver nodded, but kept looking straight ahead. Which was a good thing since he was driving and all.

Marek pulled out his phone and tapped the screen. "There's a hotel in Lincoln Park."

"Won't they look there? Maybe we should look outside of Chicago."

He nodded and went back to his phone.

A few seconds later, the Uber driver's cell phone dinged, and he said, "It looks like we're heading to Evanston." And then there was silence.

Marek leaned against the seat and closed his eyes. He looked so tired. Today had been one hell of a ride. The ups and downs weren't nearly as much fun as a stomach-dropping day at Six Flags. She reached across the seat and wrapped his hand in hers. They could have caught him. And yet he'd stayed. After everything that happened to him today, he hadn't left.

Not that she thought he would.

She slid her thumb along the skin of his palm. He had such great hands. Long fingers. And strong. She loved the way those hands had carried her. How they felt on her skin, on her body. She'd missed those hands.

"What are you doing?" Marek looked at her through one eye, almost as if he were trying to get a literal wink of sleep.

"I like your hands."

He smiled and twined his fingers with hers. "They like you too."

The throbbing at her temple deepened, but she couldn't help the smile that forced its way onto her face. *Ouch.*

He lifted her hand to his mouth and placed a warm kiss on the back of her knuckles.

Another smile, another ouch, but worth it.

She forced herself to stay awake as the car drove on, along highways and city streets, finally winding through suburban traffic. Lights blinked and washed over Marek as he slept. And he was asleep. His chest rose and fell in a slow, perfect rhythm.

Up and down. She could watch him all night. Bathed in white. Bathed in darkness. He was so peaceful.

"We're here." The driver nodded at the bright lights of the hotel.

Marek didn't move. His eyes stayed closed, so Danni tapped on his shoulder. "Marek." No movement.

She shook his shoulder. "Marek, we're here."

Marek flew forward, his eyes wide.

"It's okay." Danni patted his knee. "We're at the hotel."

Marek looked around as Danni opened her door. This was it. Time to see if she could handle the simple task of walking. She stepped out of the car. Her knee buckled. The. Pain.

Fire radiated from the stitches—why had she thought four was a joke?—and her knee wobbled like Jell-O. Her hands flew to the door, and she hauled herself upright.

She. Could. Do. This.

"I'm going to check us in." She turned to Marek, who still looked a bit out of it. "Why don't you sit outside, and I'll come get you when I'm ready."

Luckily, the driver left them close to the entrance. Right foot forward. Left foot, right foot. She might have to hobble, but she was getting inside that damn hotel.

Danni barely made it through the revolving door, and limped her way across the cream tiles to the white marble check-in desk. Who thought putting it at the back of the lobby was a good idea? The elevator bank sat off to the right, past cream furniture and rugs swirled with a splash of red and green-blue. Tasteful, but not too fancy. Perfect.

"Welcome to the Evanston Inn." The guy behind the

counter couldn't have been more than twenty-five. His bloodshot eyes and overall confused expression said she'd probably interrupted a toke-break.

"Do you have a room available for tonight?"

"Sorry. There's a dental conference."

She leaned against the counter, shifting her weight to relieve some of the pressure on her leg. "There's not even one room? We've had a really long day of traveling." Like anyone couldn't tell that. She was bruised, the leg of her jeans was hanging open, and she probably looked like a train accident victim.

"Let me see." The guy poked and prodded the computer in front of him. "We do have a suite available. It has one king bed."

Suite. With one king bed.

Fantastic.

She couldn't decide if that fantastic was sarcasm at having to share a bed with Marek, or if she was truly excited about it.

"I'll take it." She slid a credit card and driver's license from the back of her cell phone case. Getting the IDs set up was always a challenge, but a few bucks to some unsavory characters and she had untraceable documents.

The boy took the card and smiled. "Deana Winchester, when will you be checking out?" He apparently didn't see the connection between her name and *Supernatural.* Not that anyone ever did.

"I'm not sure. Let's play it by ear."

She finished checking in and went outside to look for Marek. He was sitting on a metal bench, somehow still awake. Barely. "We have a room," she told him.

"I can't go in there. I'll be recognized."

"The front desk clerk is higher than the International Space Station. He won't notice you."

She grabbed his hand and helped him to his feet. "Keep your head down."

They walked through the brightly lit entrance, across the atrium, and into the elevator. In their room, it was all black furniture with silver hardware, and white bedspreads and lamps offset the dark gray walls.

"One bed?" Marek pulled off his shoes.

"Yep. We'll have to share." She still wasn't sure how she felt about that. But considering how tired she was, she could share a bed with a naked Avenger and still be able to fall asleep before her head hit the pillow. "Are you okay with sharing?" She pulled the bedcovers down. It looked so inviting.

"I can share." Marek fell onto the bed and yanked the blankets up to his chest. He was snoring before Danni even made it to the bathroom to look over her scars.

She needed a plan. She still had to find out who used her code and did all of this to Marek. She was getting closer to him, which wasn't good. Not while she was trying to solve the mystery without him finding out. But having him so close was torture.

She just wanted to touch him. And maybe she could. Since his marriage was over and she was in between relationships, they could actually make it work. Once they figured this crap out.

She needed a computer. Tomorrow, they'd have to get her laptop. Somehow. But that was tomorrow's issue.

Today was about sharing a bed with Marek and not accidentally jumping him in her sleep.

SEVEN

DANNI'S EYES CRACKED OPEN. The clock on the side table said eleven, and streams of light escaped the edges of the drapes. A muscled male arm wrapped around her, her back to his front.

Marek.

She hadn't done this in years. *This* being Marek's arms around her. Not that she was complaining. She liked sleeping in, and she loved sleeping in with Marek even more. They'd slept in a lot when they were dating due to middle-of-the-night sexy shenanigans. Not that this was anything like that. There'd been no sexy shenanigans.

Not out in the real world, at least. In the real world, it was dangerous shenanigans with pain. However, in her dreams? There were no bad guys chasing them, and her leg didn't radiate with misery. Her dreams were a lot more fun, and slightly X-rated.

Marek's hand moved. Ever so slowly. Fingers slid up and down her stomach, touching skin. Each feather-light caress moved higher under her shirt until his hand rested on her breast. Rubbing. Her nipple pebbled until it could cut glass.

All the pain she felt in her leg disappeared when his fingers brushed against hot skin. Every other nerve ending probably forgot how to fire. Her brain forgot how to think.

She bit her lip to stifle a moan, her heart banging against her ribcage. All the blood drained lower and lower in her body. Each knead and stroke made her forget. Then he leaned in. And that was it. She couldn't even remember what she was forgetting.

His breath was hot against her neck, pulling her body closer and closer to his. No one might be able to tell she had morning wood, but she could tell he did. And the pressure of him behind her felt so good. The warmth of his body soaked into her skin.

Lips met her shoulder. Soft. Warm. Need zipped through her body. A groan built in her throat, so she bit her lip again. She didn't want to wake him. And then his hips pushed toward her, and she *needed* to wake him.

Her hips moved back and forth, wanting to turn around and feel him against her core. Everything throbbed.

And then everything stopped. His hands. His hips. His arm disappeared.

She turned to see his face. Eyes wide open and staring at her. Shock. Confusion. All the reactions you didn't want to see when you woke up grinding on a guy.

"I'm so sorry." Another thing you didn't want when you woke up grinding on a guy—him telling you he's sorry. "I didn't mean to do that."

Didn't mean to do that. Just shoot her now. All she needed was a look of disgust and the humiliating picture would be complete.

She inched farther away from his strong, warm arms. Strong? Warm? That was her first mistake. Getting sucked in by Thor arms...and his hammer. Okay, the hammer was her second mistake. She jumped from the bed. Well, she *tried* to jump from the bed, but with her leg it was more of a hobble.

"I'm going to take a shower." She continued her hobble across the room as if she were being chased by her own stupidity. Doing the walk of shame without actually having sex. How stupid was that?

She flew through the bathroom door and slammed it shut. With a turn of the lock and another turn of the shower spigot, she was alone with her thoughts.

She braced her hands against the white stone counter. She didn't want to look too closely, but the mirror spanned over half the wall. Her reflection was hard to miss. Redness crawled up her face. Well, up one side of her face. The other side was still a hodgepodge of blue and purple.

What was she thinking, rubbing against him like a lap dancer looking for college money? Enjoying him like a cheap floozy. No dinner. No movie. Just some early-morning booty call that he obviously didn't want.

"Oh, God." She was like a horny Chihuahua, humping any leg she could find. And no leg ever wanted a horny mini-dog hanging from it.

Steam finally overtook the glass, making it impossible to see. She felt unclean. Deep-down dirty that even a shower wouldn't fix. Good thing there was a shower all warmed up and ready to go.

That made two of them.

Maybe if she used enough hotel soap, she could clean the shame from her skin. And then maybe, just maybe she could walk out of the bathroom and face Marek again. Although, right now, the thought of facing him was about as welcome as looking in that mirror again.

WHAT THE HELL JUST HAPPENED?

Marek had been in the middle of the most amazing dream. He was with Danni, her hands running up and down his body. And it felt so good and real.

Then she groaned. Actually groaned, and his eyes popped open. He was wrapped around her body. In real life, not just in the virtual reality of sleep.

Waking up to the look of horror on her face about broke his heart. He'd obviously woken her up with his tentacle-hands. It didn't matter that he was asleep. He'd groped her, even if he didn't mean to do it. All that mattered was his hands were all over her body, and she didn't want it.

She ran for the bathroom like the bed was on fire. With the heat swimming through his veins, maybe it was on fire. He looked down. The bed wasn't smoking, his body wasn't engulfed in flames, but he was sporting some heavy-duty morning wood.

Painful. They never told you about the pain. Not that knowing it was coming would stop it. He'd been dealing with blue balls for years. And he needed to deal with it. The way Danni ran out of the room made him think his current condition wouldn't be welcome when she got back.

Her walking in on him "dealing with it" wouldn't go over very well, either. Then he'd be more of a creep. He needed a distraction. Too bad there wasn't any noise in the room, just the sound of water hitting tile coming from the bathroom. The sound deepened as water hit her skin.

Water sliding over soft skin—the skin he'd been touching just five minutes ago. Imagining what was going on in the next room didn't exactly fall under "distraction".

He could only think of one thing to calm him down. Sitting up, he grabbed the remote. He found a news channel and waited. It only took a few minutes until he heard his name.

"Obrona Security is undergoing an investigation in conjunction with the data breach..." His body recoiled, the excitement slowly draining. *"According to a confidential company source, Mr. Skala is the primary suspect..."*

And that was it. His body was no longer an issue. Someone from the company was talking about him. What source?

Son of a bitch.

Who from the company even knew all the details? It had to be someone high up in the company. Which meant it was someone he trusted.

"This story just keeps getting stranger. Mr. Skala was seen with an unidentified woman at the Blue Line Monroe stop last evening..."

A grainy picture of Marek and Danni splashed across the screen.

"Speculation as to his relationship with this woman and whether she's in danger requires further investigation..."

Further investigation. Well, at least Marek had that. The vultures hadn't figured out who Danni was. Yet. If there was a leak in the office, it wouldn't take long.

The bathroom door clicked open and Danni walked

out, wet and determined, wearing yesterday's clothes. Her eyes didn't meet his as she ran a hand through her hair.

"How was your shower?" Great opening line after he'd practically mauled her. Maybe he should've opened with "How's the weather?" Pathetic.

"Fine." Fine was never good. Fine with an attempted smile was even worse. Well, attempted was a stretch. It looked more like invisible fingers pulled the corners of her mouth until they were stretched like a psychotic clown's.

"Danni?"

Her eyes were on everything and anything in the room. Except him. Couch. Ceiling. Fuzz on her shirt. Apparently she was ignoring him, too, because she said, "I need to run and get my computer."

He wanted to jump up and down. Wave his arms. "Danni, we need to talk about it."

"Nothing to talk about." Her fingers slid through the back of her hair and snagged. She pulled but couldn't seem to get them out. That still didn't get her to look his way. "Do you have a brush?" Her fingers jerked back and forth, probably making the existing knots into super knots.

He shrugged, and then she finally looked at him. Dammit. He liked it better when she was staring at the fuzz. Then at least he couldn't see the pain.

"I'm sorry." The words just kind of fell out, but he was sorry. He didn't want to upset her. Ever.

"For what?" Her fingers stilled, as if she were waiting for something. Her eyes were on his now. Something hung in the air. Expectation?

Damn. He was starting to sound like a headshrinker, reading too much into everything. "I somehow ended up sharing a bed with you and got a little excited this morning. I didn't mean to touch you."

She shook her head, and the hair vines released her hand. "No big deal. Maybe I should go alone." She walked over to her side of the bed and sat down. She pulled on her gym shoes.

Alone. "Where are you going?"

"To get my laptop."

"Can we talk? Tell me what's wrong."

She sighed. "You're sorry you got a little excited. That you touched me."

He wasn't sorry he touched her. He wanted to do it again. "I didn't mean it like it sounded. I just meant I'm sorry you woke up to some guy groping you."

"Some guy." She nodded and laughed, but it sounded hollow. Like she didn't think it was all that funny.

Honestly, neither did he. "I keep saying the wrong thing."

"Then don't say anything." She grabbed her credit card and stuck it in her bra. "I should be back soon."

"You're not seriously going alone."

"Why not? I'm walking fine." She proved her point by walking across the room and picking up her phone. She began typing.

"They've seen you. You can't just go running around by yourself."

She turned off the phone and slid it into her pocket. "I'll be fine. This is my job."

"Danni."

She walked toward the door.

"Danni!" He intercepted her before she got there. "I'm going with."

She sighed and grabbed her hair with one hand, twirling it and draping it over her left shoulder. "Fine."

Fine. He hated that word. If he'd learned anything, it

was that when women said fine, it was never fine. He got his cellphone and the spare cash he'd taken from his desk last night. He wasn't sure how long they'd be able to use credit cards. They hadn't connected Danni to her fake credit cards, but no one was looking. Yet. Eventually they would, and then the credit cards would lead the cops and anyone else to them.

They'd have to talk about when they should switch to another hotel—one that his modest roll of cash would cover. That was a conversation for later. Like when she didn't look at him like he'd kicked her puppy.

EIGHT

THE BUS BUMPED and shook down the streets of Chicago, and the leg of Danni's pants flapped open when the bus hit yet another pothole. She needed a safety pin or twelve, or maybe just a new pair of pants. At least she could pick up a pair when she got home.

The bus bounced again. Of course, grabbing her clothes and laptop wasn't going to fix her transportation issue. She missed her car so much it hurt. The dull ache in her chest, singed raw around the edges, had to be about the car, and not about Marek and his stupidity.

I'm sorry I touched you.

I'm sorry you're an ass. She'd almost said that out loud, but she refused to give him the satisfaction. When they'd originally parted ways after his ex-girlfriend announced her months of mono turned out to be pregnancy, Danni had licked her wounds and hid away and cried. A lot. Her heart was broken, but she'd managed to move on.

Well, move on was an overstatement. She'd managed to deal. And she swore she'd never let a guy get close enough to cause her to lose her shit like that again. Then Marek and his magic hands showed up, and she was young and dumb again.

That had to stop. She wasn't that same naïve twenty-year-old anymore. She'd seen what he could do to her. And she refused to let it happen—no matter how magical his hands were.

"Where are we going?" Her magic-handed shadow sat across the aisle.

She wasn't dumb enough to share a seat with that man. See? Not the same naïve twenty-year-old.

"My place." The bus slowed, and stopped at Fullerton and Western. Just a few more blocks to her condo.

"Are you sure?" He leaned across the aisle, whispering. "They might have tracked down your address. The press had your picture all over the TV this morning. It was grainy, but someone might recognize you."

"Who would recognize me? The only ones who know I'm with you are Jalen, Dave, Enrique, and Jessi from my office. I know Jessi won't talk."

"I guess." He said it like he wasn't so sure.

"Do you think one of them would talk to the press?"

"No. They're loyal."

"Are you sure Dave didn't throw you under the bus?" *And then back up and try to run you over again?* She wouldn't put it past the man. But she might be biased.

Dave had always hated Danni. He thought that she distracted Marek—and that was the nicest thing he'd said about her. Like it was any of Dave's business what she did with Marek.

Maybe if Dave could find a woman who could tolerate him for more than a few hours, he'd get a little *distracted* himself. But Dave didn't do women. He didn't do men either—Danni had made sure to ask him that at one point. He'd just whined about distractions.

"I don't know why you hate him so much," Marek said.

"Maybe because he called me a *code bunny*." And had asked how many beds she'd hopped into before landing in Marek's. Jackass. Not that she'd tell Marek all of that. She never wanted to come between the two of them. And she wasn't about to start now.

Marek shook his head. "Why would he call you that?"

'Cause he's a dick. "Because I went from dating Jalen to you."

"You weren't exactly dating Jalen. You went on like two dates and didn't even sleep together."

Did she mention Dave was a dick?

"Sometimes he pisses me off." Marek shook his head again. "He's such a dick."

The singed edges in her chest cabled together and warmed. When she was younger, she'd thought she was the problem. Now? Thankfully, she had that whole wiser thing going on.

"But no matter how big a dick he's been," Marek went on, "he wouldn't hurt the company. He wouldn't hurt me."

Danni nodded. She would have agreed with that a few days ago. Now? Maybe. Maybe not.

"If he was the leak, then those assholes chasing us would have found us," Marek said.

"Not necessarily. I don't own anything. Deana Winchester owns my credit cards and my car. Harmonie Granger owns my condo."

"Let me guess, a know-it-all with mad wand skills."

It was almost like he was describing himself. No. She wasn't going to start thinking about him and his wand skills. They were finally talking without the awkwardness of the morning. Not that she still didn't feel the sting. Rejection was never pretty. And his rejection hurt deep.

The apology didn't help.

"Yep. Neither are traceable back to me." The bus jerked to the side, stopping at Fullerton and California. "We're here."

She jumped from the seat and headed toward the front of the bus. The door whooshed open with the grind of gears and they both stepped off onto the curb.

They walked toward her building. Normally, the sidewalks were quiet, but people stood around, some in their muumuus, staring down the block and whispering. A crowd had accumulated at her building, the kind generally seen on the five o'clock news.

Her phone rang, and she hit ignore. She needed time to think. She needed time to figure out how to get to her condo without all of these people seeing her. And she definitely couldn't let them see Marek.

"Is it normally like this?" Marek slowed down, to avoid the people who were gawking.

Danni's feet refused to move when she heard a familiar wail. The crowds parted as a police car turned down her block, lights blazing. Now she could see the other cop cars lining the street. What the hell?

She turned to Marek, holding up a hand. "Wait here." Danni looked at all the strangers lining the block. She didn't know anyone. These were her neighbors, and she had no clue who any of them were. She wasn't exactly part of the neighborhood coffee klatch.

And then she saw a mess of curly gray hair pulled

back in a bright pink plastic headband. Mrs. Stivak. The old woman had been there to talk to the cops when Danni's car was stolen. She'd also been there to deliver a pie when Danni had a very public breakup with an ex-boyfriend. Mrs. Stivak knew everyone—and everything about everyone. If the old woman knew how to blog, the whole neighborhood would be screwed.

"Mrs. Stivak, what's going on?"

"Oh, Danni, it's your building." She shook her head. "They won't tell us what's going on."

"I think they're looking for someone." An older man walked up, his dark bald scalp glistening between little sprigs of graying hair. "My grandson heard them talking about a shooting, and some guy plastered all over the news. Look, here's another news van."

Sure enough, the Channel 7 minivan, complete with a satellite dish on the roof, pulled along the curb up ahead. *Shit.*

"Thanks." Danni headed back to where Marek stood and whispered, "We have to go."

"What did they say?"

Danni slipped her arm through his and drew him back the other way. They had to put as much distance between them and that news team as possible. "We'll have to get my laptop from the office. They found my place. They're looking for you."

"How did they find the condo? It's not in your name."

She shook her head as they walked to the Fullerton bus stop. "I have no idea how. And how did they put us together? Dammit. Dammit."

Danni's phone rang. She hit ignore again.

"It's okay. I'll grab an Uber." Marek's fingers flew over his phone screen. "Let's get back to the hotel. Regroup."

"What if they figured out the names on my credit cards?" The phone in her pocket dinged. She couldn't ignore it any longer. Well, she could, but she ran the risk of someone taking out a missing person ad.

Maggie. All three missed calls were from her. Danni accepted the current call.

"Danni, are you okay?"

"Yeah. I'm fine. Shooting was exaggerated. The bullet only grazed my leg."

"What?" The high-pitched end of that sentence said that maybe she hadn't heard about the shooting. But that was what the old man said. "What shooting?"

"Nothing." If she didn't know about the shooting... "Why are you asking if I'm okay?"

"Do you want the whole list? You told Jessi to leave yesterday, and you ran out of here with some strange guy after turning off the phones. No one has heard from you since. Oh, and there was a standoff at your building. Some guy was holding his girlfriend and her family hostage with a gun. Haven't you seen it? It's all over the news. Wait. Are you shot?"

"Not really. Did they mention Marek?"

"Marek? The tech guy? What about him?"

The news. That's what they were talking about on her block. The standoff on the news. It had nothing to do with Marek or Danni.

"Car's here." Marek stood over a Prius, holding the door open.

"Sorry, Maggie. I'll call you back."

"Don't you dare—" Maggie's words came out on a hiss. Which made it that much easier to hit the end button. She was going to be pissed. She was probably swearing like a sailor at this very minute. And the next time Danni talked to her, she was going to be a huge pain in the ass.

Danni slid into the back seat, next to Marek. "Everything okay?" he whispered.

"There was a standoff in my building. Some guy and his girlfriend's family." There hadn't been many wins since Marek showed up. She'd take this one.

He sighed, relief flooding his shoulders as they dropped. "Let's stop somewhere and pick up some clothes, and then go back to the hotel and figure this out."

"I need to get my computer, but going to the office might be a bad idea." She wasn't willing to risk Marek—or herself—again.

"Could your friend bring it to us?"

"My friend?"

"The one on the phone."

"I don't think so." Which was tragic, since Maggie was her go-to person, but the frantic in her voice told Danni she would not understand. And there was no way Danni was going to bring Maggie around Marek. The whole cop's-girlfriend thing made her unpredictable.

But maybe Jessi or Leti could bring the laptop without gaining a tail. Oh, and without telling Maggie. It was worth a shot. Danni settled on Leti as the car sped north on the tollway.

Can you talk? she texted.

No dots appeared. No response. She'd just have to wait. And waiting was not in her wheelhouse.

MAREK'S ARMS were loaded with junk food as he headed back to their room. He would have liked to have gotten real food, but the onsite restaurant was closed. That left them with coffee, machine jerky, and chips. Breakfast of champions. And it was breakfast—at one in the afternoon.

They'd run out in such a rush that they hadn't grabbed a meal or anything. Not even coffee. Which would explain why Danni's head was on the verge of spinning around while she vomited pea soup.

He paused outside their room, making sure the door was still wedged barely open before he tried to get in, the coffees in his hand sloshing.

Overall, it was a nice room. Light blue carpet with maroon swirls. A bed with white bedding and a matching dresser sat on one side of the room. A glass table and green chairs sat on the other side. It was an interesting combination. But it was clean, and it had Danni.

"I have sustenance," he announced.

Danni leaped off the bed, grabbing one of the coffees. "You are a god." Her lips wrapped the edge of the cup. She inhaled half the contents and groaned.

In his visions of Danni groaning and calling him a god, the steam wouldn't have been coming off a cup of coffee. There would have been nakedness, and those hands fondling the cup would be fondling...

His brand-new pants turned uncomfortable, his pulse racing a path his body was in no position to finish. His hands were filled with vending machine snacks and drinks. And even if they weren't, he didn't think Danni would appreciate him rubbing one out while they watched the afternoon news.

He couldn't take his eyes off her as she tipped the cup back, getting every last drop. The new jeans hugged her legs and hips, and the T-shirt reminded him of everything he'd barely gotten to touch. He drank coffee, but not with the fervor she did. She'd always been a java junky.

"Do you want some more?" He offered her his cup and she took it.

"Are you sure? Don't you need the caffeine?"

He drew one of the Monster Energy drinks out from the crook of his arm. "I'm all set." It was his biggest vice. He ate well. He exercised. He took care of his body, except for this. He'd picked up the energy drink habit in college to get through long nights of coding assignments. Now he used it to get through long nights of coding. "Any word on the laptop?"

"I sent Leti a text, but she hasn't responded yet."

He would ask about the other partner, Maggie, but given the look Danni gave him the last time he'd made that suggestion, he figured that was a touchy subject. Something must have happened on their last call.

Danni didn't appear to want to talk about it. And Marek wasn't about to push.

"There's food." He dumped everything he'd bought onto the table. All the food groups were represented— salty chips, sugary candy, and dried meat. His arteries sputtered just thinking about it.

She drank down the second coffee, and selected a bag of chips and the other Monster from the pile on the table before sitting back down on the bed. "Thanks."

"Sure." He sat at the table, and took a Slim Jim.

Danni smiled as she slid a potato chip in her mouth. Salty crumbs lined her lips. Her tongue slid out to gather them in. He tried to stop watching, but her tongue roamed her lip, leaving behind a glaze. A kissable sheen that begged him to taste.

And he wanted a taste. But that would be stupid after

the way she'd reacted to him this morning. Who could blame her? He couldn't even share a bed with her without getting grabby.

"Can I ask you something?" Uh-oh. She sounded serious.

He was hoping she would pretend this morning hadn't happened, or at least they'd save the discussion for later. Much later. Maybe never. "Ask away."

"What happened with Jill?"

This wasn't where he thought the conversation was going, but he'd take it. "We divorced a couple years ago."

"You mentioned that." She took another chip out of the bag. "But why?"

It wasn't a secret he'd only married Jill because of the pregnancy. "She had something called vasa previa. It's rare. One day we were getting married and picking out baby clothes, the next we were burying our child. I don't know if you heard, but it was a son."

Her eyes crinkled in sympathy. "I didn't know."

He hadn't wanted a baby at that age. He definitely hadn't wanted a baby with Jill, but the idea of a family and a home was too much to resist. "He bled to death. Inside Jill. They tried to do a C-section, and they couldn't get him out fast enough. None of it helped. In the end, he just lay there. His skin was so cold. Barely skin. I touched him when they weren't looking."

He hadn't talked about this in years. Every time he thought of his son, he smelled the antiseptic. His chest ached. It was like he was back in that room, looking at the remnants of his heart in child form. "He never got a chance to play video games. I never got a chance to teach him how to code." His chest about tore open as a laugh shook his ribs, but there was no humor. "With my luck, he would've been a jock, wanting to play baseball or hockey, and I would've sat on the sidelines, hating the whole sports thing, freezing my ass off, loving my son. Cheering. But I didn't get that chance, and neither did he."

"You stayed married." It wasn't a question. He had.

"Yes."

"Why?"

"Marriage wasn't something to take lightly. Not in my family. My parents were married for twenty-six years when I got married. They were so proud. I never told them that the only reason I married Jill was because of the pregnancy. And after she lost the baby, it was so hard." It was the lowest point in his life. He'd lost his son, his parents were heartbroken, and Jill had been swallowed up by depression. He'd been alone, and all he'd wanted to do was call Danni.

And he couldn't.

"I'm so sorry. You could have called me. How many times were you there for me when my parents threw chicken salad at each other?"

He attempted a smile. Her parents were always entertaining. "They did like to throw things." Marek cleared his throat. "How are Bev and Stan doing?"

"Well, my dad flipped over my graduation cake because my mom told him the caterer was cheap. Then my mom dumped a bottle of red wine on his office couch when she found out I was leaving the Chicago Police Department to go into business with my friends."

"Why was she in his office?"

"She went there specifically to yell at him. Apparently, me being tired of the bureaucracy and political bullshit was all his fault."

This time, Marek's smile felt more real. "You have to admire her dedication."

"Admire wasn't the word I'd use. But things have been okay. Although I haven't done anything to provoke their ire lately." She glanced down at the crumple chip bag, and back up at him. "You should have called me. I would have been there."

"And say what? That after I left you for my ex we lost our son and my new wife was glued to our bed? For months, my parents couldn't be in the room with me without crying. What would have I said to you? Asked you to listen and then went back home to my wife?"

Danni winced, but looked him right in and the eyes and said, "Yes." She sounded like she really believed that would've worked.

"I couldn't do that to you." To himself. He wouldn't have wanted to let her go.

She stood, tossing the chip bag into the plastic garbage can in the corner before sitting in the chair across from him. Her hand settled over his. The warmth of her skin and the warmth in her gaze drifted through him. Just that touch gave him the strength to tell her the rest.

"After that, I started the company with Dave and Jalen, and Jill finished school. It worked for us. For a few years. We pretended. We pretended to love each other. Went through the motions until she just couldn't do it anymore." He'd been so alone back then. "She's remarried and happy. The guy's nice." He'd thrown himself into work. It was all he'd had. "And I have Obrona." But maybe not for long.

Her hand wrapped tighter around his. "We'll figure out who's doing this. You won't lose your company."

He didn't want to be such an open book, but he didn't

have the energy to fake it. Without Obrona, he had nothing. He dragged a breath from the black hole where his heart and lungs used to be. "I hope you're right."

"I am." She smiled, and dammit if he didn't want all the crap just to disappear. He wanted to keep looking at her lips and believe what she'd just said.

Except deep down, he knew this wasn't going to end well. Someone was going after him and his company. He still had one thing, though. He had his freedom.

Until they took that away too.

NINE

DANNI SAT NEXT TO MAREK, wishing she could take away his pain. But it didn't look like anything could help—except clearing his name. He couldn't lose his company. He'd be lost. And Danni couldn't let him be lost. No matter what might have happened between them. She still loved him.

Love was a strong word. She liked him, she'd loved him once, and that never really did go away. It never did when you truly loved someone.

She'd always wanted to know what happened after he'd let her go. She thought it would make her feel better. It didn't. Knowing he had been in pain didn't make her feel okay. It made her feel empty.

Strong fingers ran along her skin. It felt so good to have him close again. The emptiness almost felt full. Almost.

He looked so tired. Worn. He sighed and stretched out his legs under the table, bumping hers. She cringed as the past twenty-four hours came back one throbbing flash at a time.

"Oh, sorry." Marek drew his legs away. "It's time for your pain meds, isn't it?"

"I'm going to try to go without the pain meds."

"Why be a hero?"

"I need to be coherent when Leti calls."

"But she hasn't called yet." He picked up an amber medicine bottle and shook it at her like a maraca. "So why not take care of your health and your sanity till then?"

Danni glared at his outstretched hand, and he got the message because he put that bottle down and selected another one. "How about antibiotics? Are you going to try and go without?"

Smartass. "No." She smiled, and waited while he read the side of the bottle.

"One pill, every twelve hours." Marek shook one pill out and set it on the table. "Let me get you some water." He went into the bathroom and came back with a half-full glass of water. Danni took the pill, and Marek watched as she emptied the glass.

"Do you need more water?" He was so attentive and adorable. And so close.

The whole process should have been sweet. He was taking care of her. So gentle. He'd always been the first to jump in and help. Those strong hands could be so soft when she'd needed them to be.

She couldn't calm the electricity pulsing in her belly. Maybe that was why she wanted him to kiss her. And not just because his face was so close, and he looked so good.

He smelled good too.

She never thought she'd be this close to that face. Not again. Yet, here he was. And she wasn't making a move. Not that she would after the fiasco this morning. But maybe she could make it easier for him to make the move.

She leaned to the side, bringing her face closer to his. Hint. Hint.

His eyes darkened. Her pulse leaped. She leaned farther. Hint.

She bumped her leg against the table, and everything went red. "Son of a mother fuck buckets."

"Maybe you should take a pain pill?" His eyes were the size of saucers as he watched her swear a blue streak and grab at her leg.

Yes. Please God, yes now. She nodded because the words she wanted to say were stuck behind the pain-ball lodged in her throat. She hobbled over to the bed and lay flat. Took in a deep breath. One. Two. Three.

Slowly, the pain-ball disappeared, opening a path for another blue streak of creative profanity.

Marek came out of the bathroom—apparently, he'd gone in there—with a horse-sized pill and more water, and then disappeared back into the bathroom. Bottoms up. She took the pill and drank the water. The only sound in the room was the rush of the water coming from behind the door.

She lay back down and waited as the pain slowly receded. The throbbing stuck around, but the needles were losing their pulse. The lack of pain, of noise, enveloped her. Her eyes closed as the running water stopped, leaving only silence.

Beautiful silence.

They had too much to do. She shouldn't fall asleep. But her head dipped. Her body was weightless, and then there was darkness.

DANNI WOKE to the crinkle of paper. Did anyone use paper anymore? Her eyes roamed the room—hotel room. If she remembered correctly, Marek was somewhere in here. Bingo.

He sat at the table, flipping through a magazine, the late afternoon light from the open drape surrounding him like a halo. "Morning," he said, closing the magazine.

"No it's not," she grumbled.

He smiled. It was one of the most gorgeous things she'd ever seen. Gah! She was starting to sound like a Hallmark movie. Thankfully, she hadn't said that out loud. And she couldn't blame the drugs. Not really, anyway. She'd only taken one, and that had been—she checked the clock—a few hours ago.

The corners of his smile curved until his eyes positively sparkled. "I'm gorgeous?"

She'd said it out loud. Fantastic. "I meant the sun. You know, the halo around you. The sun, it's gorgeous." *Great save.*

"So I'm not gorgeous?" He somehow managed to smile wider.

Stop saying the word gorgeous. "You're okay. It's okay. I have to run to the washroom." Although she was going to skip the running.

She gimped from the bed to the bathroom, which almost took a millennium. They could have gone to the moon and back in the time it took her to cross to the comfort of the closed door. She stood in front of the mirror and sucked in a breath. She'd woke up so normally, then her mouth took everything to shit.

It was like that with Marek. She turned into a babbling idiot. Not all the time, just when she was too tired to fight off his sexy vibes.

Sexy vibes? There was something seriously wrong with her. And not just the bedhead that was currently her hair. She needed to relax. She needed to breathe. She needed her computer. Work always kept her grounded.

Maybe Leti had texted.

With a hand or two through her hair to tame the bedhead, she walked out into the room and straight to her phone.

"Everything gorgeous, or maybe just okay?" He was giving her shit.

She couldn't help her scowl. Although she probably could have helped the middle finger that flew up to greet him. But why?

He laughed. Deep and delicious. It didn't matter that it was at her expense. The sound went straight to her girl parts and pulsed.

He was so damn sexy. Even when all he did was laugh.

She grabbed her phone and checked the screen. Leti had texted an hour ago. *Shit.*

Fingers flying over the screen, she asked Leti to call her. She added an ASAP just to be safe, then watched the screen. Nothing. No dots for an incoming text. No ring for an incoming call.

"Are you going to watch that all night?"

"Maybe." If he didn't like it, she could show him that finger again.

Paper crinkled in his hand. "Nice outfit."

"Thanks." She looked down and regretted it. She was wearing underwear, but nothing else. When did that happen? And not just underwear. Harry Potter boy shorts. Boy shorts with a fucking wizard and owl on them.

So not sexy. She gave up on pulling the shirt down

over the golden snitch covering her snatch. Nerd level ten. Not that he didn't know she was a nerd, but some people grew out of it.

He probably didn't have Hobbit underwear or anything like that. He grew up. She apparently did not. Ugh.

She usually waited until the fifth or sixth date before she upped her nerd quotient. Thank goodness this wasn't a date. Although that didn't explain why she was practically naked. "Where did my pants go?"

"You tore them off while you were sleeping. I folded them and put them on top of your bag."

"Thanks." She dove for her pants, and then made the mistake of looking at him. Her pants hung in the air as she watched his eyes eat her up. And his lips. His tongue peeked out the side of his mouth and slowly slid along his lower lip.

Dear Moses.

Damn, those lips were her kryptonite. And her kryptonite had folded her jeans while she lay on the bed wearing boy shorts. It was sweet. Although the look he was giving her right now wasn't all that sweet. It was hot. He was looking at her like she was the last snitch on earth.

She wanted to cross the room and jump him. But she knew better—she didn't need a live replay of the rejection from this morning. Although her snitch was slow on the uptake.

Stop.

He was taking care of her. It was nice. Sweet. Kind. It made her feel all gooey inside. And she hadn't done gooey in a long time.

Her phone chirped. Good phone. This was what he did to her. And she knew she should hate it. She knew she should tell him to go to the other side of the room. She could put her own bandages on. But something kept her quiet. Probably looking at those damn lips.

Damn kryptonite.

DANNI'S PHONE CHIMED, and she checked the screen. A few keystrokes and she put it down. "Leti's bringing my computer, but it may take a bit. She's in the middle of some accounting thing." The cringe as she said the word *accounting* was adorable.

"Accounting thing?"

"Yep. That's the technical term." She huffed—probably at Marek's laugh—and picked up the phone. "Fiduciary audit for some bank. Blah. Blah. Whatever it is, it sounds unremarkably boring."

"So, do you normally help Leti with bank audits?"

"Not really. Thank God." She slipped on her pants and sat on the edge of the bed.

His eyes nearly teared up as Harry Potter disappeared from view. Those underwear were amazing. They'd be even better balled up on the bedroom floor.

New topic. Or maybe he needed to focus on the old topic. What was that? Finance. "So, not really? How do you help with bank audits, then?"

"Mostly setting up the FTP sites with the banks so we can transfer information securely. Every once in a while, she'll ask me to help with the data, but she generally spares me from that nightmare. Sometimes, I set up a backdoor access so she can analyze spending patterns." Which was just a nicer way of saying she hacked them.

"What about Maggie? How do you help her?"

"I manage the network, backdoor for information, and troubleshoot. If there's something to be done with the computer, I'm the one doing it." Danni's work was fascinating. It was the stuff they'd done back in college. It was edgy. And it made him respect the hell out of her. He walked over to the bed and sat down next to her. "So, you're a jack of all trades. Or a Danni-of-all-trades, as it were."

"Yeah." She smiled.

He was close, and he should pull away, but his body wasn't moving. He rested his hand behind her and leaned in. Waiting for her to tell him to go to hell.

"What about you? Besides owning a multimillion-dollar company, what do you do?"

Sometimes he wondered the same thing. "Jalen codes. Dave runs the day-to-day stuff. I sign shit and look pretty."

He tried to make it sound like a joke but, based on the look she gave him, he didn't think it worked. And it wasn't a joke. The company would do just fine without him. Hell, they were currently testing that theory, and it wasn't going to work in his favor.

"Really?" She was feeling sorry for him. He could see it in the pity-laced frown.

"Sometimes it feels like it." He added a laugh as he got off the bed. He needed distance—distance from that look and distance from the way he felt. Her gaze stripped him raw, like the rest of the world had beer goggles and she was the only one who saw the real him.

Her hand stopped him. "I'm sure you do more than that."

He wished. "In the beginning, I helped Jalen code while Dave got the business off the ground. Now Jalen has a whole team, and we have enough staff to run the place." He sank back onto the bed. It was so easy to talk to her. Maybe because he already felt like she could see him to the bone. It was easy just to let it all out. "If I had been smart, I would have found my own specialty. But I was so busy doing it all, everyone just sort of passed me by."

She slowly slipped her fingers through his. "So what you're saying is that you're a Marek-of-all-trades."

He laughed. She would see it that way. "There's a difference. You are single-handedly running IT at your company." His thumb traced along the soft skin of the side of her hand. Their fingers curled together. "I'm not running anything."

"I don't believe that. You understand the restrictions on the developers, the regulations, the marketability of your product. You see the big picture that no one else can see."

"You do all of that, and everything else."

"Yes, but I ignore most of that." She smiled. "That's *my* job."

He'd missed this. Having someone to talk to. No, not someone. Danni. She got it. She understood what it was like. She might not run a company, but she came damn near close with everything she did at Busted. She was the glue.

Her fingers left his and ran along his arm. "Jalen and Dave would be lost without you." It was like she knew what he was thinking.

"What about you?"

"What about me?" Her hand moved back and forth on his biceps.

"Are you lost without me?"

"I was. For a long time."

"I still am." He hadn't admitted that out loud in a long time. Back when Dave was telling him he'd be better off without her. But he hadn't been better off. "I *am* lost without you."

He put it all out there in five words. If he'd thought he was bare before, he'd just handed her a magnifying glass.

The tears lining her eyes told him she didn't like what she saw. And could he blame her? She was an old friend helping him, and he was bringing up history. History that neither one of them wanted to face. He should walk away now before she ran screaming from the room.

She'd taken a chance on him once. Why in the hell would she take that chance again?

He needed to get away. Maybe if he ran fast enough, he could use the centripetal force to keep his heart in his chest instead of flying out through the cracks splitting him open.

TEN

DANNI GRABBED his arm and kept him on the bed. "Where are you going?"

He didn't say anything as he sat down next to her, just looked at her with those big sad eyes. She was here. He needed her. Why was he sad about that?

She traced the lines along the side of his frown. God, she missed him. His face. His body. She missed having someone to talk to, someone who...who just understood.

He closed his eyes when she rested her palm against his stubbled chin. A day and a half worth of beard covered his face, and she liked it. Although she liked his face without it too.

She wanted to pull him close. Kiss him, but she didn't want him to regret it. Not again.

His right hand found the nape of her neck. Rough skin against soft. His hand big and warm curving around her as he leaned in.

His lips hovered above hers. "May I?"

She should say no. They needed to talk before they

did anything crazy like getting sucked into lips and teeth and tongues—dear God.

His tongue slid along his bottom lip. Her tongue mimicked the movement, and she could swear she could taste him on her lips. But she couldn't. Not yet. And she wanted to. Screw the talking. Screw the crazy.

This was what she wanted. She wanted him. She closed the distance, her lips bumping against his. Hot, urgent kisses. Hands feeling arms, abs, everything. Her mouth wrestling with his, his tongue invading and crashing with hers. Nothing gentle. All want and frenzy.

Fire ignited every nerve. Her core throbbed. Her body needed to be touched. To be explored by him. His hand moved down her throat and skimmed her breasts. Slowly moving lower, until his hand cupped her...

Somebody thumped a fist on the door. "Danni," a voice said from the hallway.

The hand was gone. The lips were gone. Cold engulfed her as her body thrummed like a well-played guitar. But the notes were incomplete.

"Danni, are you in there?"

"I take it that's Leti." Marek sat sideways and rested his elbows on his knees. Breath sped in and out of his lungs.

Yeah, she could understand that. "I'll get the door." She stood and took one of those speeding breaths. In and out. In clarifying breath. Out blue balls.

Another knock rocked the door. "Danni, are you okay?"

Oy vey, Leti was about to have a panic attack. Danni could hear it in her voice. "I'm coming."

Danni checked through the peephole before she cracked the door open. She wasn't sure if she should introduce Leti to Marek. He was a wanted man, and Leti wasn't exactly someone who lived on the wrong side of the law. That was Danni's job. "Hey, Leti." Danni rested her head on the doorframe.

"Hi." Leti narrowed her eyes and craned her neck to look past Danni.

"Thank you so much for bringing me this." Danni tried for the laptop bag on Leti's shoulder, but Leti just stood there.

"Can I come in?" Leti held tight to the laptop bag. "Or are you here against your will?"

Danni shook her head and held back a laugh. Against her will. Like Marek would ever do that.

She sighed. There was no way around this. Danni stepped out of the way and Leti walked in the room. As usual, Leti towered over Danni—mostly because of the demon heels she wore.

"Why are you limping?" Leti asked, sounding horrified.

"It's fine. The bullet just grazed the skin."

"Bullet? What bullet?"

For cripes sake. Didn't her partners ever talk? Maggie knew more about the bullet then even Danni wanted her to know. "It was just a graze."

"You were shot?" Leti's eyes widened to CD proportions.

"Grazed." Danni turned to Marek, and her eyes were met with gorgeous skin. His muscles bunched as he sat on the bed. Nearly naked. Although Danni loved the view, she didn't think Leti would appreciate it.

"By whom?" Leti's voice rose. Okay, so maybe street cred was overrated.

"By the people chasing Marek." Danni tossed him his T-shirt. "Leti, this is Marek. Marek, Leti."

Marek pulled the shirt on and stood up. "Nice to meet you. I've heard a lot about you." He held out his hand. His hair had finger tracks. His lips looked puffy and thoroughly kissed. And Danni would take bets that she probably didn't look that much better. Not to mention Marek's missing shirt. It had all the makings of a conjugal visit without the actual conjugal visit.

Leti looked him up and down as if he were Satan's drug dealer before she took his hand. "I've heard nothing about you." And her tone said she didn't want to hear anything.

"He's a friend from college," Danni told her. "Thanks for bringing the laptop." She held out her hand again.

"I think we should talk." Leti swung the bag around behind her back and stared at Danni. She had this gift. She was like Danni's mother, with those beady penetrating eyes guaranteed to make a teenager squirm. Thank goodness Danni wasn't a teen any longer.

"Okay, talk." Danni's blood boiled. Her computer was being held hostage by a Latina with judgy eyes.

"Alone."

"Whatever you have to say, you can say in front of Marek."

"I'm going to run to the ice machine." Marek picked up the plastic ice bucket and started toward the door.

"You can stay," Danni said.

"I'd rather not." He paused at the door and nodded at Leti. "It was nice to meet you."

Leti snorted after the door swung shut.

"What?" Had Danni mentioned the judgy Latina thing?

"I expect this from Maggie, but you?"

"Expect what?"

"You following around a man—a wanted man. I watch TV. I've seen him. And you're making out with him."

"Not that it's your business who I make out with, but he's my friend."

"With benefits?" Leti smirked. "And will these benefits keep going once he's in prison?"

"He didn't do anything. It's a big misunderstanding."

"How can you know? Have you even seen him since college? People change, and rarely for the better."

"I know him. If you're just here to give me shit, then leave. I don't need your judgment." Danni sat down at the table. If Leti wouldn't hand over the laptop, she'd buy a new one. She would need to recreate some of the programs, but she'd done it before.

Leti sighed. "I'm not judging you."

"Could've fooled me."

A small smile landed on Leti's face. "Okay, I am. But I'm worried about you. This guy shows up out of nowhere, and you disappear." She waved a hand. "You leave Busted, turning off the phones and scaring Jessi. You don't show up at the office the next day and then you text, looking for your laptop like it's life or death. But, oh yeah, it might be because you were shot. Oh, so sorry, *grazed*."

Sounded familiar. Leti and Maggie were complaining from the same handbook. Even if they hadn't fully discussed everything.

"Are you done?"

Leti stared at her for a second and blurted, "And you hung up on Maggie."

"I knew that wouldn't go over well."

Leti's chest shook as she laughed. She sat in the chair across from Danni. "Not well? Oh, my good-granola. Not well doesn't even scratch the surface. She used swear-words in combinations I've never heard before. She tried to put an APB out on you, but Chase calmed her down with stories of misappropriation of resources. And his potential firing for said misappropriation. She's worried."

"I'm fine." Danni rested her hand on Leti's. "I've been friends with Marek for years. I know what he's capable of. I know what I'm capable of. I can help him. Wouldn't you help a friend in trouble?"

"Of course, but..."

"There are no buts. I need to follow this through and help him. It's what I'd do for you or Maggie or Jessi."

Leti squeezed her hand. "Are you sure this guy's okay? Maybe he's changed."

"Not that much." Danni knew it deep in her bones. No man could change so much that they would destroy the one thing they built. Well, some men might, but not him. "I need you to trust me. Tell Maggie to give me a little time to work this thing out."

"I'll try. I think she only speaks in swear words now, so it might be hard." Considering Leti's aversion to swearing, that could be an interesting conversation. Leti stood. "Is there anything I can do to help?"

"Just keep Maggie calm. Let me handle clearing his name."

Leti set the laptop bag on the table and stood up. "I'll do what I can. "Be careful. I can't lose another friend to a pretty face."

Danni didn't know the whole story, but from what she could get out of Maggie, Leti's best friend ran off with Leti's husband. And Leti had never forgiven her. Then, a couple years later, the friend died from cancer. Leti never got over that, either.

"I'll be careful," Danni assured her.

Leti hugged her. "Call me if you need anything," she said as she walked out the door.

"Of course." Danni let out a relieved breath and sat back down. It was time to clear Marek's name.

She booted up the laptop and found the jump drive. She had some work to do. Then this could be over, and she could go back to the office. It would be good to have all this behind her. But Leti had brought up a good point about the benefits. Would the benefits continue when this was all over? What about the friendship?

She'd lost him once, and it about destroyed her. She'd never survive losing him again.

MAREK STOOD at the end of the hall, holding a bucket of ice. He could have just walked out and skipped the ice, but he felt like an idiot just standing there. He had to do something.

Danni's friend had been pissed, so the conversation going on in there could take a while. Not that he blamed her for being mad, worried, scared. He could admit he'd felt all of those things for Danni before, too. And the fact that his bullshit was what was putting her in harm's way was killing him.

She deserved better than this. She deserved better than him. Always had.

The door swung open, and Leti came down the hall. When she saw him, she stopped.

"I got ice." Did he really just say that?

She smirked. "Did you carry a watermelon?" Her smile held a hint of humor, but mostly contempt.

Still didn't explain why he'd be carrying a watermelon. "What?"

"*Dirty Dancing* reference, sorry." Leti sighed. "Just, uh, keep her safe. Take care of her. And if she gets hurt, I'll find you. This is Chicago, there are a lot of places to hide the body."

The glint in her eye said she wasn't joking. She'd apparently watched *The Godfather* one too many times—and *Dirty Dancing*. Maybe she should have focused on the movie without the bodies sleeping with fishes.

"Nice to meet you." Her high heels thumped on the carpet as she walked toward the elevator.

"You too."

She looked over her shoulder and smiled. He could admit the woman was gorgeous. Not like Danni was gorgeous. Different. Not bad, but not the type he would normally go for. He liked Danni. He liked her type.

He knocked on the door to their room. In his urgency to escape the body-hider, he hadn't grabbed a key.

"You're back." After Danni let him in, she sat down at the table with her open laptop and tapped at the keyboard.

"You're working already."

She smiled. He swore his heart stopped, but since he was still alive, that couldn't be true.

"I'm analyzing the data we found at Obrona."

"Is there anything I can do?"

She pushed back from the table. "Not really. Not until the program finishes running."

"So we're waiting."

"We're waiting." She crossed her legs, her jeans

hugging all that smooth skin. And he knew it was smooth. He'd had his hands all over her just an hour ago.

"What are we doing while we wait?"

"Whatever you want?" She licked her lips.

He wanted to do that too. He wanted to lick her lips, her thighs, her...

She stood up and raised the bottom of her T-shirt. Her fingertips played over the revealed patch of skin, showing just enough to see the bottom of a red lacy bra. She gathered the shirt in one hand before lifting the cotton over her head. Gorgeous taupe skin greeted him. The barest of mesh covered her breasts. "Why don't we start where we left off?"

She pulled down her jeans and kicked them off to the side. Her fingers played at the elastic of her boy shorts. Slowly. Painfully slow, she hooked her thumbs in the material and then pulled them down. The cotton landed at her feet, and then there was nothing but Danni and all of her gorgeous skin.

His pants tightened as she stood there. Practically naked. Waiting for him.

He moved closer.

"Wait." She stepped back, palm out. "I showed you mine. You show me yours."

Wait? He didn't want to wait. He slid his fingers through hers, drawing her hand up to his mouth. He rubbed the satin skin against his lips. An evil trick he learned when they were together. She never could resist his mouth.

Her eyes hooded as her tongue slid along her bottom lip. *Damn.* He forgot. He never could resist her mouth, either.

Heat zipped through his veins. He needed to kiss her. He needed *her*.

Before he could lean down and claim her, her hand found his shoulder and slid down his chest. Lower and lower it went until she reached...

Nothing. Well, there was something to reach, but she pulled her hand away. His body pulsed, but without her, it was cold and lonely, nearing pain.

She ran a hand up her hips. Slowly. Those fingers slid back down, stopping between her legs. "Lose the shirt."

Seriously? He thought about ripping the thing off Hulk-style, but this was Danni. Not a wham-bam kind of woman. He'd been waiting—more like hoping—for this moment for years He wasn't going to rush it.

He would not rush her. He lifted his T-shirt with one hand, the other one rubbing down along his abs and unsnapping the button on his jeans.

She stared at the button. Her lips parted, and he swore he heard the tiniest sharp inhale of air. It felt so good to know she was feeling the same way he did. And from the heat in her eyes when he lifted the shirt over his head—yeah, she was feeling it too. "Do you like what you see?"

He wanted to hear the words. He wanted to know for sure. He needed to know he wasn't alone in this.

She smiled and moved closer. Her hand found his zipper. Her mouth found his. "Yes."

One word. That was all it took to set his blood to boil. His body burned for her. He needed her. He lifted her and laid her down on the bed.

It was time for him to explore every curve of her body —his hand slid along the satiny skin of her breast—inch by inch.

ELEVEN

MAREK SWORE HE HEARD CLICKING. He couldn't even sleep without dreaming about the clacking keyboard. His eyes popped open, and the clacking stopped.

It must be night still because the sun wasn't sneaking through the cracks in the drapes. The rest of the room was dark. The only light came from the open laptop on the table. The clacking began again.

"Did you sleep at all?" Marek asked.

"Sleep is overrated." Danni's fingers flew over the laptop keyboard, and she frowned at the screen. How many times had he sat in front of a computer in the same state? Tired but unable to sleep.

Although he would have thought with all the exercise they'd shared, she would have slept a little bit. "Come back to bed." Thinking about last night made him want to revisit it.

"I just need to figure this out. The way they code—it's really strange. I don't know whether to say they're a complete idiot or a mad genius. Either way, I'll find them. I'm better."

"Naturally." He couldn't keep the smile out of his voice, even though his body was disappointed. Recreating last night didn't seem to be on the agenda. But watching her work was fun too. She was always an amazing programmer—and she knew it. But she was also competitive. She had to be.

Back in school, she'd been the only female in a class of thirty, unless her friend Cherise was in the class. She'd always had something to prove. Which was probably why she was up in the middle of the night, tracking this programmer down. She had to be better than whoever compiled this code. And she was.

He had faith in her.

"I found some information. They disabled the server logs first, then launched the attack. Remember how Professor Blake was all about the server log? And the IP address. I did some research, and they used a port sweep in Germany. But I can't find the origin of the original attack."

"Dave and Jalen just went to Germany to talk to MetalWolke."

"Your computer security company?" The computer dinged. "Hmm..."

Hmm? What hmm? The whole Germany thing was a coincidence. It was a huge country. "Yes. It's probably a coincidence."

"Probably." Her tone said she didn't agree at all. "Hmm..."

"What hmm...?"

"Oh, nothing." She poked at the keyboard and shook her head.

She was driving him crazy. Between the head-shaking and the hmms and the "nothing," he was ready to scream. "I need to get some work done."

"Okay." She nodded, still staring at the screen. Not getting it.

He needed to be more specific. "I need the computer so I can send a few emails."

She shook her head. "Use your phone. I'm working on something."

"So am I." He got out of bed and crossed over to the table. Loomed over her. Maybe she'd let him use the thing for a half hour if he moved into her space. God, she smelled amazing. Not her usual vanilla, but something else—maybe hotel shampoo. "Did you take a shower?"

"Yes." She didn't look up. She didn't seem to care that he stood over her. She didn't seem to care at all—not good, not bad. Good thing his self-esteem was strong, or he might take offense. Especially since standing this close was setting his blood on fire.

"Hmm..." Her tongue slid along her top lip as she leaned into the computer.

Fuck. She tilted her head, showing the soft skin of her long neck. Skin that begged to be kissed, to be touched. Before he could stop himself, his hand slid down the side of her neck. Soft skin met his rough hands. Maybe if he got close enough, they could revisit the whole revisiting thing.

"What are you doing?" The words were gruff, but the quick intake of air as her eyelids fluttered shut told him she was enjoying his touch as much as he was enjoying touching.

"Getting you back to bed."

She looked at the computer, and he leaned down. His

lips found the place on the side of her neck that was obviously attached to her core. The happy path that always led to her squirming in her chair back when they were dating.

And it didn't disappoint. She shifted in the seat. Her eyes closed, and her breath stuttered in her chest. Her hands fisted on the armrests as a groan flew from her lips.

Yeah, that's it. He moved his arms around her and whispered along her skin. "Come to bed, sweetheart."

She nodded.

And then they did a whole lot of that revisiting.

DANNI WOKE to the tapping of keyboard keys. It felt too early for all the clicking. "What time is it?" She pulled the comforter to her chin. It was feathery and soft and warm.

"Ten." Marek's voice was deep but distracted.

She'd slept eight hours. She never got eight hours of sleep. She should do it more often. Maybe if she had a blanket like this, she'd stay in bed longer. "Why didn't you wake me?"

"You needed to sleep."

"And you didn't?" She threw the thick comforter off her body, and the cold tickled her skin. Naked. She was naked. And Marek was not.

He'd put on jeans and a T-shirt. Which made sense since he was sitting in front of the laptop. Her laptop. The one she'd been working at in the middle of the night. The one he'd wanted to use to send emails.

"Are you working?" she asked.

"Yes." His eyes focused on her. They were cloudy and hungry. If looks could talk... Well, the words would be X-rated. It felt nice. It had been a while since someone looked at her like a bag of Garrett Popcorn.

She dragged the blanket up over her body. "So, are you enjoying my computer?"

"Absolutely. She's a nice piece of apps."

"Anything new?"

"Not much yet. I sent a few feelers out. Still waiting to hear back." His attention moved back to the screen. Apparently, her body wasn't nearly as exciting when it was covered in an inch of feathers. Which wasn't surprising. He tended to like her in her birthday suit. Although he seemed to like her just fine last night when he was begging to use her computer.

Maybe if she rubbed along his back, she could lure him away from the table, and she could jump on... sounded familiar. "Did you sleep with me to get to my computer?"

That got his attention. "I'm hurt. Would I do that?"

She got out of bed, dragging the comforter with her. "You would." And he totally would. He once bribed her with donuts to get her to skip class. Although to be fair, she would've skipped that class without the donuts. Anything to get out of Advanced English.

"Trust me. I don't need motivation to want you in my arms."

"No motivation at all, huh?" She came around the end of the bed, and let the blanket fall to her waist.

"That would do it." He stood and slowly moved toward her.

The heat in his eyes almost stopped her. But what

was the saying? All's fair in love and war. Danni edged back toward the bed. All she had to do was get around him and the empty chair was hers. She inched forward.

Marek grabbed the blanket. He was so close and smelled so good. His body angled toward her. One more second and his mouth would be on hers. One more second and she'd fold like a polymorphic function.

Marek tugged and she spun, leaving the blanket in his hand. She immediately claimed the chair.

After opening her email, she checked the open tabs. Email. Tor query. Marek had been looking through the code. Same as she'd done early this morning. "Did you find anything new?"

Marek didn't say anything. He just seemed to stare, blanket in his hand.

She looked over at him. He stared back, blanket in hand. "What?" she asked.

"You're naked."

"True." She sifted through her email. Someone had to have some sort of information and gotten back to her. "I am naked."

"And you're all the way over there." He actually seemed upset.

She didn't want to upset him. "I am. We need to find this person so you can get your company back. So we don't have to hide." So she could fix what she'd done. She wanted to fix it before he lost everything. He'd never forgive her for stealing his code, and she'd never forgive herself.

"I get that." He tossed the blanket on the bed and sighed. "I just thought we would wait for our contacts to get in touch, and get to know each other again. You know, talk. I've missed that."

The lump in her throat grew. She'd missed that too. She wanted to get to know him again. Be with him mind, body, and soul like they'd been in the past. She wanted that again. She wanted him.

She stood, and walked over to him. Lifted her hand to his biceps. His heat. His strength. It had been everything to her. And it still was.

He patted her hand and dove for the table. "Maybe we could braid each other's hair, too." He smiled as he picked up the laptop before plopping back on the bed. He set the computer on his lap and laughed. "Two can play at that game."

"That was cold." And she felt that cold all the way to her core.

"Come here." He smiled and patted the bed. "I don't ever want you to feel cold."

Danni crossed her arms. She wasn't going anywhere near him and his laptop-stealing ways. Jerk.

Marek set the laptop on the mattress and crept across the bed. He pulled her down as he fell back, and her arm wrapped around him. It was instinctual, but who wanted to cuddle with someone so jackassy?

Even though it was against her will—instinct and all—she couldn't seem to pull away. His body was still warm, still strong. Her cheeks flushed. She missed this.

He handed her the laptop, and his smile was gone. "We're in this together. We need to work together. We need to share."

"I'm not good at sharing." And she wasn't.

He laughed. "I know. But we need to. It's you and me."

"Against the world." She smiled. It was so easy getting back into it. He knew her. He wasn't surprised by her idiosyncrasies. He didn't expect her to be someone she wasn't.

He rested his lips on hers. "I'm going to take a quick shower, sweetheart. Keep an eye on my email."

Sweetheart. He'd called her that last night, but today she was coherent enough to revel in it. Her body reacted like a pervert at a porn convention. She never thought she'd be the type of woman who liked cheesy pet names, but somehow when he said it, her knees and other parts of her anatomy went squishy.

The splatter of water came from the bathroom. Visions of Marek taking a shower danced in her belly like Gene Kelly. Her feet angled off the bed, turning toward the bathroom. She could use a shower. She took one earlier, but there was no such thing as over-showering. Right?

Maybe he wanted to be alone. A few hours of phenomenal sex didn't mean he wanted to share the soap. The water hit a lower octave as the shower curtain rumbled on the track. He was underneath the spray. And she was out here thinking about the shower she *needed*.

To join him or not to join him, that was the question. The noble thing to do would be to join him. Water conservation and all.

Before she could change her mind, she jumped from the bed and slid into the steam-filled bathroom. Through the translucent shower curtain, she could just make out a very wet and very naked Marek rubbing his hand down the front of his body.

She pushed the plastic out of the way.

His fingers slid through wet, dark hair. "Took you long enough."

She smiled and replaced his fingers with hers.

God bless water conservation.

TWELVE

DANNI SCROLLED through the results on her phone and sighed. There were a million pizza places in Evanston. All of them claiming to be the best. This one won this award. That one won that award. If she could find one that said *No stupid awards, just really good pizza,* she'd jump at it.

But so far, none had met that particular requirement, so she sighed, scrolled, and tapped. "We're getting Giordano's."

"Deep dish?" Marek sat at the computer instant messaging with one of his contacts. They'd been working on the code for the past hour, which meant they were both clothed. That wouldn't be so disappointing if they'd actually found something.

"Of course deep dish." If you were going to eat at Giordano's, might as well get the good stuff. "Green peppers and mushrooms?"

He smiled. "You remember."

"Like I could forget fungus pizza." She clicked the

order button and selected veg and fungus for Marek's half of their pizza. Pineapple, sausage, and bacon for her half.

"Fungus is better than fruit. Fruit does not belong on pizza." He remembered how she liked her pizza. A fuzzy, happy feeling warmed her chest.

She sniffed. "You're just jealous because my side of the pizza balances the sweet of the pineapple with the salty of the meat. It's a perfect combination."

"Perfect combination of gross."

Submitting the order, she laid the phone next to her leg on the bed. "Well, if I like gross then I guess that makes you..."

His eyelids lowered, and his mouth curved a little. "Did you want to finish that statement?" He wanted her to finish it. He wanted to pounce.

"I wasn't saying you were gross. You said it. I can't be held responsible for conclusions based on the transitive property of equality."

"The transitive property of equality, huh?" He let out a low chuckle. The pouncing cat was gone, all that was left was amusement.

"If I like pineapple pizza and pineapple pizza is gross, then I like gross. I like you; therefore, you're gross. You said it, not me."

"Your theory is wildly distorted."

A giggle vibrated in her chest. This was the Marek she missed. He made her laugh, and he pushed her to up her game.

Her phone buzzed. Probably the pizza place. "Maybe they ran out of fungus." She clicked without looking. "Hello."

"Danni? Are you okay?" Maggie sounded frantic.

Again. *Oy vey*, this woman was driving Danni nuts. "Are you still with *him*?"

The disdain with which Maggie said *him* was not lost on Danni. Leti must not have reported back happy thoughts.

"This is Danni. I'm okay. And I'm not sure who 'him' is, but if you mean Marek, then yes."

"Danni, this is serious. It's all over the news."

Great. What now? "What's all over the news?"

"His partner, Dave, was shot."

Wait. "What? Is he okay?"

"Last night. Dave's in critical condition. They're saying Marek did it."

"He couldn't have done it. He was in bed with me."

Silence. Judgy, critical silence. Danni checked her chest to see if she had a scarlet letter anywhere.

"They're saying he's armed and dangerous. You need to go to the cops."

Danni shook her head, not that Maggie could see it. "He's not, Maggie."

"No offense, but your judgment in this is distorted. The cops can help."

"I don't trust them." Danni hadn't trusted the cops before she worked at the police station. Working there only proved she was right. Not that they were all bad. Most were fine, upstanding people who wanted to do good. But that sliver of shitty cops made it hard to trust anyone. And besides all that, she'd know if Marek had a gun, which Maggie would know if she stopped freaking out for two seconds.

"You trust Chase. He can help."

"No, *you* trust Chase."

"We'll help you." Maggie was on the verge of begging. "We'll make sure Marek is heard."

"They're after him. They've already shot at him twice. I can't put him in a cage where he'll be a sitting duck."

"He'll be in the jail surrounded by cops. You can't get any safer than that."

"Tell that to Poussey."

"Who?"

"*Orange is the New Black*. She got smothered by a cop."

"You're talking about a TV show? This is real life. He's dangerous. And if he's not, he's a thief. He destroyed these people's lives. One of the women whose pictures were stolen was fired. A school teacher lost her job because of what he did."

"It's awful for them, but he's a victim here, too."

"And you're so sure about that?"

"I'm sure he's a victim. Are you sure he's not?"

"I don't know him." Maggie sighed. "But I do know that you're with him and not protected. You should have come with me to learn self-defense or to learn how to shoot..."

"Maggie, I do know him. And what would change if I had learned how to shoot? I don't have a gun."

"But he—"

"Doesn't have one either. I know."

"Danni, this isn't putting us in a good position. I know you're not thinking about yourself right now. And that's admirable. But think about Busted. We work really closely with law enforcement, and our clients need to trust us."

That sentence felt ominous.

"We can't be associated with someone performing illegal activities," Maggie said. "It scares off the clients."

What a load of crap. They represented and found information on plenty of people engaged in illegal activity. But if that's the way Maggie wanted to play it? "Then I quit. I wouldn't want to hold back the company we built." Saying the words was a knife in her chest. She loved her job. She loved Maggie. Normally. Right now, Danni had this incredible urge to dropkick her best friend.

Maggie sighed. "That's not what I'm saying."

"What are you saying?"

Maggie took sighing to a whole new level. The air seemed to stream out for days. "I'm just worried. You're not looking at this, at him, clearly."

"Look, I'm sure Leti told you what's going on. I'm trying to find the person who really did this. The real criminals here. That is what we do. Right?" Danni didn't wait for her to answer. "So, trust me, and let me help my friend. Great talking to you again, Maggie."

Danni hung up the phone and flipped on airplane mode. She was done with the judgy calls.

"That didn't sound good."

"Maggie." That was all she needed to say.

Dave. The purpose of the call flooded back. Shit. Marek must not have heard about it, or he'd be more concerned or sad or something. "Are you done over there?"

"I can be, sweetheart." He rubbed his hands together. "What did you have in mind?"

"Nothing. I just need your undivided attention."

The playful grin on his face dimmed as he took in the look on her face. "What's wrong?"

"Dave was shot last night. He's in critical condition."

Marek stared at her as if she were talking another language, eyes narrowed and body still. "Who did it?"

"They don't know." She slid off the bed and knelt in front of him. "They're saying on the news that you did it. That you're armed and dangerous."

The look of horror on his face would be funny if this whole situation weren't so messed up. "So they're not looking into this at all?"

"Well, they're looking into you."

He nodded. Staring off at nothing. He must be in some sort of shock—complete life-fucked kind of shock.

She laid her hand on his, sliding his fingers between hers. "We'll get through this together. I'm here." And they would. They would get through this as long as they had each other.

MAREK STARED at their joined hands. He should pull away. He should get as far away from her as possible, but he was a selfish prick. Tears bit his eyes when he thought about Dave. Whoever they were couldn't get to Marek, and now they went after Marek's friends, his family. And Dave was his family.

The skin at the back of his neck itched until it didn't fit the area around his shoulders. Muscles bunched and twisted until he couldn't breathe.

Pretending that Danni was safe here with him at the hotel was ridiculous. She wasn't safe. No one was safe. Whoever they were, they weren't going away.

Danni squeezed his hand. "We'll get through this together. I'm here."

No. She wouldn't get through this. Not with him. He was the problem, not the solution. He pulled his hand away and stood up. "You've done enough. I think I need to handle this on my own." He went to the dresser and got his wallet. He didn't have a lot of money left, but he'd get by. Luckily, Danni had used her credit card for the room the past few nights. That had helped.

"Why?"

"It's my fight, not yours."

"You're just going to leave." The disappointment in her tone was heartbreaking.

"Yeah."

"Where are you going to go?"

"I don't know, but I can't stay here." He didn't have time to answer all the questions. He needed to be as far away as possible when the shit splattered against the fan. But he could tell she wouldn't let up. She never did. Tenacious was synonymous with Danni.

Decision time. He could keep going as they were, or he had to make her leave. He'd have to push. Turn off the charm. He slid his T-shirt over his head as he stared at the door. He couldn't look at her. If he did, he'd crack. And he couldn't crack. Her safety was at stake.

"So you're just going to ignore me?"

Yes.

"Dammit, Marek, talk to me. How are you going to get away?"

"What's with the third degree?"

"Because you're not thinking."

"I'm not thinking. Really?" He slammed his wallet into the pocket of his jeans. "Are you thinking? Dave is in critical condition. They couldn't find me, so they went after Dave. Who knows what they'll do next? But more than likely they'll find me. And they'll kill me and anyone else in their path."

"That's why we should—"

"There is no we. There is me who is in deep shit and you who should be running far away." He sighed. "Let me ask you something. The conversation with Maggie. What did she want? Why were you both yelling?"

"We weren't yelling."

"I could hear her through the phone."

"She thinks you should turn yourself in. But she doesn't know you, and she's just worried about me."

"She's right."

"But if you turn yourself in, you'll be a sitting duck."

"She's wrong about that. I can't turn myself in, but I shouldn't be dragging you down with me. She *should be* worried about you."

"So you're just going to bail on me."

"I'm not bailing. I'm going to find out who's behind this, and when it's all clear, I'll find you."

"Unless they kill you." The fear in her eyes was too much to bear.

He wanted to touch her, comfort her. "I won't let them. I won't let them hurt me."

"Then I can stay with you and help. If you won't let them, you're not in danger."

"Danni..."

She scowled. "Don't 'Danni' me..."

A loud thump hit the door. "Police Department. Open the door."

Marek froze, his eyes locking with Danni's. Neither of them moved—like maybe if they didn't move, the cops would go away. Marek wasn't sure he could move even if he wanted to. And he didn't want to.

The keypad on the door beeped and the door flew open. It all happened so fast. Too fast. There wasn't anything he could do to stop it. Cops in riot gear swarmed into the room. "Let me see your hands!"

"We're unarmed." Marek pushed Danni behind him and lifted his hands.

"Get down on the floor." The officer pointed his gun toward the floor as he shouted the order. There was no question in his voice. There was no reasoning.

So why Marek yelled into the rug, "She has nothing to do with this," he had no idea. And from the way they were pushing Danni down, they didn't care.

"Don't move," the female cop with her knee on Danni's back yelled.

"She has nothing to do with this." A knee dug in his spine as they wrenched his arms behind his back. Pain spiraled down his wrists and didn't stop until his shoulders, which were jacked so far back he was amazed they were still in their sockets. His breath sputtered. His face was plastered to the carpet, his chest pressed between the floor and a hard ass.

He bucked, trying to remove the boulder on his lungs. It fucking hurt. And if they were hurting him, they were hurting Danni. All the pain in the world couldn't get that out of his head.

He sagged against the carpet. He wasn't making it better by fighting them. He was making it worse. For him and for her. "Let her go. It's not her fault."

"Shut up," someone said. Probably Hard Ass, but it could have been anyone. The room was crawling with cops. He could hear their boots scuffing the floor and drawers opening. Not that there was a lot of contents of said drawers to search.

Danni groaned. "He's not fighting back. Stop it."

Dammit. He should never have involved her. This was all his fault. The weight on his back disappeared. His chest filled like a crunchy balloon.

The room tilted as hands wrapped around his forearms, pulling him to his feet. People in blue uniforms swarmed around him. Men in SWAT attire stood to either side of him and surrounded Danni as she sat on the chair, arms behind her back.

He couldn't tear his eyes away from her. She wasn't crying. But dammit if it didn't look like she was about to. He should have put some distance between them. He shouldn't have waited.

He always knew they'd find him. He just didn't think it would be so quickly.

"Let's go, Skala." Hard Ass pushed on Marek's back, shoving him out into the hall and all the way to the elevator. They passed people wearing everything from swimsuits to business suits. All of them looked at Marek like he was trash. And he was.

There was no innocent until proven guilty. In everyone's eyes, he was guilty. Hell, half of these people probably didn't even know what he was guilty of. Yet they were so willing to judge.

He walked past the front desk. The clerk didn't hide the scowl. No one hid their disgust. He had been so worried about the guys that wanted to shoot him. Fuck. Maybe he shouldn't have worried. Because living with this was a hell of lot worse.

THIRTEEN

HOW THE HELL did they find us? That thought ran on a loop in Danni's head. Watching him flop around and get his ass beat by the police had not been pleasant. Now Marek was gone, and she couldn't see what the hell they were doing to him.

Thankfully, he'd calmed down, and she hoped he would stay that way. Freaking out wasn't going to get him released any faster. And she needed that to happen right away. She needed to make sure he was safe, out of the cell where anyone could get him.

They needed to play nice and get him the hell out before someone realized where he was. Not that she could think about that now. If she actually thought about the danger he was in, she might get sick.

She was helpless. Here alone. Arms pinned behind her back.

When the cops dragged Marek out of the room, she'd wanted to jump up and stop them. Explain. But the look on the cops' faces told her anything she said or did would just make it worse.

A short cop with a blond ponytail and black tactical gear stood in front of Danni. She was five-foot-nothing, but when it had been Danni against this girl, she'd kicked Danni's ass.

They were all in tactical gear, with all different official patches. Great. A joint task force to apprehend Marek. No wonder they pushed through the door five deep—every cop sporting a SWAT tag had been called in, from Evanston to Chicago. When Danni worked for the Chicago PD, she'd seen these units in action. Although usually she was on the other side of action, behind the cameras. Being on this side sucked. They took the whole "armed and dangerous" thing seriously, except Marek had neither been armed nor dangerous.

"Where are Marek's guns?" One of the cops leaned over her. He was tall. His shoulders were broader than her arm span. Probably steroids. "The guns?"

Guns? Like he had some sort of arsenal. "He doesn't have a gun." Let alone plural. "Don't believe everything you see on TV."

"Where the fuck are his guns!"

She arched backward away from 'Roid Rage and the spittle coming from his mouth. Maybe if she closed her eyes, he'd disappear.

"Back the fuck up, Simms." The little ninja stood in between the white Hulk and Danni. She might be small, but she was standing toe-to-toe with this guy.

"Why? We need his fucking guns."

"His guns. Not hers. According to the tip, she was held here against her will. She's not a perp."

They talked about Danni as if she wasn't sitting right here. In cuffs.

"Skala said the same thing. He said she had nothing to

do with it." Another cop in tactical gear nodded as he followed 'Roid Rage out of the room.

Nothing to do with it? There had been so much going on at that point, she thought she'd imagined it. But no. Marek *had* said that. Danni was sure it was to keep the cops off her back. Even while his face was pressed against the carpet, he was thinking of her. "Where are they taking him?"

The short cop looked over at her and tried to smile. It was more a cringe, something that said *look at the pathetic woman with Stockholm Syndrome*. The radio on the cop's shoulder crackled. "Skala is en route to Chicago PD."

He was gone. Marek had left the building. Probably why Danni felt so cold and panicked.

"Is this your computer?" The other cop sat at the desk and clicked the mouse.

Danni nodded. The dread in her chest pulsed until she watched him close the laptop. Thank goodness. Not only was it encrypted, if anyone tried to hack the thing a Trojan horse would erase the data.

The cops had thinned out at some point—probably when Marek left. There was the one at the computer and the tiny ninja standing over Danni. Overall it was quiet. Too quiet.

Gave her time to think. Today started out so well. She and Marek had some nighttime playtime, then they woke up and eventually fought. But there were plans to have pizza. How did a pizza party turn into this? How did anyone even know where to find them? Only one person knew where they were, and she wouldn't...

Oh God, please say she wouldn't. Leti wouldn't have done this to her.

"How did you find Marek?"

Ninja cop stood over Danni. It was almost creepy how intently the woman watched Danni. "I think a tip came over the line."

No shit, a tip. "From whom?"

Ninja didn't say anything as her shoulders bumped up. She didn't know. Of course, she didn't know. Why would anyone know anything?

"Where is she?" The quiet was engulfed by a loud voice. A voice Danni recognized.

"Oh, thank God you're okay." Maggie ran into the room and wrapped her arms around Danni. "Why are your arms behind your back? Why does she have these cuffs on? She's the victim here." Maggie looked like a mother hen ready to peck someone's eyes out. She sure had the clucking down. And Danni might find it adorable if the implications didn't break Danni's heart.

"We were waiting for orders?"

"Orders from who? I'll find them." Maggie was pissed. Her eyes were narrowed, her fists clenched. "I told you she was the victim. Why is she being treated like a criminal?"

Whatever anger Maggie felt didn't hold a stick of dynamite to the anger building in Danni's chest. She did it. She fucking did it. She called the cops on Marek. Leti probably told Maggie their location, and she opened her big-ass mouth to her cop boyfriend.

After all the years they'd had each other's back. After all the times they'd believed in each other.

Fuck. The pain in her chest burned. She didn't have a lot of people in her life that she trusted. And she'd just lost one.

"She's going pale. Please get those off."

Danni looked at Maggie through a veil of tears.

Funny. Maggie was complaining about Danni going pale, yet she was the one who caused it.

Ninja looked around the room and then nodded. She took a key off her belt and unlocked the cuffs. "Are you okay?"

"Fine." Danni stretched her arms around to the front of her body and rubbed her wrists. Having those damn bracelets off was actually a good thing. Not that she'd thank Maggie. Those damn cuffs would never have been anywhere near Danni if not for Maggie and her big mouth.

"Can she leave?" Maggie offered a hand to Danni. Maybe she thought Danni would take it.

Danni didn't. Earlier, she was disappointed that she and Marek had been clothed, but it turned out to be a blessing. She couldn't have imagined going through all of that naked.

She would never have imagined going through it at all.

"She's needed for questioning," Mini Ninja said.

"Do you have to take her?"

"Yes."

"Then we'll wait outside."

Danni followed Maggie out of the room. Anything to get out of the clutches of the interdepartmental police party.

And this party had sucked.

When they hit the lobby, Danni stopped and retrieved the phone in her bra. She'd managed to stuff the thing in there before her hands shot up. The cops hadn't frisked her, so they'd missed it. Thank goodness. She needed to get out of here.

Maggie turned around. "Why are you stopping? I'll

just take you to the police station. My dad won't mind." Maggie's dad the chief of police might not mind, but Danni did.

"No thanks." Danni sat on a bench and waited for a cop to appear.

"Why? I'll drive you."

"No offense, but I'd rather walk." Danni really hoped Maggie took offense. Offense didn't even cover it.

"Why?"

"Do you really need to ask that?"

Maggie looked about ready to cry as she walked up to Danni. "I'm sorry, but what was I supposed to do?"

"Nothing, Maggie. Nothing. I had it under control. Marek didn't hurt Dave. He didn't hurt me."

"What about getting shot?" Maggie's eyes widened, but the tears stayed in place. "Leti told me about your leg."

"The people chasing Marek shot me. Not Marek. And now he's stuck in jail with those guys coming after him."

"I didn't know—"

"Dammit, Maggie, I told you. You didn't listen."

"I know how he hurt you. He's your kryptonite. I didn't think—"

"No, you didn't. You didn't trust me either." She watched as the ninja cop walked over to the bench where Danni sat. Her salvation and her escape from this conversation. "I needed you to trust me like I've trusted you. I needed you to have my back and not sharpen the knife before you slid it in."

"It wasn't like that."

"Yeah, it was. When you needed my help with Chase, I didn't question you. I've never questioned you. Wire-

145

taps. Account information. Hacked email accounts. That's why we worked. Because we trusted each other. At least, I thought we did." Danni didn't stick around to hear another word. There was nothing Maggie could say right now to change the way she felt.

Because, honestly, Danni didn't want to change the way she felt. The wound in her back was too fresh, too raw. She needed space. Although with what Maggie did, Danni wasn't sure enough space could make her forget.

MAREK SAT on a folding chair in a small room. The smell of sweat and something like mold hung in the air of the precinct. No wonder these cops had such a shitty attitude. They were surrounded by rotten smells and fluorescent lights. Fluorescents sucked the life out of everyone.

He'd worked for three years under those crappy lights after college. Once he'd built his own company, he'd banished them from his part of the building.

"So, you were mad at your partner. Is that why you shot him?" Detective Perry Flores pulled the rest of the peel off another orange. A pile of peels sat off to the side. The smell was trying to cut through the nasty of the air. Although, after three of them, one would think the air would be clean as well as his bowels. Even with that much fiber, it didn't seem healthy to mainline oranges.

"Isn't that much vitamin C lethal?"

Detective Chase Montgomery laughed, but stopped when Flores glared.

"I won't get scurvy." Flores separated another slice. "But that doesn't matter. So, why did you shoot Dave Nelson?"

They'd asked the same question over and over in different ways. The answer wasn't going to change.

They'd been at this for over two hours, although it felt more like two months. And it wasn't just the smells. People came in and out. They asked the same question and seemed confused when he gave the same answer.

"I didn't shoot him." If Marek had his cell phone, he'd just record his voice. *I didn't shoot him. I wasn't even in the city that night.*

"But you were mad. You needed to make him pay." Montgomery stood off to the side. "I get it. The guy was a traitor. How could he say all that shit on TV about you? He practically made it sound like you ripped off your own company."

"I didn't rip off my own company." And, yeah, he was pissed at Dave for even implying it. "I was mad at Dave for going off script with the reporters, but I didn't shoot him. I was at the hotel all night."

Flores picked a seed from a wedge. "Just because you didn't pull the trigger doesn't mean you didn't shoot him."

Actually, that was exactly what that meant. But who was Marek to argue with the scurvy-free cop?

"It doesn't mean you didn't have something to do with it." Montgomery grabbed one of the open chairs and sat. "You said you were at the hotel. Did anyone see you there? Can someone corroborate your story?"

"Dannielle Stein was with me the whole night." His stomach growled. Couldn't they have at least waited until they'd gotten their pizza before the cops busted down the door? Pizza sounded so good right now. And it would probably smell a hell of a lot better.

"The woman who helped you?"

"She had nothing to do with it." He had to put some

distance between them. She'd get in trouble for aiding and abetting. He watched TV. He knew that was a thing.

"So she's your alibi, and you were with her the whole night, but she had nothing to do with it." Montgomery leaned back, with a look that said he didn't believe a word coming out of Marek's mouth.

"That's what I said."

"She claims you're old friends."

"We are. Why does it matter why she was there? Just leave her out of it."

"I'm just trying to get the story straight." Montgomery sighed, most likely in frustration. Join the club. "But the story doesn't seem to match."

"Why don't you spend more time figuring out who shot Dave and why?"

"That's why we're here."

"Well, I'm sure Danni told you I was with her. So why are we still talking?"

"Because the way she talks about you, she'd do anything for you. Maybe even lie about where you were. The gunshot residue test will be back soon. We'll know more then."

Marek couldn't keep from shaking his head. "You will, and you'll know I had nothing to do with it. She wouldn't lie for anyone." That wasn't exactly true, but they didn't need to know that.

Montgomery laughed. Maybe he did know her well, then. "I wouldn't call Danni a liar either. But she's loyal."

Wasn't that the truth.

"Look, I'll tell you anything, just leave her out of it."

"Tell us why you shot Dave." Flores leaned forward.

"I had nothing to do with shooting Dave." Fire spit down Marek's throat as he tried to pull in a breath. Every second they wasted on him was another second they weren't looking for the real bad guys. "I was shot at twice. Have you looked into that?"

"We're looking at all angles."

"Then focus on that and stop wasting your time with me and Danni."

"This is going nowhere." Marek had to agree with him on that.

Flores shook his head and gave Montgomery a look. Montgomery shrugged and nodded. "I'm done," Flores said. "Come with me." He stood, and wrapped his hand around Marek's upper arm, leading him out the door. They walked down dingy yellow-gray hallways, and through another set of doors.

Loud screams and thumps came from in front of them. If Marek thought the interrogation rooms stank, this was a whole new level of nasal persecution.

Flores nodded to the uniformed cop at the desk and then gave Marek a hard look. "Maybe you need to sit and think." Flores guided Marek around the desk, and they followed the cop down the hall to a set of bars painted plain blue.

The cop slid a key into the lock pad. With a clink and rumble, the bars rolled to the side, leaving a gap wide enough for Marek to walk through. Not that he wanted to walk through it, but Flores didn't give him a choice. The doors gave an angry bark as they slammed shut after him, making Marek jump.

This was so far outside his comfort zone. He'd seen jail on television, but TV just didn't do it justice. The screen didn't give you the smells and the drafty, moldy feeling—and there was an actual feeling. The wet air seeped through his skin.

The room wasn't even empty. The cell had two benches, one toilet and sink, and three guys. Good thing he didn't need to take a leak, since one guy sat on the toilet, legs spread wide so his junk hung down in plain view. Another guy lay along one bench, groaning.

The third one walked over to Marek, pushing his long, knotted hair behind his ear. "You holding?" His breath hovered between decay and death.

"What?"

"You holding?" The gaunt, pale face leaned closer, giving Marek a better sniff of this guy's stench. It was closer to death. The guy rubbed a hand down the back of his neck and twitched. "C'mon, man."

Marek didn't know much about drugs, but the dilated pupils and spasms screamed druggie. "Sorry. I'm not holding anything."

"Nothin'? You holdin' out on me?"

"He said he don't got no drugs. Shut up," the lump on the bed yelled, raising his hand from his forehead for a second before letting it flop back in place.

"Shut it, sugar tits. No one asked you." The druggie clawed at his arms, and Marek could see the tracks lining the insides.

"You did ask me, hophead, and I didn't have nothing either. None of us got nothing. All our shit is with Officer Dickless." The lump sat up. He was a heavyset man in a tight T-shirt, his light-brown skin was an interesting shade of green. Trying to sleep off an afternoon of binge drinking, perhaps. "Screw this." He laid back down and rested the arm over his eyes.

"You can bring shit in if you try hard enough." Druggie twitched and moved across the room. "I gotta pee."

That last sentence was aimed at the dangler on the toilet. "Too fucking bad." The guy was large and bald. He had enough muscles to ensure Marek wouldn't be pissing him off anytime soon.

Marek sat down on the unoccupied bench and kept his eyes trained on the blue bars. Maybe if he kept his attention on the bars, he could pretend he wasn't here.

His lawyer should be here soon, even though she'd chosen this weekend to visit family in the upper peninsula of Michigan. Once she showed up, he'd be out of this godforsaken jail and home where he belonged.

Maybe not home. He still had the problem with the people who wanted to kill him. But "anywhere but here" fit the situation perfectly.

FOURTEEN

MAREK'S HEAD HUNG DOWN. Any minute, he swore it would swing and fall to the floor. His shoulders and neck were fractured glass just waiting to crumble. He'd been sitting in the holding cell for at least an hour. Although...maybe it hadn't been that long. Time slowed to a crawl in this place. Maybe it had been fifteen minutes. Or maybe it was two hours. He had no idea.

"Marek Skala." A uniformed officer stood outside the cage. Must be time for questioning, round two. If he'd actually done anything wrong, he'd consider confessing just to get out of here. But he wasn't about to take responsibility for something like this, not when Dave's shooter was out there doing God knew what.

And Dave was in that hospital alone.

"Skala?"

"For fuck's sake." The lump on the other bench raised the arm from his eyes. The druggie and bald guy had long since left, but the lump was still around. "I'll say I'm Skala if you shut the hell up."

"Yeah. Sorry." Marek creaked onto his feet and

walked over to the bars just as the cop turned the key and popped them open.

"Follow me." This cop didn't sound like he'd be as much fun as the orange-eater and his partner.

"Where we heading?"

Silence. The cop kept walking.

"Where are the other cops?"

Nothing. This guy not only didn't smile, he didn't speak. This was going to be another joyful couple of hours. This guy not asking questions and Marek answering the same over and over again.

Marek followed, but the cop was practically running. Like he was in a hurry to get back to that tiny room where they'd both silence each other to death.

"Are we in a hurry?"

Sunshine looked at the watch on his wrist. "Yes."

Marek sighed but moved a little faster. Maybe the cop would be more prone to listening if he wasn't pissed at him. Then again, the two he'd talked to earlier hadn't started out pissed, but nothing he could say would've made them happy—apart from confessing to something he didn't do.

The front desk was chaos. A cop talked on the phone as the cops on the other side of the counter held back a prisoner.

"Fuck you, pigs! You're not taking me in that hell-hole." The prisoner flailed his arms around while cops engulfed the area.

"We need to get this transfer complete, per the mayor's orders." The cop with Marek nodded at a piece of paper on the desk. So the guy could talk.

"We're kind of in the middle of something." Another

scream came from the perp as he chomped his teeth at the cops like freaking Jaws.

"I have orders. You have the letter. What more do you need?"

"Sign this." The cop at the desk tapped a piece of paper.

The cop with Marek grabbed a random pen on the desk and scrawled his name. and the desk cop took the paper without looking at it. He pushed a button, and a door clicked. "Exit is to the left."

Marek let the cop drag him by the arm down the hall on the left. "Am I getting out?"

"Shut up."

"But—"

"Do you want to get out and see your partner? Shut up and let's go."

Marek wanted to complain. He wanted to say something. Anything. But he'd seen enough cop shows to know that complaining wouldn't help. And he was going to see Dave. He could put up with a lot of crap if he had the chance to see his friend again.

They headed to the parking lot. Sometime between when Marek walked in the door of the precinct and now, the sun had set. It was quiet at this time of night—whatever time it was. If he had to guess, he'd say dinnertime, since the traffic on the street was still in full swing.

An awaiting dark blue Chevy Impala idled at the door. He opened the trunk and took out a flashlight. "Get in."

Marek could've sworn the guy said to get in. But that was ridiculous. It was a trunk. "I'm free, right?"

The cop laughed. Something hit the back of Marek's head.

He turned toward the side. What hit him? Another thump. Pain shot through his temple and throbbed as it traveled down his cheek and enveloped his head. The tail-lights dimmed. The cop in front of him blurred.

His body crumpled like wet paper. Stiff carpet slid against his face. The world went black.

FOUR HOURS. She'd sat through four hours of questions and random bullshit. Question after question. It was like they were too dumb to understand the answers. She shook her head.

She knew it wasn't stupidity. She'd dealt with half these guys when she'd worked in the reform management division of CPD. She might have only run reports and occasionally helped the cops find information online, but she knew the bullshit they tried to play. They were trying to get her to change her story or trip up. But a funny thing happened when you were telling the truth: your story remained the same. They must have figured it out about twenty minutes ago because they finally let her go.

"Danni."

She knew that voice. She actually liked that voice. Too bad that voice was dating her knife-wielding ex-best friend.

Chase looked upset. He really was a nice guy. "Don't be too mad at Maggie. She was worried about you."

Danni wasn't ready to hear about traitorous Maggie's virtues. She didn't want to hear how Maggie cared. She wanted to be mad. And until she had Marek back, she was going to be mad. "I'm worried about Marek. That's all I care about right now."

Chase nodded. "Go to receiving. Tell them Montgomery is allowing a visit. They shouldn't give you a hard time. But have them call me if they do."

Worry balled up in her chest. She wanted to see Marek. No, *needed* to see him. And Chase was willing to make that happen. "Thank you, Chase."

He smiled and nodded before turning down the hall. When she'd worked for Chicago PD, she hadn't explored receiving all that often, but she knew the general direction.

She walked into chaos incarnate. The screaming. The scuffling. She stood off to the side as the crazy whirled around her.

"Get him in a cell!" Six cops surrounded a guy who apparently didn't want to go to jail. Surprise.

The guy growled, and what Danni would like to think was pasta sauce rimmed his lips. Of course, the huge teeth-mark shaped gash on the cop's shoulder holding the guy's arm told another story.

The cops converged, and bracelets ratcheted onto the guy's wrist. Four officers led him back behind the desk and through a locked door.

The cop at the desk picked up the phone. "It's all under control... Yes, ma'am... I'll tell them." He hung up the phone and looked over the room. "You all saw what happened. We need a report from everyone."

There were grunts and nods as the room emptied. The threat of a report chased them all away. The uniform behind the counter sat at a computer and started typing.

"Excuse me. I need some help."

"Picking up or dropping off?"

Dropping off? This wasn't exactly her stomping ground back when she'd worked here. They'd kept her in a small cubicle in the back. Would someone drop off here? Never mind. She was getting off track. "I need to see Marek Skala."

The guy poked at the computer. Didn't say anything to indicate he was helping her. Just poked.

"Excuse me."

"I'm looking." He sighed. Yeah, sigh away. If he'd taken two seconds to tell her he was paying attention to what she'd asked, she wouldn't have to throw out another excuse me.

"I'm sorry, he's been let go."

What? "Let go?"

"Transferred." The cop didn't look up. "Order of the mayor."

"Transferred where?"

The cop raised his shoulders in the universal "who the hell cares" move.

She ran out the front door, but Marek wasn't on the street. She checked the corner, but the remnant of rush-hour traffic was all she could see. He could be anywhere. And given the situation, she couldn't blame him for not hanging around.

Why hadn't Chase told her he was being let go? She would have made sure she was there. But now he was in the wind. And there was no way to find him. Why would Chase do this to her?

She stomped back inside the building and headed for the bullpen. If this was some kind of joke, she was going to kick the shit out of Chase. She might get arrested for punching a cop, but to hell with it. Nothing was going her way today, what was one more cluster to add to an already shitty day.

At the bullpen, she navigated the narrow walkway

between the crowded desks until she got to Chase. "Why didn't you tell me he was transferred?"

Chase looked up from his computer, head tilted and eyebrows squished together. "Who?"

"Who do you think? Marek."

"Marek wasn't transferred. His lawyer will be here in twenty minutes, then we'll start questioning him again." He was either a really good actor, or he really didn't know what was going on.

Of course, neither did she. "The guy in receiving told me he'd been transferred by the mayor."

"The mayor doesn't transfer people." Chase pushed his chair back and walked away, Danni on his heels. The cop behind the counter she'd just left was still staring at his computer.

"I need to see Skala." Chase stood at the desk waiting to be buzzed in.

"He was transferred."

"To where?"

The officer behind the counter looked just as confused as Chase. "I don't know. We got an order from the mayor. A cop from District One had a letter like the one we got last month for that Henri Piaget."

"Henri, as in the guy who was caught shoplifting and had diplomatic immunity so everyone from the mayor to the US State Department came breathing down our neck to release him before an international incident? That Henri?" Chase's nostrils flared. He was one scary dude when he was pissed. She was almost impressed with the way Maggie handled him and didn't back down. Except then she'd have to admit Maggie had good qualities. Right now, she wasn't willing to do that.

Chase leaned over the desk. "Why would you think

the mayor had any interest in Skala? He was in here for assault with a deadly weapon."

"Look." The guy slapped the letter on the counter. "We were dealing with Macon when this came in."

"Doug Macon. The addict who likes to show his privates in soup kitchens."

"Yeah, he came in agitated and bit Bartley."

"Since when does Macon bite?"

Danni tried not to glare at Chase. This was interesting and all, but he needed to concentrate on Marek, not pervy biter dude.

"He was jacked up on something. It took six guys to bring him down. We have him in the padded cell."

"He's never even raised his voice at the cops before, let alone bit an officer. I need to see him."

"Sorry, medical staff has to clear him before anyone gets time with that guy."

"Okay." Chase nodded. "Did the cop that took Skala say where they were going?"

"Nope." The cop shrugged, and Danni leaned in to look over Chase's shoulder at the piece of paper. She wanted to laugh, but the fact that this left one less clue made her blood cold instead. "I don't suppose Iron Man came through here."

"We'll check the security footage, but probably not," the guy behind the counter said, giving Danni a dirty look.

She rolled her eyes and tapped the signature. "Tony Stark. Really?"

"What?" The guy shrugged. "That could be his real name."

Chase shook his head. "I need to look at the security footage from today, outside these doors."

"Talk to Lieutenant Bartley. Oh, wait, you can't. He's on his way to the hospital with a freak bite."

Chase's nostrils flared. Somehow, he managed to contain whatever was flying through his mind. "Did Skala and Officer Tony Stark say anything while they were here?"

"Skala stood there and the officer signed."

"That didn't seem weird?"

"No. The cop had a letter."

"Which in itself is weird."

"But it happens."

Chase jerked his head at the door. "Let's get someone to show us the security camera footage on the back door. Maybe we can get a license plate." He nodded at Danni.

It was a sweet gesture. Enough concern and pity and determination to make her feel a bit better.

"Oh, yeah, I forgot," the cop behind the desk called out. "The cop said something about seeing Marek's partner."

"Marek's partner." Chase frowned. "We have a security detail on him right now."

Danni's feet stuttered to stop. Marek would be going to see Dave. Which made sense. He was dying to check on his partner. Poor choice of words. But what did Iron Man have to do with it?

FIFTEEN

DANNI STAYED on Chase's heels as he opened a door and crossed one area of the precinct. Did it again. The lull between day shift leaving and night shift kicking off was over, and the rooms were swarming with people.

Chase opened the door to the bullpen and stopped. Just stopped. Danni swerved and hung on by her toes as she pulled back from becoming a sketch in a comedy show.

And then Danni saw why he'd stopped.

Maggie stood in front of Chase. He grabbed her shoulders when her whole body wobbled. "Whoa." He held onto Maggie until she stopped channeling her inner Weeble.

"We have a problem," Maggie said, as Leti appeared on her left. Jessi to her right. The gang was all here.

"What's going on?" Danni asked.

"Follow me. All of you." Chase headed for his desk, pausing at an open office door. "One second." He stepped inside and closed the door.

"Are you okay?" Jessi patted Danni's arm.

"No." Danni almost sneered at the question. Of course, she wasn't okay, but it wasn't Jessi's fault.

"He's innocent, right?" Leti said. "They have to release him soon."

"They'll question him and let him go. They can't legally hold him for longer than forty-eight hours." Maggie apparently hadn't heard what happened, and neither had Leti.

Of course they hadn't. The only two people who knew that Marek's life was now a Liam Neeson film were Danni and Chase.

Maggie kept talking. "That's why I wanted you two to come in—"

Maggie had ratted them out. She'd done this. She hadn't trusted Danni. She hadn't been her friend—at all. Her eyes burned from tears, but she refused to cry because Maggie didn't deserve it.

"So this was *your* plan." Danni knew she hadn't planned this, but Maggie just stood there all high and mighty with her—her arrogant face.

"Umm..."

Yeah, umm. "Marek isn't here. Some cop came in saying he was from another department, and now Marek's gone. Was that all part of your master plan, Metatron?" Maggie did like to act like the scribe of God, why not call her on it.

"He's gone?"

"Yes. The exact reason we didn't want him in jail just happened. This asshole—not a cop, in case you were wondering—took him god knows where, and is doing god knows what to him." A vise clamped around Danni's chest, and those tears started to fall. He was being held by people who could hurt him—who *would* hurt him. And she was here waiting. Every second, he was getting farther away. What if they'd already killed him?

Her lungs stopped. Her body froze. Except for the tears that kept running over her cheeks.

"Breathe, sweetie." Leti took in a deep breath and pushed it out. Like Danni didn't know how to breathe.

Maybe she didn't. Because her lungs burned, and she couldn't seem to get them to work.

"It'll be okay. We'll find him." Jessi hugged Danni.

"What if they do something to him?" How or why Danni said those words, she had no idea. She didn't want the answer. She couldn't handle if something happened to Marek. She'd just found him again.

Maggie handed Danni a tissue from who-knew-where. "I'm so sorry. I didn't know. We'll get him back. I swear."

Chase came out of the office with a smile. At least someone was happy. "Okay ladies, let's move."

SOMEHOW, they made it to the basement. Danni wasn't sure how. Leti and Jessi guided her down stairs and through corridors. They finally came to the nerve center of the precinct. It looked like Danni's old office.

A guy sat behind a grouping of monitors in the teeny room. It was the size of one of the cubes in the admin section, but with walls. "Chief said you needed the Receiving exit camera about twenty minutes ago."

"Yes." Chase scrunched in behind the computer guy.

"It's not normal to have this many people in the room." Computer guy didn't look all that thrilled to have five people in a two-people room. Danni wasn't all that fond of it either, but Leti did smell nice. The hair hanging over Leti's shoulder was pasted against Danni's face, so she'd gotten a good whiff.

"Click start, please." Chase didn't seem to have the patience to wait, which Danni appreciated. She wanted to see this guy who took her man, get the license plate, and then go find him. Maybe kick him in the nuts a bit.

The grainy picture on the computer flickered to life. Marek talking with the cop as they came through the receiving door. At least she thought he was talking. His lips were moving, but there was no sound. "Sound?"

"The microphone broke last year, so it's really hard to hear." The guy said it like that made total sense.

And she supposed it did. When she worked for the department there was never enough money to cover all the things that needed to be fixed. Or just needed. Try finding an identity thief when your internet connection was practically dialup.

The cop's face wasn't visible as he approached the back of a dark blue Chevy Impala and popped the trunk. With the dings and rust, the car had seen better days and the license plate was only partially visible. The cop took a flashlight out of the trunk, and Marek and the cop talked. Well, Marek's lips moved. They still couldn't see the police guy's face. All she could see was dark blond hair, slightly long and curled right above his shoulders. Kind of like a reject from *Point Break*. He wore a black uniform, and his holster was on the left-hand side. "He's left-handed. Look at the holster."

The cop hit Marek over the head with the flashlight. Twice. Marek spun toward him, his face filled with pain and confusion before his body slumped. The cop pushed his falling body into the trunk, folding him like a fucking towel.

After he slammed the trunk closed, the cop got behind the wheel and took off. The whole thing couldn't have taken more than thirty seconds.

And Danni still had no idea what the guy looked like. "We need to find another angle. We have to see his face."

Chase was already on the phone calling in the APB as the office door opened. Chase's partner, Perry Flores, stood in the doorway.

The computer technician turned an interesting shade of green as Chase bumped into the guy's shoulder. "No one else is coming in this room," tech guy said.

"Dave Nelson is at Edward Hospital in Naperville," Flores told Danni.

Chase ended his call. "I put an APB out on the car, and Pete here is going to see who owns it." He touched the technician's shoulder, who must be Pete. "Everyone out."

Jessi and Maggie walked out into the hall after Perry. Leti stood there waiting for Danni to move. Danni wasn't ready to leave yet. "I need to see the guy's face."

Chase smiled at her. "Pete'll go through the footage in the jail and send me a picture after he gets an ID on the owner of that car. Right now, we need to see if they're heading toward Dave Nelson. We don't know if they're planning on hurting him."

Danni nodded. He was right. They needed to check on Dave, and hopefully they'd either find Marek there or intercept the car along the way.

Chase herded them all down the corridor and out to where the cars were parked. "Flores, take Jessi and Leti down Ogden. Maggie, Danni and I will take the expressway." Smart. Those were the two most direct paths to the hospital way out in the suburbs. "We need to get Marek back here as quickly as possible."

Splitting up might be genius, but bringing Marek back here was not. Danni needed to go out on her own, make sure he didn't end up right back here. Of course, that plan meant she needed a car. And going back to the garage to get hers would take time. Time she didn't have. Maybe Leti or Jessi drove here. "Shouldn't we split into three groups, cover more ground?"

Maggie nodded. "That's a great idea. Leti, why don't you go with Chase and take Roosevelt. I'll take Danni down 290."

Driving around town, alone, with Maggie. Not exactly Danni's idea of a good time. But sending Leti and Chase down another main street to look for the car was a good thing, but if Leti could drive...

"My car is the only one here, and I'm driving it," Maggie whispered to Danni. She knew Danni didn't want to get into a car with her. She knew Danni didn't want to talk to her right now.

Despite that, Danni climbed into the passenger side of the gray Crown Vic as Maggie slid in the driver's side. Losing Maggie would be a hell of a lot easier than ditching one of the cops and getting Marek to safety.

The cars all peeled out of the police lot and headed west, taking their assigned routes. Maggie and Danni rode in silence. Not comfortable silence. More like the edge of silence, because Danni knew at any minute Maggie would open her mouth and try to apologize or whatever.

Danni looked across the front of the Crown Vic. How many times had she sat here with Maggie, driving around, going on stakeouts, and complaining about working at Chicago PD? How many times had Maggie had her back when one of the cops tried to tamper with evidence and blame Danni? When another cop tried to tamper with Danni and got Maggie's knee to his balls?

That's why the whole situation hurt so much. She'd trusted her.

"Stop looking at me like I kicked your puppy," Maggie said.

"Did you kick my puppy? That seems to be in character these days."

Maggie's lips pursed as she pulled onto the ramp for the expressway. Conversation over. Danni, one. Maggie, zero.

Danni stared at the cars on the road. So many cars. She focused on the dark blue sedans. The ones in oncoming traffic sped by too fast to see clearly. They passed the ones going their way at a nice clip as Maggie ignored posted speed limits. *Thank you, Maggie.*

Maggie's phone rang, showing Chase's face, and Danni hit the speaker button.

His voice carried through the silent car. "We have a problem."

Of course, they did. Danni sucked in a breath to wait for the inevitable.

MAREK BUMPED his shoulder as his eyes flew open. Darkness. Where the hell was he? He tried to straighten his legs, but an extended fetal position was the best he could do. Exhaust infused the air as he flew up, bumping his shoulder again.

The rug under his face was scratchy, and he'd bet it was dark blue. Like the car. The cop. The car hit another hole on the road, sending his arm into the trunk lid. Again.

Dammit.

He slammed his fist on the trunk. The metal didn't budge, and pain slithered down his arm. He needed to get the hell out of here. He turned onto his back and pushed at the trunk. Again nothing.

How did the damn things work? Didn't they have a trunk release on the inside for situations like this? His eyes slid along what he assumed was the front. His body bumped up against the lid again, but this time his hands stopped him from hitting too hard. The small space closed in on him. Short choppy breaths pulled air into his lungs. There wasn't enough. He closed his eyes.

Breathe. Relax. He needed to get out. He needed a plan.

The car slid to a stop. *Shit*. He was running out of time. His hands slid along the wall of the trunk as the car lurched forward.

He still had time to get out. And then he could go into hiding. Maybe find a way to check on Dave. Clear his name. A short list, but each thing seemed next to impossible alone, without Danni.

She was no longer in danger. Which was good. But somehow that didn't make him feel any better.

He slid his fingers along felt and metal. Edges. Dips. It would really help if he knew what the hell he was looking for. A little green button glowed next to his hand. That had to be it.

The car jostled as they hit another bump. From the impact, they were obviously going pretty damn fast. He couldn't jump out of a moving car, but maybe once the trunk opened, they'd be forced to stop. Right?

Before he could think too hard about it, he pushed the button. The trunk lid flew up, wind whipping into the space. The car swerved, rolling Marek to the side. His legs bent as his body slid. He reached up and grabbed the rim of the open trunk just as the car slowed.

Car horns honked. Concrete barriers flashed by as the car pulled over to the left side of the expressway. Stones crunched beneath the tires and cars whizzed past. The guy should have moved over to the right shoulder, but he probably thought Marek wouldn't jump out of a car in the middle of expressway traffic.

The guy didn't know Marek very well.

Slower. If he waited until the car stopped, the driver could jump out and stop him. All he had was the element of surprise. This was his chance. He swung his legs over the edge and grabbed the rim of the trunk with both hands. Pushed hard, shoving his legs out and down at the same time.

Step. Trip. Lunge. He barely kept himself from planting his face on the asphalt conveyor belt.

Cars swerved. Horns honked. Fingers flew up, aimed at Marek as he ran for the center of the road. Like he wanted to climb out of a trunk in the middle of the expressway.

Good times. Not.

The guy would be jumping out any minute. Marek had to go. He scanned the concrete wall on the other side until he spotted an opening. A staggered wall left a hole big enough for him to get through. He just had to cross three lanes of fast moving traffic to reach it.

Bang. "Stop, you son of a bitch."

Marek had no idea if he was hit, but he didn't have time to figure it out. Gunfire plus the yelling meant the car had stopped. Which meant the fake cop was chasing him. Which meant Marek had to hurry the fuck up. His strides lengthened as he dodged cars like a 3D version of Frogger.

A truck barreling down the road slammed on the horn. Marek's nose came close to the grill, but he managed to jump out of the way before he became embedded in the grate. He stumbled, stopped before he ran into the tail end of an SUV.

Tires squealed. Horns kept honking. Somehow, he made it across without going splat. Somehow, he found himself climbing a small grassy hill near the opening in the noise barrier.

He looked over his shoulder as he slid through the gap. The fake cop stood in the center of the road—probably trying to decide if Marek was worth chasing.

The guy took a step forward, looked monumentally pissed. Shit.

Move. There was a Best Western in front of him, and a church behind it. Ducking into the Best Western was the obvious choice, which meant it was the first place anybody would look for him, but he'd never make it to the church in time. Unless...

He ran for the front door of the hotel, sliding inside at the same moment the fake cop came through the noise barrier. Shit. Another gunshot, but Marek didn't wait to see what happened next. He run-walked through the lobby, hoping everybody figured he was late for something, and down a side hallway, heading for the back of the building.

Doors lined the hall. Gym. Conference space. All locked. He kept going, looking for an exit, and finally whipped open the farthest door. He pushed it closed as quietly as he could and ran from across to the church parking lot, where he found a propped-open back door that led to a small office. The office door was open, but he closed and locked it before sitting on the couch.

He just had to wait this out.

The doorknob jiggled. Marek held his breath. Fists hit the door and then stopped, followed by raised voices. He couldn't hear what they were saying over the jingling of keys.

He was so screwed.

SIXTEEN

"WE HAVE A PROBLEM," Chase said on speaker-phone. "A car matching our description was spotted on 290. A man jumped out of the trunk and ran off the expressway."

"That's good, right?"

"From the 911 call, he made it across the expressway without an accident, but there were shots fired."

Shots fired? "Is he okay?"

"Not sure. A man with a gun was chasing him. They were last seen running toward the Best Western."

"Hurry up." Danni felt an urge to slam her foot over Maggie's to get the car moving. "We have to find him before the cops."

Maggie sped up. It still took hours to get to him—okay, the clock said it took three minutes, but it felt like hours. The navy-blue car was stopped in the middle pull-off of the expressway.

"Pull over. That's him." Danni looked near the road for the hotel sign. "There's the Best Western."

Instead of parking behind the stopped car, Maggie

rolled onto the shoulder. No dodging traffic. Good call. "There's an opening back there." Danni swung the door open, which thankfully wasn't toward traffic, snapping her arm as the force almost took her with it. She jumped out as Maggie pulled to a stop and ran along the shoulder, up the grassy hill to the opening.

"Wait." Maggie ran behind her.

"I need to find him."

"I needed to grab my gun." Maggie's longer strides and overall better health meant she caught up to Danni easily. "We don't know what we're going to find out here."

That was true. A bad guy was running around trying to shoot Marek. A weapon was needed, and all Danni could wield was a deadly compilation of code or a sharp tongue. Not really going to help here.

They ran across the frontage street and through the parking lot of the hotel. Another car, complete with flashing lights, came barreling around the corner and into the lot. Damn cops.

Chase and Leti jumped out of the cop car. They ran into the hotel, behind Danni and Maggie. People in suits and dresses milled around, taking advantage of the hotel happy hour after a long day of work, no doubt. Chase flashed his badge. "Have you seen two guys run through here?"

"That way." A couple of people pointed toward a back hall.

"Thanks." Chase ran where they pointed, with Danni right behind him and Maggie and Leti behind her.

"Marek," Danni called out to the emptiness, hoping he'd come out if he heard her.

"We don't usually call out to the bad guys when in pursuit." Chase jiggled a door handle.

"Good thing he's not a bad guy." Danni tried a door, glancing down the corridor to the exit. Through the glass, she could see a building behind the hotel. A church.

That's where he would go. Close enough, but not too obvious. And she could check it out and ditch the boy scout. "Shouldn't we get the keys so we can make sure Marek or the bad guy aren't in these rooms?"

"Good idea." Chase headed for the front desk, and Danni made a break for the church.

"Where are you going?" Maggie called from behind her.

"Just checking outside." Danni opened the door and stepped to the side—out of sight of her friends—and ran across the lot. At the church, a back door hung open. She ducked inside and stopped. A dark-skinned man towered over her.

"May I help, my child?" Another dark-skinned man, with a pleasant smile and tab collar, came over.

"I'm looking for my friend."

"You don't belong here." Tall Guy was the opposite of welcoming. Whatever that was.

"Now, Chris, everyone is welcome. My name is Pastor Williams."

The tower, who apparently went by the name of Chris, grunted. "Are you here for Bible study?"

"I'm sorry, no."

"Then you don't belong here."

The pastor smiled at the tower. "Chris, why don't you ensure our other guest left."

Other guest? Marek?

Chris the Tower left out the back door, freeing up some of the oxygen in the small hallway.

"I apologize for Chris's manners. We've had too many instances of vandalism. We need to be cautious."

Cautious. A church? The fact that they even had to think that way made Danni's stomach curl. "I'm not here to vandalize. I promise. I'm hoping you can help me."

"What can I help you with, my child?"

"The other guest. What did he look like? I'm looking for my friend, Marek." She reached for her phone to show him a picture. Wasn't that what you did when looking for a missing person? Except she didn't have her phone. Crap.

"Let's go in my office." The pastor pulled some keys from his pocket and unlocked a door, holding it open for Danni. "Please, sit."

She chose the couch instead of the two chairs near the desk, and sighed. This was taking too long. The cop squad would eventually figure out those rooms at the Best Western were empty and would come this way. Then whatever clues that were here would be found and they'd be off searching for him. They couldn't get to him first. The cops or the bad guys.

"So, who are looking for?" the pastor asked her, still standing by the door.

"I'm looking for my friend Marek."

"And your name?"

"Danni Stein. I need to find him."

The pastor nodded. "Well, if I see anyone by that name, I'll contact you."

If? "What about the other guest?"

"I'm sorry, his name was not Marek." Pastor Williams stepped to the side and gestured at the door. Why bring her in here if he was just going to kick her out?

"Did you get his name?" It wasn't that easy to get rid

of her. She was like malware being shielded by a rootkit. They might see her, but she was hard to remove. Especially when Marek's life was on the line.

"I did not, but I believe Chris did."

The idea of talking to the Tower of Chris was not high on her list, but sometimes you had to pull up the big girl pants and do scary things. "Can I talk to him? My friend's life is in danger." She could feel the tears stabbing at her eyes, but she refused to cry. She didn't have time.

"Have you tried calling him?" The pastor's face was drenched in sympathy.

She ran a hand over her cheeks. No tears. She must just look pathetic. "I don't have my phone and I don't know his phone number." Dammit. She stood. "Thank you for your help."

"Don't cry. I'm sure you'll find him."

She tried to give him a smile. Not that she was crying, but she was thinking about it. She had been so sure Marek had run this way. But she'd been wrong. Maybe she didn't know him as well as she thought.

———

WHY WAS SHE HERE? That was a dumb question. She was here because she was looking for him. Why wouldn't she just let it go?

The fake cop had all but tried to beat through the locks, and the pastor had been good enough to show him to the door. But then Danni showed up, and Pastor Williams led her into the office. The office where Marek was hiding. Well, hiding was a stretch. He'd just stepped into the private bathroom, waiting for the fake cop to go away.

"Thank you for your help." Danni sounded defeated. Marek didn't want to defeat her.

"Don't cry. I'm sure you'll find him."

Crap. Marek also didn't want to be the reason she cried. He stepped out of the bathroom and into the office. "Danni, what are you doing here?"

"Oh, thank God. Are you okay?" She eyed him up and down. He must've looked worse than he thought, if her wince was real.

"I'm fine." And he was, for the most part.

Danni barreled forward, wrapping her arms around him. Yeah, he was fine now. All he could do was close his eyes and enjoy. With her all soft and warm, wrapped around him, it was hard to feel guilty. He didn't regret bringing her back into his world.

He'd been without her all afternoon, and it had been a hellish, lonely existence. Maybe a bit dramatic, but he'd been in lockup all day, so shoot him.

"I'll let you two be alone." Pastor Williams walked out. He was a nice guy. His friend with the muscles was a bit frightening, but considering that guy scared away the fake cop, Marek wasn't complaining.

Danni pulled away. He was almost upset until she pressed her lips to his. Then his thoughts disappeared. Nothing outside mattered. Just her.

His hands slid along her jaw, her neck, curving past her collarbone. He deepened the kiss. Wanting more. A groan rumbled in his chest. No. It was more than want. It was hunger. He needed her.

She answered every dip and glide, opening her mouth to take everything he had to offer.

His hand lifted her T-shirt and skimmed along the soft skin of her side. She felt so fucking good. A soft gasp escaped her lips. Or maybe it came from him. He didn't know where he ended, and she began. And right now, he didn't care.

His body was on autopilot—so hot and ready for her. And given how her hands moved up and down his body, stroking his back, his front, and everywhere in between, she was just as ready.

Somewhere in the back of his mind, he knew he should stop, but he couldn't remember for the life of him why. Each sweep of her tongue. Each press of her body. His brain was one big fuzzy mess. And he liked it. He liked her. A lot.

"Num." Danni made a cute little sound as she leaned her head back, giving him easy access to the skin at her throat.

His teeth grazed the skin before his tongue came back and licked each spot. She tasted salty. Delicious. Her groans got louder.

"Ahem." Not Danni.

Marek suddenly remembered where he was. A church office. Hiding. With the door wide open and his hands practically down Danni's pants. *Shit.*

Danni caught up before Marek. She'd already pulled away.

He looked over to the doorway—afraid of what he'd find. Either a cop who'd want to take him back to jail or a bad guy who'd want to take him god knew where.

Cop. The one from the interrogation earlier. Montgomery. He currently had a gun pointed at Marek's head. Marek's hands flew up in the classic response.

A woman who almost looked like a cop, but not, stood next to him in the doorway. "I'd ask if you were okay, but unless he was giving you mouth to mouth, you're fine."

The glare Danni threw her way said this might be the infamous Maggie. Unless Danni glared at everyone like that.

"Hi, Marek. It's nice to finally meet you. I'm Maggie." She put her hand out, and Marek reached for it. Danni blocked him, and Montgomery grunted. Since he held the gun, Marek's hands resumed the position.

"You can't do this," Danni snapped.

Maggie's face fell. "Do what?"

"You can't take him back there." Danni glared at Montgomery. Marek agreed. He'd spent the afternoon getting to know the detective and was not looking forward to another round of twenty questions.

"We know better now. We'll keep him safe." Montgomery aimed the words at Danni, but his gun stayed on Marek. He talked to her like he knew her.

"Safe like you did before?" Danni moved toward Montgomery, still keeping her body between Marek and the two people at the door.

"Let me do my job. For all we know, Skala staged that whole thing."

Danni's hands planted on her hips. "And he put himself in the trunk of a car and planned his elaborate escape on 290. Because playing chicken with the messed-up drivers of Chicagoland is always a good time."

"Okay, fine. He didn't stage it." Montgomery kept the gun level but ran one hand through his hair. Frustration. Welcome to the world of Danni Stein. Although nothing here explained why the cop wasn't just taking Marek on a perp walk. Why did he care that Danni stood in the way? The cop could take her. "Danni, we can keep him safe. We know that there's a threat now."

"You knew it then. I told your cops that in interrogation. I told Maggie before you grabbed him."

Maggie leaned over and rested a hand on Montgomery's arm. "She did tell me that."

"And you didn't tell me?" Montgomery stepped back like he'd been slapped. Or betrayed. The pieces started coming together. Maggie and the cop were dating. That's how the cop knew Danni.

"I didn't know it was important." The color drained from Maggie's face as she looked from Danni to her boyfriend.

Montgomery sighed. "Everything is important."

"I know now. I'm sorry." Maggie shook her head. "This is all my fault."

"Chase, he didn't do it," Danni said. "I need you to please trust me. Let us find the person who's trying to frame him."

"I can't..." Chase looked torn. Marek sort of felt bad for him, trapped between Danni and Maggie. Then he thought of the interrogation room. Or maybe not.

"Please, Chase." Maggie stood next to Danni, blocking Marek from the gun in Montgomery's hands. "This is my fault. I did this. I should have trusted Danni. She's never given me a reason to not trust her. You either."

"I can't let a known criminal just walk away," Chase said.

Marek wanted to fight for his right to find who was doing this, but the two women seemed to have it handled so he just stood back and let them take care of things. Plus, the way Maggie and Danni were now on the same side felt huge for their relationship.

Maggie squeezed Danni's hand and then stepped in front of Chase. "You know deep in your heart that what

Danni and I are saying is true. If you didn't, you would have pushed us both down and taken Marek."

Chase lowered his weapon, but his eyes never left Marek. The cop might be listening, but he was still on high alert. To be fair, Marek was a bad guy in his world, so his guard should be up.

"Let him walk away. Let's go look for the guy who took Marek." Maggie was talking in a tone reserved for hostage negotiations. But that almost fit.

"The other cops are looking into that." There were other cops? Fantastic.

"Chase. For me." Maggie's voice wobbled. Marek didn't know her well, but she didn't seem like the type to cry.

"They'll never get away on foot." Chase was right. Especially if there were cops, plural, outside looking into the expressway thing.

"Danni." Maggie reached into her pocket and pulled out a set of keys. "Take my car."

Danni's eyes grew to the size of saucers. To be honest, so did the cop's. Then Marek remembered Danni's driving.

"Go. Find the guys who are doing this." Maggie took Danni's hand and put the keys in her palm, held on for a second. "Please check in once in a while."

"I don't have a phone."

"What—" Maggie shook her head and handed Danni her cellphone. "It doesn't matter. Take mine. I'll grab Leti's. My passcode is—"

"I know your passcode."

Maggie opened her mouth, Shut it. Shook her head again. "Never mind. I don't want to know. Contact me if you need any help. And call if you need the police or if you get shot at again. And take care of my car. And—"

"Maggie." Danni smiled and slid the cell phone in her back pocket. "I'll be careful."

Maggie smiled, but it didn't quite reach her eyes. To Chase she said, "We should go look for a man impersonating a police officer and shooting into traffic."

Chase nodded and glared at Marek. "Do not make me regret this, Skala. Or you, Stein." He walked up to Danni and kissed her forehead. "Next time I see you, I'm bringing you in, so make it count."

"Thanks, Chase."

He and Maggie left the office, and silence descended. "You didn't have to do that," Marek told Danni.

"I did." She worried the keys in her hand. "I have to go get the car."

"Catch up with Maggie." His heart broke a bit at saying the words. But it was probably better if she didn't want to be with him right now. His life was dangerous. "This whole thing is freaking me out. I don't want you to be stuck in the middle."

"I'm not freaking out. I'm worried that you'll run away while I'm getting the car."

A burst of happiness lodged in his chest. She didn't want to leave him. She was afraid he'd leave. Like he could. After today, he'd realized how much he needed her.

"Go get the car. I'm not going anywhere. I'll never get anywhere on foot, right?" He leaned into her and covered her lips with his. Soft and gentle and filled with so much love.

Not that he loved her. It was too soon for that. Probably residual love left over from when they were together before. Fuck. Or maybe he'd never stopped loving her.

She stepped back. "We have to go before the other cops come this way."

"Go." He sat down on the couch.

"Meet me at the back door in five minutes."

He smiled. She'd be back in five and then they'd sort all of this out. For the first time in a few days, things were looking up.

SEVENTEEN

DANNI RAN out of the church with a huge smile on her face. He was sticking around. He wasn't running. Which didn't stop her from running. Well, not running. More like walking really fast. She didn't want to give him time to think about running away, but she also didn't want the cops thinking she was up to something.

She power-walked from the back of the church to the front lot of the hotel, where the cherries on the cop cars swirled, painting red and blue streaks over everything. A lot of lights. A lot of cars. Which meant a lot of cops.

Her heart thumped from the speed walking or from the fact that she was closer to the cops she wanted to avoid. She stumbled. Her leg throbbed. No amount of street cred was worth the pain, but somehow she kept going until she reached Maggie's Crown Victoria.

"Hey. What are you doing?" A uniformed cop walked up, his hand on the gun at his hip.

She stuck her hands in the air. She thought about waving them, but he was jittery, and she didn't care to get shot by a young jumpy rookie. "I'm getting my boss's car."

"No one in or out."

Shit. Shit. Shit. Her heart beat faster, and not from the almost-acrobatics she'd managed to live through. "Officer, sir. Maggie, my boss, told me I could borrow her car." She pointed at the Crown Vic like he didn't know what car she meant. Like he cared.

"I don't care what your boss said." See, he didn't care. He unsnapped the flap over the gun. "Keep your hands up."

She inched her hands higher and dragged in a breath. Passing out in front of this guy would not be advisable. He'd probably see it as an act of aggression. She didn't need another bullet wound to add to her street cred. One graze was enough to make her all kinds of badass.

"Officer." Chase walked over with his badge out. "Detective Montgomery, with Chicago Police Department. I asked Danni here to pick up my girlfriend."

The officer nodded. "Oh, sure. Sorry."

"I think they need help inside." Chase pointed to the hotel. "They're looking for guys to start blanketing the neighborhood."

The guy snapped his gun flap shut and jogged toward the front doors.

"Thanks." She smiled at the man who managed to save her ass more than once today.

"Go." Chase nodded at the car. "And don't let me see you again."

"I'm not here." She flung open the driver's side door and slammed it shut behind her. She drove like her grandmother on the way to the synagogue, crawling from one parking lot to the other. Inching past parked cars, cops, and onlookers. *Nothing to see here.*

And she had to drive back this way to get out. With Marek. *Crap*.

Marek eased out the back door of the church just as she jumped out of the car and popped the trunk. "Get back here."

"Not going to happen." He slid into the driver's seat.

She grabbed the car door. "You can't drive. There are a million people out front looking for you. And you're a complete mess." She couldn't believe she hadn't noticed that earlier. To be fair, her hands and her eyes were too happy to be near him to care. He was covered in dirt and various other nasty shit—probably from his joy ride in a trunk. "You need to hide."

"No." He unfolded from the driver's side. "I'll ride in the back, but I will not get in the trunk."

"But—"

He reached around her body for the back door handle. "No trunk. I would rather listen to Chase and his partner ask me the same question using every different possible word in the English language than get in another trunk."

"Okay."

He laid down on the floor, wedging himself between the front and back seats. Or wedged as much as a six-foot-tall-plus man could wedge.

"Trunk?" Danni asked, eying his deformed downward dog position.

"No." He squirmed, angling his face toward the back seat and curling his legs into his chest. "This is good." His breath was labored, and his voice was strained, but it was the best they were going to get.

She went to the trunk and took out the blanket Maggie kept for cold nights before slamming the lid.

"This should cover you." She flicked it open and spread it over Marek's body. "I'll try to get through all the cops quickly."

She shut the back door and climbed in the front. In the rearview mirror, she could see the blanket jostle. She drove slowly along the side of the church. The alleyway was empty, but the rest of the parking lot had managed to double with people.

Where did they all come from? She rolled toward the exit. People stood around watching a large group of cops walk out of the hotel. Crap.

"Stay down," she hissed to the back seat.

"I am down."

"If you were in the trunk you'd be more down." She didn't edit the words before they flew out, but she knew what she meant.

"What does that even mean?" Apparently, he didn't.

"Shut up. Back seats don't talk."

Cops were everywhere. Apparently, a lunatic shooting a gun in the suburbs warranted a cop party. She angled past a group of onlookers. Twenty feet until the lot exit. That was it. She just had to get him twenty feet.

A cop stepped in front of the Crown Vic, forcing her to stop. He walked over to the driver's side window. She might have crapped herself as Marek's blanket vibrated like a PlayStation controller during an airstrike. Was he about to sneeze, or was he having some sort of fit?

"Hi, officer. What a lovely day." She said it too loud and definitely with more cheer than the greeting deserved.

"Where are you going?" The gruff tone and overall attitude made her stomach clench. He was big. Brick shit-house big. And when his crabby ass noticed Marek, she had a feeling Ralph would totally wreck it.

"My boss—"

The officer she'd raised her hands for earlier called out, "Detective Montgomery sent her to get his girlfriend."

"Oh, okay." The brick shit house nodded and stomped back to the gaggle of officers.

Danni stepped on the gas and turned right out of the lot, down the frontage road along the expressway until she hit a main road. She headed west. She might not know exactly where they were going, but away from Chicago was a good bet. "Where are we going?"

"I need to see Dave." Marek's head popped up from the floor as he slid onto the back seat. "If you've got a shower somewhere in your back pocket, I could use one of those."

"Do you really need a shower?"

"I have jail and exhaust all over me." He sniffed at his arm and cringed. "I need a shower."

"Then let's get you a shower." She turned onto the expressway. This would get her away. Faster. And she knew exactly where she'd stop to get him cleaned up.

MAREK LEANED FORWARD and looked out the windshield as Danni pulled into a space next to a big building with a gym logo on the side. "Are you a member here?"

"No."

"Then why are we stopping here?"

She took the keys out of the ignition and opened the door. "My mom and her husband are members."

"So they're meeting us here?" That didn't make sense. "Why don't we just go to their house?"

"I'm not subjecting either of us to them. My mom will tell me all the things I'm doing wrong with my life while she dotes on her husband."

"So, things still aren't okay between you, your mom and the step-dad?"

"I don't think that's gonna change. She still hates my dad, and anything or anyone that reminds her of him. Especially his daughter. And my step-dad—he's just weird. I see them for holidays. That's enough." She turned around and leaned over into the back seat. Her lips inches from his. "We're going inside. Trust me."

Trust her. Trusting her was easy. He followed Danni into the gym. The smell of sweat and plastic soured the air.

"Hi." Danni walked up to the front desk. "We're looking to join and want to get a tour."

"That's fabulous. My name is Shreya." A woman in spandex came around the front desk. Her black hair was pulled back in a ponytail. "If you'd like to follow me, I can show you the facility."

Shreya pointed at the metal equipment standing in rows. "The machines are grouped by muscle targets. The treadmills are along the wall..." She kept talking, but Marek blocked her out until she said, "Here are our locker rooms." She pointed at two large doorways, one with a sign above it saying men, the other one saying women. "I can't go inside the men's locker room, but I can get someone to give you a tour."

"No, I think I can poke around on my own." Marek leaned into Danni. "Keep her busy."

"Be fast."

"I will."

"Faster." Danni whisper-yelled before following Shreya into the women's locker room.

In the men's locker room, a good hundred or so gray lockers lined the walls, some with locks. He quickly stripped off his T-shirt. Black liquid smudged his hands. What the hell. He flattened the tee and peered at something resembling oil or blood from Jabba the Hut. He couldn't wear this.

He ran his hands over his jeans. Dirt. More of the black stuff crusted on the ass. His clothes were fucked.

He threw them into the garbage can and grabbed a gym towel from a stack on a table. Past the lockers, steam came from around the corner. Showers. Some of the fabric shower curtains were shut, and he heard water hit the walls.

Marek found the first open stall and hung his towel up before turning the water on and letting the hot water beat against his skin. Soft pounding. Rhythmic. It felt so damn good. So damn relaxing. He leaned his head back, the water sliding down his face and shoulders. Every muscle sagged. A groan stuck in his throat. If he weren't in a public shower, he'd just let it go.

He ran a handful of soap from the wall dispenser through his hair. The water sluiced through the strands, rinsing away more grime. He'd give anything to stay under the waterfall, but Danni was going to be coming in here soon and hunting him down if he didn't get his ass moving.

He stepped out of the shower, turning off the spray

under protest. He ran the towel up and down his body, drying as much as possible. The other showers were now silent. The locker room was silent. Everyone must have left while his head was under the spray of the shower. Which would make him searching through the lockers a lot easier. Since his clothes were toast, there had to be something he could wear in one of the lockers.

He wrapped a towel around his waist and checked the first locker. Empty. He tried all the unlocked doors. Nothing. Of course. When he was looking for an empty locker, all he ever found was other people's clothes. Now that he needed clothes to be left unlocked—nothing. Then he found a Nike bag and checked inside.

Tank top. Small. Shorts. *Short* shorts.

Nothing else. He couldn't wear this. He went back to the lockers and opening all the other unlocked doors. Empty. All empty.

He could put his old clothes back on. They weren't that bad. He walked over to the garbage and tipped open the flap. The heavy scent of exhaust and filth came from inside. He hadn't even put his nose to the clothes, and they smelled that damn bad.

Shit.

He walked back over to the bag on the bench. The bag with the shorts and the tank. He took a breath and slipped them on. After one look in the mirror, he sighed. This was better than being naked. But barely.

EIGHTEEN

MAREK TUGGED at the leg of the shorts, praying that he didn't start showing his...baggage out the bottom. The hospital staff and patients didn't need to see that. Hell, no one needed to see that.

He was one step away from playing soccer with his balls. The people at the gym had given him several sideways glances, but the woman giving the tour had her back turned when he'd snuck out.

He tugged again, and the tan shorts inched down. A breeze hit his stomach. He stretched the striped green and red tank top down until it barely covered his belly button.

Thankfully, he was hiding in a doorway while Danni asked about Dave's room and made sure there wasn't a wanted picture posted at all the nurses' stations. If anyone recognized him, that would lead to cops and another trip to jail. He couldn't end up in jail again. Not in these shorts. He'd be way more popular this time around if he ended up back in lockup. And not in a good way.

A giggle came from behind him as Danni came from the information desk.

"I'm glad you find this amusing."

"This is beyond amusing." Danni let a loud cackle fly as she headed down the main hall. "Those clothes don't leave much to the imagination."

"And still you laugh."

Her laugh turned into a snort. "I didn't mean it that way. You're very sexy." She stopped and ran a hand along the edge of the tank top. He didn't want to enjoy it. She had just been laughing at him. Loudly. But the feel of her fingers along his skin—so close to... Ouch.

The tight shorts strangled any reaction to her touch. And she was so right, that reaction was not left to anyone's imagination. It was all there in polyester glory.

He pulled her hand away. "Maybe we should finish this conversation after the hospital." Or after he burned these shorts.

"Fine." She smiled and turned down yet another hall. The hospital just kept going. Hall after hall. He followed Danni through a set of doors and past patient rooms. One officer stood outside Dave's door. "I forgot about the security detail."

"How do we get in?"

"We get them away from the door." Obviously.

He looked around. "I don't think we'll be lucky enough to have another patient freak out and pull them away."

"Probably not. But maybe we can get Chase to help." She pulled out her cell phone. "Or at least Maggie." She stuck the phone to her ear and turned away from the cop at the door. "Leti, is Maggie... Hey, Maggie, can you help us get the cop off Dave's door at the hospital? Marek just wants to make sure he's okay... I do... He's in Room 421."

Danni ended the call and slid the phone back in her pocket.

"You two seemed to have worked out your issues," Marek said. He didn't want to come between Danni and anyone, let alone her best friend and business partner. Danni might not have acknowledged her friendship with Marek, but he wasn't an idiot. She cared about the woman, whether she wanted to admit it or not.

Danni shrugged. "We aren't ready to kill each other, so there's progress."

The phone rang in Dave's room. The cop at the door went inside, and the ringing stopped. A couple minutes later, the cop walked out and made his way to the nurses' station, telling the nurse on duty, "I'm heading to lunch. I'll be back soon."

The cop walked away. Just went to lunch. Marek looked at Danni for some sort of answer. Danni shrugged and pulled out her phone. Her fingers flew over the screen, and she laughed.

"Maggie's with her dad, who's the chief of police. She used his phone to tell the cop to take his lunch."

"And it worked?"

"Apparently. But we need to hurry." Danni tipped her head into his room and waved Marek in. "He's alone."

Marek hurried through the open door and stopped. Dave looked pale and fragile propped against the white sheets of the bed. He wasn't moving, and his arm was wrapped in gauze. Machines buzzed and whirred. An IV dripped above his head.

Marek couldn't find breath in his lungs. This was Dave. His best friend. Hell, his family. Dave had been there through everything. Dave had gotten him shitfaced when Jill and Marek lost the baby. He'd made sure Marek was drunk off his ass when Jill left.

Apparently, they'd spent a lot of time drinking while dealing with shit. But that was okay. He trusted Dave. He needed Dave.

"Go talk to him." Danni pushed on Marek's back.

"What do I say?"

"Hadn't you thought of that? You wanted to see him." Danni leaned up against him and slid her hand in his.

Somehow her support gave him the strength to move forward, to see his best friend like this. It nearly broke him.

"Hey, buddy." He walked to the side of the bed as Dave's eyes flew open.

"You two are at it again." Dave shook his head. His glassy eyes closed and reopened. "I'm glad you're still together. So, we can graduate together."

Graduate? It had been five years since graduation.

"How are you feeling?" And how did Marek get some of whatever he was on?

Danni smiled. "How do we get some of the good drugs?"

Exactly.

"Not like Jalen and Cherise." Dave used his good hand to push a piece of hair away from his eyes. "They shouldn't stay together."

"They're not together." Danni shrugged when Marek looked at her. Jalen and Cherise had never gotten together back in college. No matter how many times the two were thrown together, it just didn't stick.

"Yes." He rolled his eyes and pouted. Dave might pout, but the man didn't roll his eyes. Of course, his eyes were usually stuck to a phone. "They were kissing in front of the Dragon."

Kissing in front of the Dragon. They didn't have the Dragon in college. Either Dave saw something, or the meds were making him a bit loopy.

Dave whispered, "Don't even get me started on the unicorns." Loopy it was. He leaned his head on the pillow and closed his eyes. Talking about the unicorns was exhausting. Obviously.

Danni held back a laugh. "I really could use whatever he's having."

Marek nodded. Couldn't they all. They stood there for a few minutes as Dave slept and smiled.

He'd seen his friend was okay. He could go. Preferably before the cop showed back up. "We should go," Marek whispered to Danni.

Dave opened his eyes and lifted his head. "Marek and Danni. When did you get here?" He glared at Danni. The smile and overall goofy haze had left his eyes. One minute he was hopped up on drugs, the next coherent. Maybe Marek didn't want some of what he had.

Danni must have noticed the change. "I think that is my cue to leave."

She turned and walked out. As the door closed, Dave looked Marek up and down. "Why are you here, and what the hell are you wearing?"

"I'm here because you're my friend." Asshole. He left that off since Dave was in the hospital.

"Sorry, of course, you are. It's been a rough couple of days. I don't know what the hell happened. One minute I was heading toward my car, the next there's a loud snap, and I wake up here."

"As long as you're okay, man. I was worried."

"I was worried about you. You just disappeared."

"Yeah, I had to. We didn't know who we could trust."

"We? But you could trust her." The pain in Dave's voice was coming across loud and clear.

Marek didn't want to hurt him, but... "Yeah."

Dave shook his head. "All right. I'm not fighting it anymore. I'm too damn tired."

"Why fight it? I like her." It was as simple as that.

"I don't know. I never liked her, and then she just left when you found out about the pregnancy."

"I told her to go away. I thought Jill and I would make it work."

"But why would she listen?" Dave shook his head and groaned. "I never understood how she could just walk away. You and Jill were a train wreck. It was never going to work."

"What?"

"You never loved her the way you loved Danni."

Marek smiled. That was true. "Why didn't you say anything?"

"You were hellbent on giving your child a father. I couldn't take that away from any of you."

Marek felt his chest expand. Dave did care. He wouldn't have turned on Marek. Never. "You really do like her, don't you?"

"Danni? No. But you do, and that's all that matters." Dave laughed. "Now, about the clothes."

Marek didn't even know how to respond—from emotional to seventies basketball shorts in two seconds. He pulled the shorts down with one hand and covered his stomach with the other. But he'd wear this ridiculous outfit again and again if it would get Dave to laugh. The man hadn't done that in a while.

DANNI WALKED DOWN THE HALL. She'd originally thought she'd stand outside the door and guard it, but knew she looked like she was casing the joint for a robbery, so she figured a small side trip to grab a cup of coffee was on the agenda.

Thank God for Apple Pay. She found the coffee machine and used Maggie's passcode to buy two cups. She'd pay Maggie back once Danni grabbed some cash and could be in the same room as Maggie without her boyfriend arresting Marek.

She walked down the hall, the cups sloshing in her hand. The hot coffee burned down her fingers in tiny rivulets.

Dammit. She put a cup down on the counter by the nurses' desk and shook the moisture off her hand. She grabbed a handful of tissues from a box on the corner and dabbed her fingers before wrapped the tissues around the cup. She turned, and her breath caught in her throat. Blue uniform. A gun at his hip. A cop. Not the cop who was at the door previously. In fact, she recognized him. "Charlie?"

"I'm sorry?" He squinted at her.

"Charlie Horton?" She waited for him to nod. "Danni Stein. I went to school with your sister, Cherise."

"Yeah, Danni." Charlie smiled, but his gaze kept locking on Dave's door. He must be the next guard. Or he was checking on Dave. Which Danni respected. She wanted Dave safe. But she also wanted Marek to get out before the cops got hold of him.

"I thought you were in the Army." She needed to distract him with small talk.

"Nope."

"What have you been up to?" He was a cop, what else would he be up to? "Well, apart from your job change, what's new?"

"Not much."

Not much was a bit more than nothing. Couldn't he at least humor her with the *not-much* things and not just *not much*?

"How's Cherise doing?" Danni was reaching for small talk straws, and he was not sipping. But she needed to keep him away from that door. And if bringing up his sister did the trick, she'd take it.

"She's fine, just started a new job. Maybe you should call her once in a while." He scowled at her. True, Danni hadn't been a good friend lately. Over the years, Danni and Cherise had grown apart. She'd been so busy working, she hadn't reached out. If Danni were a better friend, she wouldn't have let it happen. Being a better friend would have to wait until she lured Charlie away from Dave's door so Marek could leave.

"Work has been crazy, but you're right. I need to call her." She gripped the tissue-wrapped coffee tighter, and the words just rambled from her lips. "We used to be such great friends. I miss her." *Stop rambling.* "But you probably don't, you see her all the time, now that you're back." *Stop talking.* "And you're a cop. How cool. Did she tell you I worked for the police after college?" *Shut up.* "It was super exciting, but now I work for a PI." There, she was shutting up now.

He didn't seem all that impressed with her resume. He probably thought she was nuts. That happened a lot.

"I guess," Charlie said. "You two always did like drama. Visiting someone?"

She nodded. "A friend of mine."

"Dave Nelson?" His gaze went back down the hall to Dave's room, like he was going to head over there. And find Marek.

She needed to create a distraction. Preferably one that would make Charlie go away. "Yeah, he went to college with Cherise and me." She bumped one of the cups of coffee against the other, and they both went flying to the ground. "Shit." Brown liquid pooled on the white tile. "Oh, darn, our coffee."

"Our?" He looked suspicious. She needed to nip that in the bud.

"One cup was for Dave."

"Is he allowed coffee?"

"Don't tell." She pushed a smile onto her lips. "Contraband. It's inhumane to make him stop cold turkey."

"Very true." Charlie smiled. "If you want to run and get him another cup, I'll watch the door."

Ummm...no. That was the exact opposite of helpful. What happened to chivalry? If you drop something, a man offered to get another one or to clean it up. Movies were flooded with heroes saving heroines.

Of course, in the movies, there was a damsel in distress. She needed to be the damsel. She tossed the tissues and the empty cups in a trashcan next to one of the rooms and sighed. "I have to get back to work. We're swamped." She frowned and looked back at Dave's door. She was going for longingly, but who knew what Charlie was seeing. Danni sucked at this crap.

But maybe contact would convince him of her sincerity. She reached for Charlie's hand. The best way to describe it was moist. And she hated that word. But his hand was an experiment in humidity.

She blinked again and again until her eyes were wet, willing a tear to fall. She sucked at this, so the best she was going to get was watery eyes and a frown. "Can you please run and get Dave his coffee? My boss is all over my ass. She's threatening to fire me. I just couldn't go into work today without seeing Dave was okay."

The threat of tears must have done the trick. Charlie squeezed her hand. "Sure." He tried to smile, but it came out all grimace-y.

"Thank you so much." And she meant it. Charlie must have changed, because he was such a dick when they were in college. He sponged off Cherise and stole from their mother. He'd spent most of his time under the influence. For him to turn himself around like this was amazing. They should run an article in the *Tribune*.

Especially since Cherise never mentioned her brother got his shit together. She never mentioned him becoming a cop. In fact, the last Danni heard he failed out of the Army. How you failed out of the Army, she had no idea, but that was a few years ago. The last time she'd talked to Cherise. She really needed to reach out.

"I'll be back in a minute." He turned around. His blond hair curled just above his shoulders like a *Point Blank* reject. His holster sat on the left side of his black uniform.

Holy shit.

No wonder Cherise never mentioned he'd gotten his shit together. He hadn't. He was the guy that kidnapped Marek. And he was here, maybe to hurt Dave or Marek. She didn't know. But she needed to get Marek out of here now and get the real cop back to Dave's door.

She ran into the hospital room and glanced at Marek, hoping her eyes were intense enough for him to see she wasn't messing around. "We have to leave." She leaned over Dave, pressing the call button at the same time. "Tell the nurse you saw the man who shot you. Make them get the cops. The bad guy is here."

"In the hospital?" Marek got to his feet.

"Yes. I distracted him, but we have to go now." The two of them hustled out of the room just as a nurse came down the hall. Danni heard Dave yell at the nurse, "The man that shot me is here in this building. Where's the police officer from the door?"

Danni and Marek bolted down the stairs. In Danni's case, more of an intense hobble. Her thighs burned. And she didn't care. The farther they could get away from this hospital, the better she'd feel. Even if her thighs didn't quite agree right now.

NINETEEN

AFTER AN EXCURSION TO find some clothes and food, Marek sat fully clothed—without the nut-hugging shorts—on a motel bed with the entire McDonald's dollar menu spread out on the bedspread. He bit into a cheeseburger and felt his arteries clog. At this point, who cared? If the burger didn't kill him, Cherise's brother was going to do it. Why give the asshole the satisfaction? Especially when this tasted so damn good.

The door to the room swung open. "Apparently, they don't have a business center or any type of computer access." She grabbed a box of chicken nuggets off the bed. "Thank goodness we paid by cash or who knows how we would have paid."

"We could've found a way. They rent rooms by the hour, and he seemed to like you—"

"Do not finish that thought." She shoved a nugget in her mouth and narrowed her eyes. After wiping her hands on a napkin, she pulled out Maggie's phone. "We'll have to use this for research."

"What do you know about Cherise and her brother?" Marek asked around some fries.

"Not much. He said something about her having a new job. If that's true, he must have reached out to her recently. But that's really all I know."

"Didn't she tell you?"

"No. We kind of lost touch when I started the PI firm with Maggie." Her eyes locked on the phone.

"Lost touch? But you two were inseparable."

She shook her head. "I put all my money into the firm, and we were killing ourselves trying to make a name. I even started taking odd coding jobs to stay afloat. I didn't have time to go clubbing or meet for lunch anymore. So she stopped asking."

"Yeah, but now Busted is a big name. I've heard good things."

"We went from famine to feast. It's just a lot of work. I'm the only one who knows how to operate the computers past the start button, which is great because I like to help, but it leads to a lot of long nights."

She didn't say the word lonely, but he knew that feeling. He was surrounded by his friends, sometimes day and night, yet he went home alone. He reached for her hand. She was so delicate and soft. "You have me now." He felt those words all the way through his chest. She did have him, no matter how hard he'd tried to fight it.

She slid her fingers through his as her gaze took on a faraway look. Something was either on her mind, or she wasn't feeling him the way he was feeling her. *Please be something on your mind.* "Everything okay?"

She shook her head. "Yeah. Sorry. We should find Cherise." She clicked on the small screen in her hand, pulling her other hand from his. Whatever had been swimming in her eyes was long gone. "Let's see. She's living in Aurora. She has a dog named Peaches. She hates Maroon Five."

"Where are you getting this?"

"Facebook." Her eyes widened. "Bingo." Her fingers flew over the screen. "She took Peaches to the vet for an ear infection." More clicking. "There's one in Aurora on Galena."

She put the phone on speaker and brought up the website for the vet. The ring-back tone chirped, and a woman came on the line. "K-9 Animal Hospital. Merina speaking. How may I help you?"

"Hi, Merina. This is Cherise Horton, and I brought Peaches in to see the doctor a few weeks ago."

"Of course. How's Peaches doing?"

"She's doing well. We took her to the dog park last week and she's fine." The real Cherise had, according to the pictures on another internet tab.

"That's great. What can I help you with? Is she sick again?"

"No, she's fine. There was supposed to be a rebate for the antibiotic ointment they sent me home with. But I haven't received it yet. Do you have my correct address?"

"I have you at 1523 Henry Avenue."

"That's right. Oh well, it must have gotten lost in the mail."

"I don't think we have any active rebates for antibiotics." Merina sounded so disappointed. "I can find out for you?"

"That's okay, I should go. My mom's calling." Danni's hand hovered over the screen. "Bye." She ended the call and smiled. "1523 Henry Avenue."

She tapped on the screen some more. "Half hour

away." She took a cheeseburger from the stack of food. "I don't know why people insist on putting all their personal information online. It takes two minutes to piece everything together."

Opening the wrapper, she raised the burger to her mouth. A groan came from between her lips. *For heaven's sake.* Her eyes closed as she chewed, obviously savoring every bite. Her throat moved as she swallowed. Her tongue shot out and slowly licked at her bottom lip.

He might have visibly gulped. He wasn't sure. All he was sure about was that he had a weird desire to be that burger.

Danni was staring at him, the burger hovering inches from her face. "What?"

You look hot when you eat a burger. I can't help but want to see if you'd look that hot eating me. Uh, no. He couldn't think of one way to say that and not sound creepy.

He sighed. "Nothing."

"I think we should go over there tonight." She took another bite of the burger.

This time he turned away. He didn't have the mental capacity to watch that again. "Where?"

"To Cherise's."

"Why?"

"You really want to stay here any longer than we have to?"

He glanced around the room they were renting by the hour. The dark stain in the corner looked like it might have come from a drug deal gone wrong. The bedspread had weird blotches that he'd like to believe were caused by excessive bleach, but he had a feeling this room hadn't seen bleach since the release of Windows Vista. "No."

"Then let's go talk to Cherise." She stood and tossed the burger wrapping in the bag. She was right. They had to get out of this place and get back to their real life before they walked away with crabs or worse.

DANNI STEPPED out of the Crown Vic and checked the address. "This is it."

"This is where she lives?" Marek came around the car and stood in front of the double-wide trailer with white siding. It looked clean, although the sun was long gone and it was hard to make out anything with the faded street lights.

She laughed at the look of horror on Marek's face. "Yes, princess, people don't always live in penthouses in the city."

"I didn't mean it like that. I meant... Hell, I don't know what I meant."

"Let's go." Danni walked up the short driveway and turned onto the sidewalk. When she thought trailer, this wasn't what she thought. Garage. Driveway. Sidewalk. All permanent-type things, leading to a house that could be hauled away at a moment's notice.

She went up the stairs, which were covered in fake grass. Or a rug that was supposed to look like grass. The locked yellow screen door bounced when she knocked on it. Flowers sat in pots along the front of the trailer. In the sunlight, the place was probably colorful and cheery. At night, it looked creepy.

Or maybe it was the neighborhood. Now who was being the princess? Or it could be the fact that the family of the guy trying to get Marek was inside. And maybe he was even inside. She really needed to get a gun. And learn how to shoot it.

A woman whipped open the white inside door, a cigarette hanging from her lips. Danni had met her a bunch of times over the years, and although her skin looked worn, time had been kind. Her muscular legs filled bright blue spandex leggings. Her black tank top hugged generous curves. She was still pretty. She just looked a few years older.

"Mrs. Horton?"

"Do I know you?" Her eyes went from dull and cold to sparked with recognition. "Oh my. Dannielle Stein. Look at you."

Mrs. Horton wrapped her arms around Danni and squeezed. Danni almost forgot the woman was a hugger. Like, a crazy hugger. A personal-boundary antagonist who got off on constant touching.

"And who do we have here?" Mrs. Horton eyed Marek, her hand resting on Danni's arm.

"Old friend from college." Danni smiled, hoping that was enough information and she wouldn't push for his name. "Is Cherise here?"

They might want Charlie, but asking about Cherise seemed to be the better bet.

"She's still at work but should be back soon." Mrs. Horton stepped back and opened the door wide. "Would you both like to come in and wait?"

"Sure." Danni stepped through the open door, and a little dog with golden fur barked at her feet. It was the cutest bark and the cutest ball of fluff. The little thing looked like a teddy bear with dog-like tendencies.

"That's Peaches. She likes to think she's badass, but she's not." Mrs. Horton led the way further inside.

Holy crap. It was so much bigger inside than it was outside. Danni saw a large family room, a formal dining room, and a small den off the front. A kitchen was visible through a chest-high opening in one wall that had with a counter, and a hallway led from the family room, probably to bedrooms.

"This is really nice," Danni said. And it was nice, mixed with a dash of old-lady. Flowered couches covered in clear plastic sat in front of a big-screen television. Wooden side tables held remotes and a corded telephone. Who had a landline anymore? A plastic tree sat in the corner.

"It's home." Mrs. Horton smiled around the cigarette. "Can I get you two something to drink? I have a wonderful herbal tea."

"No, thank you, Mrs. Horton." Danni walked past a wall of frames. Charlie's face scowled back. So young and so unhappy.

"Oh, please, you're an adult now. Call me Cheryl." She sat down on the flowered loveseat.

Cheryl. Cherise. Charlie. They liked the *ch* sound. Just because his parents lacked imagination didn't mean he had to be miserable.

Danni sat on the couch. Marek sat down next to her. Plastic stuck and crinkled as they made themselves comfortable. Trying to Netflix and chill on this plastic was probably enough to make anyone crazy.

"How are you doing, Cheryl?" Danni asked.

"I'm doing well." She snuffed her cigarette out in a nearby ashtray. Peaches' little collar jingled as she pranced around, sniffing everyone's leg before sitting at Marek's feet.

"She likes you." Cheryl smiled and lit another

cigarette. "That dog doesn't seem to like anyone. We had to take her to the vet because she kept getting into fights with other dogs."

Part of Danni felt bad the dog couldn't seem to chill out long enough not to fight. The other part was glad because that's how she'd found Cherise. Now she needed to get Cheryl talking so they could figure out where Charlie was. Maybe she should start with something safe before she jumped into the whole long-lost son thing—if he was even lost.

Danni remembered all the nights she and Cherise would visit Cherise's mom at the restaurant where she worked. Those were the best meals they'd have all month. Of course, they were in college, and food was at a premium—good food anyway. "Are you still waitressing?"

"Not anymore. I'm a yoga instructor. The food they served was so full of fat and chemicals. I couldn't live that way anymore. I'm trying to focus on putting healthy food in my body."

That would explain how good she looked. The cigarette train she had going on probably wasn't the best non-fat non-chemical substitute, though.

"Does Cherise know you're coming?" Cheryl glanced at the clock hanging on the wall. "She's not normally this late coming home from work."

"I thought I'd surprise her."

"She might be with her boyfriend." Cheryl bounced as her eyes lit up again. "You probably know him. He went to school with you."

"Her boyfriend?"

"Yeah, Jaden or something like that."

"Jalen?" Danni turned to Marek. Did he know? He shrugged one shoulder and had a confused look on his face. Probably the same look she had on her face. Cherise and Jalen were dating?

"Yep. I told her I'd remember his name when he stepped up and put a ring on it. Years of stringing her along—breaking up and getting back together. They can't make up their damn minds." She shook her head. "But I guess she loves him. She always loved him. I'm glad she found someone." Cheryl eyed Marek briefly. "Have you found someone special?"

Had she? She had no idea how to answer that question, especially with Marek sitting right there. Did they have anything? He still didn't know what she'd done. And when he did would they be anything to each other? Or would he turn away? Just the thought of a cold shoulder made her insides ache. But it was inevitable.

Before she could answer, the front door swung open and Cherise walked in. "Danni. Marek. What are you guys doing here?"

"We wanted to say hi."

Cherise frowned. She wasn't buying it. Granted, she probably knew more about what was going on. When one of your friends from college was plastered all over the news, you tended to pay attention. And when that friend shows up at your door, despite being plastered all over the news, something was up.

"And we wanted to see if you knew where Charlie was."

"Charlie?" Cheryl took a deep inhale of her cancer stick. "My son Charlie?"

"Yeah." Danni nodded.

"That boy." She shook her head and tapped her cigarette a little too hard on the edge of the ashtray. "He is nothing but trouble. I haven't seen him in years. Why are you looking for him?"

"I saw him at the hospital today, but I forgot to get his number." She was making crap up but trying to keep it as close to the truth as possible. "He asked how our friend Dave was doing, and I wanted to give him an update."

"I heard about that." Cheryl nodded. "That was one of your friends, wasn't it?"

"Yeah, Ma." Cherise chewed on her pinky nail. "How's he doing?"

"Shot. He could have died."

"Do you know why?" Cherise leaned against the kitchen counter, dropping her purse next to her elbow.

Danni wanted to ask "No, do you?" but she didn't think that would go over well with her mom sitting on the couch. If Cheryl hadn't seen her son in years, maybe Cherise hadn't either.

Maybe Cherise would be just as surprised by all of this as Danni. She had to be, because even though they hadn't seen each other in ages, her best friend couldn't have changed that much.

TWENTY

DO YOU KNOW WHY? Wasn't that the question of the day. And Marek leaned forward, waiting for the answer. Although the person he thought might have the answer was asking the question.

Cherise looked the same. Older, but she still had brown curly hair that stood up in frizzy waves. Too much makeup. But that was always what he saw when he saw her. Too much. Too much noise. Too much drama.

Danni shook her head. "We're not sure what happened." What an understatement.

"What does that have to do with my brother?" Cherise asked, frowning a little.

"We wanted to tell him what was going on with Dave." Danni smiled innocently. "Do you know where he is?"

"Oh, um. I don't know."

"He said you talked to him recently."

"Well, yeah. I talk to him if he calls me or whatever." Cherise's eyes zipped back and forth—her phone, the door, Danni. "I can tell him when he calls me next."

Either she didn't know where he was, or she was evading. Considering the way she jittered, he'd say evading.

Danni kept going. "I was sort of hoping to talk to him about his new career as a cop."

"Ha!" Cheryl spit out smoke as she coughed and Cherise jumped. When Cheryl's gasping stopped, she took a drag off the cigarette in her hand. "Charlie's not a cop, and he sure as shit doesn't have a career."

Cherise made a face. "Ma."

"What? Your brother is good for nothing. I always knew there was something off about that boy. There was almost hope when he joined the military, but he messed that up too."

"Stop." Cherise sighed. "Go take Peaches for her walk."

"Why?"

"Please, Ma. I need to talk to my friends."

"Fine." Cheryl crushed the cigarette into the ashtray and stood. "Come on, Peaches. Let's go outside." She picked up a pack of smokes and her lighter. "I'll be outside if you wanna tell me more about my cop son." She barked a laugh as she followed Peaches out the door, grabbing a leash on the way. And then there was silence.

Danni stared at Cherise, who picked up her phone and came over to sit on the loveseat. Plastic crinkled as she crossed her legs and took off her red suit coat. She tapped at her phone and tossed it down next to her. "You want to talk. Let's talk."

Danni sighed. Marek understood. He wanted to sigh too. He could see how this would go. They'd ask all the questions, Cherise wouldn't give any answers. A one-sided conversation only the Joker could pull off.

"Where is your brother?" Danni was obviously done playing around. "I need to talk to him."

"Why?"

"I told you."

Cherise sighed. "You want to tell him about Dave? Why? He wouldn't know him."

"Then why was he visiting him at the hospital?"

"I don't know." Cherise shrugged. "Maybe it has to do with his job."

"What is his job, exactly?" Danni leaned forward.

"You saw him. He had on a uniform. He's a cop."

Danni smirked. "I didn't mention a uniform."

"Well how else would you know he's a cop?" Cherise shook her head and picked up her phone again. "I have things to do. Are we almost done?"

"We should go." Marek stood up. If Cherise didn't know anything, this was a waste of time. If she knew where Charlie was, she could warn him, which also meant this was a waste of time.

"Fine." Danni didn't sound as excited about leaving. "Can you call me if you hear anything from him?"

"Sure."

Danni stood and walked to the door. "Thanks, Cherise."

The front door flew open. One second Danni was standing, the next she was on the floor and Charlie had a gun angled against her head. Another guy, dressed in jeans and a T-shirt came up from behind. He looked like the wannabe cop who'd shot Danni.

"Don't move," Charlie screamed at Marek as the gun shook against Danni's head. Against. Her. Fucking. Head.

Marek lifted his arms and patted the air with his

palms. Calming. At least that was what he hoped it was. "I'm not moving."

Cherise jumped off the loveseat. "What the fuck, Charlie?"

"Shut the hell up," the guy by the door screamed.

"Jason, don't talk to my sister like that," Charlie snarled.

"Let's get this shit over with." Jason was an asshole, but Marek could understand the sentiment. He wanted to get this shit over with too.

Charlie turned to Cherise. "Do you have the password so we can do this retina thing? You said that's all we need, right?"

"I don't know."

Marek knew she was lying. It wasn't a stretch to figure Charlie would know that too.

"How can you not know?" Charlie glared at Marek. "You. We need the retina scan for the Dragon server."

"What?" Marek tried to play ignorant. Which wasn't too hard. How the hell did this guy know anything about the Dragon server?

The gun rattled, and Danni groaned as Charlie shoved the barrel harder against Danni's head.

"Okay. Okay." Marek shouldn't be pushing this guy. But the information on that server was top secret. He couldn't just give it away.

Charlie motioned to Cherise's bag. "Get your computer. We need to do this now."

"But we need to be behind the firewall," Cherise said, but still grabbed the bag.

"For fuck's sake," Charlie snarled, "we're never going to be able to get back inside that building."

"But you're the police." Marek didn't know why he

said it. This guy was no more a policeman than Marek was a Time Lord. On the other hand, this douchebag was holding his woman hostage and trying to destroy everything Marek built. It was pissing him off.

Charlie stared at Marek. "You're right. And you're the owner. Don't you have keys?"

Marek nodded, patting his pocket. He never went anywhere without them. Right now, he was regretting that.

"Get up." Charlie dragged Danni up by her hair.

Her legs scrabbled at the floor, her head angled back as Charlie held fast. "Ouch. What the fuck? I can't breathe."

"Shut up." Charlie pulled her closer, the barrel in place. "Cherise. Let's go!" He turned to Marek. "Get up."

"Why are you doing this?" Marek stood, trying to keep his movements slow, his words quiet. He couldn't watch this guy hurt Danni again. He wanted to jump this guy and beat the ever-loving shit out of him.

Cherise slung her bag over her shoulder. "I have it. Let's go."

"Start the car and take him with you." Charlie nodded at Marek, and waited for him to follow Cherise and Jason out of the trailer before Charlie came out, dragging Danni.

They were forty-five minutes from the city if there was no traffic. Forty-five minutes to figure out what the hell he was going to do. He had to figure out something.

Given the choice of handing over the key to destroying his company or saving Danni, there was no contest.

FORTY-FIVE MINUTES LATER, emergency lights were the only thing keeping the stairs and hallways at Obrona from total darkness. That didn't stop Danni from seeing the crazed looks on the faces of Charlie and his terrorist friend, Jason. With his dark spiky hair and blue eyes, Jason could've been hot. Instead, he was a psycho. Not surprising he was Charlie's friend.

"Hurry up." Charlie gripped Danni's hair all the way down the hall and into Marek's office. She was pretty sure her hair was still there. He kept pulling. Why he hated her hair so much was a fucking mystery. Her scalp was on fire. Her eyes watered. And every yank struck tears from her eyes. She wasn't fighting back and yet he was still pulling. What the actual fuck?

Not that she'd cry or cry out. She wouldn't give the dick the satisfaction.

Another yank. An overhead light came on. Darkness buzzed between the flashes as her eyes adjusted.

"I'm not a fucking cat." Screw his satisfaction. She wrapped her hand around the hair still attached at her nape and pulled the rest out of his hands. "And my hair is not a fucking leash."

He managed to latch onto the collar of her shirt, hauling her back against his chest. Her head jarred at the impact, but his breath against her neck was roiling her stomach. "Your *hair* is whatever I say it is." He shoved her toward the couch in the corner. "And what kind of sick fuck puts a leash on a cat."

She tried to catch herself before she hit the carpet, but the floor was closer than it appeared. Her knees hit first. Then her palms.

Jason laughed. "Maybe if you wanted to hang the cat." Sick asshole.

"Sit down and shut up." The words were obviously for Danni, or maybe Danni and Marek. Whatever. As long as Charlie's creepy hands and breath weren't all over her. Charlie pointed the gun at the desk and motioned to Cherise. "Set up on the desk."

Silence settled on the room as Cherise took out her laptop and turned to Marek. "I need you to turn on your computer."

"I can't." Marek sat next to Danni on the leather couch, his leg against hers. Warmth. Strength poured from that one touch. She wasn't sure how, but she was pretty damn sure she felt his concern in that small touch.

Cherise looked up from behind her laptop. "Why?"

"Dave took away my access." He shrugged. Since they'd been on the computer just the other night, he must be stalling. "And I lost my laptop when somebody tried to abduct me."

"Who tried to abduct you?" Cherise honestly looked confused. What the hell did she think was going on? Her brother and his thug were holding guns.

Marek didn't bother answering. He just looked at the two guys.

"Enough of this. Get to work." Charlie leaned against the wall, gun still aimed at Danni and Marek.

"Then find me a laptop he can sign in to," Cherise told Charlie.

"Fine." He looked over at Jason. "Watch them. But don't shoot anyone. Not yet."

Charlie jogged out of the room and returned after a few minutes. "Here." He slid a laptop onto the desk.

Cherise opened it, and dings and dongs sounded as the computer whirred to life. "Come over here," she said to Marek.

He walked slowly past the armed assholes, dragging a chair from the front of the desk around next to Cherise. He sat next to her. Slowly.

Bile balled in Danni's throat. Once they got access to the server, they wouldn't need Marek and Danni anymore. They weren't going to get out of this. There was no way.

"I have to log into the server with your password?" Cherise tapped at her computer.

"How do you know my password?"

Cherise's cheeks flamed. "I used a keystroke logger."

"How did you get access to my computer?" Marek's eyes were the size of saucers. Danni would laugh if this weren't a nightmare.

"I used Jalen's computer one night when I stayed over." She glared at Marek. "I'm not as incapable as you think I am."

"Who thought you were incapable?" Marek truly looked confused. But then again, the whole situation was confusing.

Cherise huffed. "You did when I asked to work for you."

"When did you ask to work for me?"

"Through Jalen." She sighed. "Never mind. Where's the iris scanner?"

"You don't have to do this," Marek said.

"Yes, she does. Where's the scanner?" Jason stepped away from the door and aimed the gun at Danni.

Marek got up and crossed the room, over to a wall safe. He opened it, took out a scanner, and handed it to Cherise. "Did Jalen know about any of this?"

"No." She plugged the USB cord into his laptop. "I'm

sorry." She paused for a moment and then tipped the scanner toward his face.

Marek closed his eyes. Danni wasn't surprised. This was it. Once he let them in, his company was over. His career gone.

"Open your eyes." Jason wrapped a hand around the back of Marek's neck and used his other hand to pry one eye open.

"If you gouge out my eye, it won't work," Marek said.

Cherise nodded. "I got it. Leave him alone." She typed and clicked and ran her fingers over the mouse pad. She scowled at the screen.

"What's the matter?" Jason's tone was pure dickhead. Probably why he came across as such an asshole. Or that could be the gun waving around.

Cherise didn't look up. "It's not working."

Charlie lurched toward Marek. "Put your face in front of that thing again."

Marek pushed back from the desk. "I did already."

"Stop. He did. He did." Cherise nibbled on a finger-nail, eyes fixed on the screen in front of her. Given how uneventful running code was, Danni had no idea what she was so intrigued by. "The code is erroring out. It says the trigger is invalid. Line 4532."

"What does that mean?" Charlie came around behind the desk and squinted at the screen. Like he could help.

"It means it's not working."

Charlie ran a hand over his face. "It worked before." He leaned down to his sister's ear. "Get this shit working, or no money. You'll be stuck here forever without your guy."

"I'm trying." She swiped at her eyes. "That was a different set of code. I had to make a few changes."

Charlie poked her shoulder. "Why? If it fucking works—"

Jason sighed. "This shit is taking too long. Fix it."

"I need her." Cherise pointed at Danni.

Danni went cold, then hot. *Please don't say it's my code. Please don't say it's my code.* This was really something she should tell Marek on her own. She should've told him earlier. Now he'd never forgive her.

"Why?" Charlie stepped in front of Danni like he didn't trust her or maybe he didn't trust his sister. Whatever it was, Danni wanted to be left out of it.

Please.

"She sold me Marek's code. I need her to fix it."

Danni's ears burned. She should have known it would come out. She closed her eyes, hoping and praying that Marek didn't hear what Cherise said. Or maybe that he hadn't understood.

"That's my code?"

Danni made herself look at him. His pallor told her he might actually believe she supplied the code that destroyed his company. The rest of him looked hopeful. Hoping that Cherise was lying.

Fuck, Danni wished Cherise was lying. "I didn't know the code was being used to take down your company. I swear."

"Wah. Wah." Charlie took her arm and dragged her off the couch. "Go fix this shit so we can leave."

Danni walked over to the chair where Marek had been sitting. She sat in the chair and looked back at the couch. Why the hell had she looked? All that hope was gone. Marek's face was cold, shut down. Eyes like ice. Lips a flat line.

Tears burned her lids as she tried to make him understand with a look. Just one look, her eyes pleaded. *I. Didn't. Know. I didn't mean for this to happen.*

Her telepathic ability wasn't working. But her body-language reader was on point. The expression on his face said he'd never forgive her. She'd lost him forever.

TWENTY-ONE

HE WROTE THIS CODE. He. Wrote. Marek couldn't get those words out of his head. Danni had sold his code, and Cherise used to break into his company. She said she didn't know, but given the way she reacted when Cherise said the words, she'd known.

Charlie huffed. "Are you about done?"

"I'm working as fast as I can." Danni sighed, taking a second to twist her hair into a rope and slide it over her shoulder. Normally, he'd find that attractive.

Hell, he still did. It just felt more painful than pleasureful. She was part of the reason he was losing everything. His company. Her.

He watched as her fingers flew over the keyboard. Each stroke another knife in the back.

Cherise's brother sat down on the armrest of the couch. What could he possibly gain from all this?

"Money. Pure and simple, brother."

Marek must have asked that out loud. Great. Conversing with the enemy—and they were all enemies.

"But this could put lives in danger."

"Lives are already in danger. Might as well get our piece," Jason snarled. Of all the enemies, he seemed the least hinged. "Besides, our government sells enough of our secrets to make things dangerous. When we were working in Kabul, our government traded secrets like Tic Tacs. Why shouldn't we just do what they do?"

"So two wrongs make a right," Marek said.

"Fuck that." Charlie laughed. "Two wrongs make me a rich man. Do you even know what you have here?"

"No. We don't ask our clients what they store on our servers."

Charlie laughed. "You have got to be kidding me. There's all the specs for a brand new radar-absorbent material. For fighter jets. And we'll own the technology."

Danni looked up from the screen. "So you have a buyer."

"Get your face back in that computer and shut the hell up." Jason stalked over to the desk and used one hand to Professor Snape her face toward the screen. "What we have or don't have isn't your concern."

Marek might not like Danni at the moment, but he didn't like seeing her manhandled. Not that he could do anything about the guns pointed at them. "If they catch you," Marek said, "you'll end up in Guantanamo. That can't be a good place for a discharged officer."

Charlie shook his head. "Maybe not, but I wasn't discharged, so I'm fucked either way."

"Shut up," Jason growled. The man actually growled. "No more talking."

Seconds turned to minutes turned to hours as Danni tapped at the keyboard. Well, it felt like hours. Marek just sat there waiting for the word that his data was gone. That everything he built was gone.

And then what? Would these two idiots let them go? He didn't know. But why not? It wasn't like Marek and Danni could stop them.

"What are you doing?" Jason came up behind Danni.

"I'm recreating the trigger." Danni kept tapping. She looked so intent, Marek almost bought it. There was no way it should take this long, though. Not for Danni.

Jason glared down at her. "What are you doing now?" His already tense voice was getting clipped. Angier.

"Same thing." She sighed and slammed her finger against a key. Either she didn't hear the annoyance in his voice, or she didn't care.

"How the fuck long does the same thing take?"

"It takes as long as it takes." Danni didn't look up. Which was probably why she didn't see the change on Jason's face.

Marek leaned forward, but before he could get up, Jason backhanded Danni's head. The sound of his knuckles cracked in the silence.

"What the fuck?" Marek jumped up to a symphony of *what the hell* and *what are you doing*.

"Sit down." Jason pointed his gun at Marek and then at Cherise, who'd jumped up as well.

Marek fell back on the couch, watching Danni. He might be pissed at her, but he didn't want this. Her arms covered her head, shoulders hunched.

Jason grabbed Danni's shoulder and pulled her back. "Quit fucking around and get this done."

She nodded, lip curled in a silent snarl. She tapped at the computer. "Done."

"See." Jason patted the top of her head. "You just needed a bit of motivation."

Cherise sat back down and turned the laptop toward

her. Her eyebrows drew together as she turned to Danni. Confusion. What had Danni done?

And why? Her life wasn't worth this shit. This was his problem. His company. His mistake.

Marek had been arrogant thinking he and his team could handle it quickly. They hadn't handled it, and now it was all gone.

"What?" Charlie demanded. "Is there something wrong?"

"Nope. Just checking the code." Cherise poked at the computer and stood. "Okay. It's done." She closed her computer and slipped it into her backpack.

"Good." Charlie stepped away from the wall. "Take your computer and get out of here."

"Okay." Cherise slung the backpack over one shoulder and turned to Danni. "Let's go."

"She's staying here," Jason put a hand out, blocking Danni from standing up.

Cherise stared at him. "Why? We got everything you need."

"Cherise, get out," Charlie snapped.

Cherise hiked the bag higher on her shoulder and ducked her head after one last look at Danni. There was pity and maybe regret on her face. Not that any of that mattered. Not that being friends in college mattered.

Marek watched Cherise walk out the door without another glance. They might have been close, but now she wasn't even a friend. She walked out the door, leaving Danni behind with her brother and a guy with a gun.

He couldn't believe this was happening.

DANNI WATCHED CHERISE LEAVE. She'd actually left even as her brother and his goon pointed guns at Danni and Marek. They might not have been her friends in a while, but they'd been close before. At least Danni thought they'd been.

How crazy of her.

The door closed, and a scene from a few months ago played in Danni's mind. Maggie walking into a room with guns pointed at her head. Bullets flying. Chase bleeding.

She was so screwed.

"Get up," Jason ordered.

"You don't have to do this." Marek stood.

Charlie walked over to Jason and leaned in. "Why don't we just go?"

"They know who we are," Jason said.

"The cops have figured out who you are. They were looking for you." Danni was lying, but hopefully they'd buy it. "How do you think we found you?"

Jason the asshole stared at Danni. His eyes were unnerving. It was weird. "You're lying, or they'd be here now." Or it was some horrific X-ray mind-reading thing. She better figure out how to convince him, or she was back to being screwed.

"I swear. I'm not." She was grasping at invisible straws. "They should be here any minute. Go. Before they get here."

Uncertainty swam in Jason's eyes, and Charlie looked at his friend with what Danni could call hope. At least Charlie was on board with the whole *Keep Marek Alive* operation.

"Let's go, Jason." Charlie nodded toward the door. "We got what we need."

Well, technically, they didn't get what they needed,

but who was counting. That was something for the two of them to figure out at a later date. When them and their guns were far away.

"The cops know we kidnapped them and that we shot Dave. We're already in too deep." Jason shook his head, and gestured to the side of the desk. "Come over here and kneel down."

Danni turned to Marek, hoping he had some brilliant idea. Something. Anything to get them out of here. He looked defeated.

And why not?

The cops weren't coming. Maggie didn't even know they'd gone to Cherise's. Danni probably should have told her. Or warned her. Hell, she should have kept Maggie in the loop on the bad guys. Who knew if the cops would figure out who they were.

The only reason Danni had figured it out was because she knew Charlie. They didn't. They didn't even know Cherise. How would they get to the bad guy without the information?

Voice memo. Danni just had to reach in her pocket. She slid her thumb over the fingerprint sensor and clicked the icon at the top right—hoping and praying she clicked the right app.

She put on her angry-mom voice. She'd heard it from her own mother enough. "Charlie Horton, you can't do this. Tell your friend Jason we won't say anything. Marek's company is destroyed. You have the plans from the server. You win."

"Shut up," Jason yelled. "And get down on the floor."

Danni knelt. What else could she do? She was a computer programmer, not some gun-toting private investigator. Which was her own fault. Maggie had been trying to get her to learn to shoot or take a self-defense class.

She could honestly say this was not how she saw her life ending. She figured she'd die from a heart attack after binging on Cinnabon and Jolt—probably during a week-long stint of sitting on her ass playing Fortnite.

She didn't think it would end like this. And a part of her still hoped it wouldn't. But her hope had nothing to cling to. Nobody was coming. Nobody knew they were here. But she didn't want to let it go. If she did, she'd lose her shit. If she let it go, this was the end.

She didn't want it to be the end. She had plans. She had things she needed to fix.

Marek kneeled down next to her. Speaking of fixing...

TWENTY-TWO

MAREK WAITED FOR THE INEVITABLE, on his knees next to Danni, waiting to meet his maker *Sopranos*-style. So many things he wished he'd done. So many regrets.

"I'm sorry." Danni leaned toward him, and his senses filled with her. He drank in her face, her body. "I answered an ad to write a piece of code and used some of our old stuff as a starting point. I didn't know. I swear."

Marek nodded. "I get it." And he did get it. He wasn't happy about it, but at this point, who cared. It all meant nothing. His company. His life. The worst part was that he'd dragged Danni into this.

He reached out and took her hand. They were in this together, whether he wanted it or not. And he did not want her in this. He'd never forgive himself for pulling her in. Not that he was going to have to carry around the guilt for long so there was that. He closed his eyes and waited. And waited.

The two morons with the guns kept talking. Still

trying to figure out if they wanted to kill them. If these two didn't kill him, the suspense just might.

A loud thud.

Marek's eyes slammed open. No pain. He wasn't dead. Danni?

He didn't want to look. He couldn't bear the thought of them hurting her. To have to see it would break his heart. His head hadn't received the memo. It turned to see Danni was still kneeling. She was okay. Another crash.

Gunshots.

Marek dove toward Danni, flattening her onto the floor. His body covered hers as shots whizzed by. Not that he felt the whizzing, but he heard the cracking glass.

"Chicago Police."

Thank fuck.

More shots. Glass, paper, and who knew what else rained down over them. He wanted to check on Danni, make sure she was okay, but he couldn't hear a damn thing. And he wasn't going to lift his head. He refused to give anybody a target, and he was all that stood between the flying bullets and Danni.

Pop. Pop.

And then silence.

"Clear," a voice yelled from somewhere, followed by shuffling. But no more bangs.

Marek lifted his head and checked the room. Nothing but carnage. And, shit... Jason lay there, eyes open. Blood pooled on the floor around his body.

"Mr. Skala, are you okay?" A police officer carrying an assault rifle stood over them. Marek was still on top of Danni. He could feel her, but he couldn't feel her breathing. He couldn't feel if she was injured.

So, even though it killed him, he pulled away, his eyes

roving up and down her body. No blood. No holes. "Danni, you can get up."

She didn't move. Not at all.

"Is she okay?" The cop squatted next to her.

Don't touch her. Marek wanted to knock him out of the way. He blocked the cop and slid his hand along her back. "Danni, honey. You can get up now."

Nothing. *Jesus, please get up.*

Danni's arm moved. Maybe it was more of a twitch. No, it moved. She planted one hand on the floor and rolled onto her knees. "Ouch." She shifted sideways and fell on her ass, rubbing the side of her leg where she'd been shot earlier.

"How are you?" Marek kept his eyes on her, watching every move. No blood. Nothing looked broken.

"I'm fine." Danni tried to stand, but the cop leaned around Marek and put his hand on her shoulder.

He stared at her—a little too closely. "Stay down, ma'am. You might be in shock."

The cop was right. Her eyes were big. Blank. She wasn't herself. Which wasn't a surprise. As far as he knew, she'd never been on this side of the action. Well, they'd run from gunfire, but not been in the center —helpless.

"I'm not in shock." Danni glared at the cop. The doe-eyed look was gone. In its place was fire.

Marek could admit he liked the fire a hell of a lot more. He reached for Danni's hand and she grabbed on. Her hand soft and small compared to his. He wanted to bring it to his lips. He wanted to bring *her* to his lips. But he didn't think she'd be into that. Not after what just happened. As soon as she was standing, she snapped her hand back. Like she didn't want to touch him.

The hand-holding as they'd knelt. The contact as she'd stood. It meant nothing. Comfort during a high-stress situation. Not real. How did things go so far off track? One day she was sharing her bed with him, and the next, she couldn't share a hand.

Chase flew through the door and glanced at the two bodies. "The building's secure. Danni, Marek, why don't we move into the hall." He nodded to the cop. "Stay here. Sergeant Flores will be up here in a minute."

Marek followed Danni out the door. And stopped.

Somebody was screaming. Cops pulled their guns as Maggie barreled down the hall. "Danni, where are you?"

"Put the guns away. Guns away!" Chase holstered his weapon and glared at Maggie. "I told you to wait downstairs."

Chase's glare would scare small children and the elderly. Maggie's shut the big bad cop's mouth up tight. Maggie won, hands down. Chase huffed and went back into Marek's office. Marek swore he heard the man say "Women."

Marek was on the verge of agreeing. He didn't know what to do about Danni. He liked her. Hell, he loved her. And she wouldn't give him the time of day. And it was all his fault.

Of course, getting a girl almost killed twice would do that. His only excuse was desperation. He'd needed help catching the bad guys and saving his company. The bad guys were down. His company was screwed. One out of two wasn't bad.

Right now, as EMTs ran past to look at the bodies, he didn't care about Obrona, or that Cherise had the infor-mation from the Dragon server. It didn't matter. Somewhere along the way, he'd fallen for Danni. And he'd put her in harm's way.

Something grazed his hand, and he pulled away. He didn't want to talk to anyone. He didn't want to touch anyone. He wanted this over.

That look. The way she pulled away from him after the cops ran in the room. She was never going to forgive him. But that was okay. He was never going to forgive himself, either.

THEY WERE BOTH DEAD. Jason and Charlie. Danni had never seen a dead body before. Now she'd seen two. Not something she needed to do again.

Marek's face was colorless. It took every ounce of her dwindling energy not to jump at him and hold on tight. But she'd hurt him. Nearly destroyed him. The fact that he'd pulled away when she'd tried to hold his hand earlier told her everything she needed to know. Whether she wanted to know it or not.

Danni's legs wobbled, but her heart throbbed. Breaths sputtered in her throat as tears lined her eyes. They'd almost died.

She fell into Maggie's arms. It wasn't her usual MO, but neither was getting stuck in the middle of a *Call of Duty* live-action game.

Maggie inhaled deeply. "I'm so glad you're okay."

"Me too." Danni looked over Maggie's shoulder to the man in the chair. His head was in his hands as he bent forward. He wasn't used to this anymore then she was. She pulled away from Maggie and took a hesitant step toward Marek. "Are you okay?"

"Been better." His voice was muffled. He didn't look up.

"I'm sorry."

That got his attention. He lifted his head. Those eyes. He looked sad. Drained. "Me too."

What did she say to that? "If you need me to do anything to help, I'm here."

"I need a job." He laughed, but it wasn't the sexy little rumble she'd come to love. Nope. It was cold. No humor.

"Why do you need a job? Can't you rebuild?"

"Who's going to trust me with their data? Cherise got away with everything on the Dragon."

"No, she didn't. It was encrypted, probably by Metal-Wolke. There's nothing she can do with it."

"But the files are still there. It's only a matter of time before they hack it."

"If she tries to open any of it, Maggie will get an email with the coordinates, and Cherise's computer will crash."

Maggie pulled out her cell phone. "Why my email?"

Danni's shoulders hitched upward, trying for nonchalance. "Because I wasn't sure I'd be around." The words were pretty hard to say. It wasn't often she faced her own mortality. And, honestly, she wasn't a fan. "I don't think she'll open it, though. Charlie and his friend were the masterminds behind the whole thing. We just need to find her and get the file back."

"Umm." Maggie clicked on her phone, frowning as she poked and swiped. "Is this the email?"

Dammit. *Please don't have opened it. Please don't have opened it.* Danni took the phone from Maggie's outstretched hand. The email was open, and the return email address was from one of Cherise's accounts.

Maggie, this is the location of Obrona's stolen data. Tell Chase. Danni. Map coordinates followed.

"Those would have been your final words to me?" Maggie's voice tilted up at the end. She was hurt.

Danni almost wished she'd put more. An *I'll miss you* or *Thank you.* Something other than the basics. "I had a bad guy behind me who'd just hit me in the head." Literally. Right as she was finishing the email to Maggie. She ran her fingers along the bump at her temple. She'd written what she could. Not that any of that mattered right now.

Since the email was there, that meant Cherise opened the file. Why? "She opened it a few minutes ago."

"Where is she?" Maggie looked over Danni's shoulder as Danni typed in the coordinates.

"Over on North Dearborn. A few blocks down."

"Two ten?" Marek didn't look all that good to begin with. Pallor didn't work for him. But somehow, saying those numbers, the poor guy's skin went ashen.

Danni nodded. "Yeah."

"Jalen's condo."

Ashen probably didn't even begin to describe her at this point. Jalen was in on it? How could he? Why?

"Guys, we really need to go before she's on the move." Maggie took back the phone and walked to the door of Marek's office. "Hey, Chase."

"Don't." Danni grabbed her arm.

"Why?"

Danni wasn't sure what was going on with Jalen or Cherise. But she knew they weren't dangerous. And she also knew her friend wouldn't steal information from Marek. There had to be another explanation. And she'd never get it with the cops tagging along. "I need to talk to her, without the tail."

Chase appeared in the doorway. His face was hard. The perfect cop-face. "What do you need?"

Maggie looked over at Danni, who tried to tell her to trust her with that one look. She widened her eyes, begging.

"I need to run out, get some fresh air. Danni and Marek too." Maggie leaned into Chase. "This is hard on them."

"Oh. Yeah." His face softened. The smile he threw at Danni was so kind. She almost felt bad keeping him out of the loop on this. Almost. He curled an arm around Maggie.

Danni could see they were about to suck face and get all sappy. She headed over to Marek. "I'm sorry. I didn't mean for any of this to happen. I just answered an ad for some code. I would never do anything like this to anyone, especially to you." The irony that she wouldn't yet she had was not lost on her. "Not knowingly. Anyway."

"I know." He shook his head. "I'm sorry I put you in the middle of all this."

A laugh bubbled in her chest. "You didn't put me in the middle. I did. I should never have answered that ad."

"Why did you?" Marek smiled. It wasn't a bright, sexy smile, but it was something. So what if he was smiling at her expense?

"I don't know. Sometimes I get tired of rummaging through philandering husbands' computers. I get tired of seeing the porn and the money laundering. I just want to write code. No people."

Marek's eyes held sadness and pity, just not forgiveness. He was right. Danni should have known better. She should have researched the client first. She shouldn't have used the code that she and Marek wrote as the foundation.

But Cherise had known that Danni could make that code work. She'd known she was going to use it to get to Marek.

Her heart ached in her chest. Had their friendship ever been real?

TWENTY-THREE

MAREK WALKED in the front door of the building behind Danni and Maggie. This wasn't some three-floor walkup on the outskirts of the city. This was a high-rise in the Loop. There were doormen and cameras.

"How are we getting past the doorman again?" Marek's gym shoes scuffled along the gray granite floor. Lots of dark wood surrounded the doors and windows. A high-top front desk made of more dark wood sat in front of silver elevator doors, guarded by a single doorman.

"Stay back here." Danni smiled. "And watch her. She's amazing."

"Hi, sir." Maggie tilted her head and wrapped a piece of hair around her finger. "I think I'm lost." She leaned across the front desk, chest heaving; like she'd run all the way here.

The desk rent-a-cop didn't stand a chance. His eyes were the size of the O's in Hooters. And stuck on her. He said something back, too low for Marek to hear.

Maggie giggled. "Oh my god, I so wouldn't do that."

"Let's go." Danni pulled Marek toward the elevators. She hit the up button and waited as Maggie flipped her hair and pouted.

Marek was impressed. "She has that guy completely under her control."

Danni slipped into the elevator, and Marek followed. "That's nothing. You should see when she's wearing a short skirt. Holy crap, guys just fall at her feet."

Marek could see that. The woman was hot. "I could see that." The punch to his chest took a puff of wind from his lungs. "Ouch. I meant that some guys might find her good-looking, so I get it."

Danni smiled, and it almost seemed genuine. "I'm kidding. She is totally hot."

"I agree, but I think her friend is hotter." Where the hell did that come from? They weren't exactly at a point where speculating on the hotness factor was acceptable.

The door closed and Danni hovered over the floor buttons. "Which floor is he on?"

Marek had been to Jalen's to watch football and play video games. He'd helped him move in. "Twenty-third."

She hit the button, and the car flew up to the floor. When the doors opened, they walked down the hall. Danni grabbed his hand. "Thank you."

He didn't let go. Honestly, he didn't want to. He was so mad, but deep down, he still wanted her. He also knew it would never work. Trust was so easy to break and so hard to fix. "Thank you for what?"

"Coming with me. Doing this."

"It's nothing." And it was nothing. He needed to see if Jalen was part of this. It didn't make any sense. Jalen and Marek had been close, but if Jalen wanted to sell the company out, he had enough access on his own, without Danni or her code.

"It's not nothing. I don't think I could do this alone."

"You're not alone."

Danni released Marek's hand and knocked on the door. A second later it swung open, and Jalen stood just inside. "Marek? Danni?"

"Where is she?" Danni pushed past him.

"Who?"

"Don't bother, man, we know." Marek followed Danni.

"Know what?" Jalen shut the door and trailed behind Marek. "Would someone tell me what the fuck is going on?"

"How long have you and Cherise been dating?" Marek asked him.

"Why does that matter?"

"How long?"

Jalen sighed. "We dated for a few years on and off. A few weeks ago, we broke up."

"You broke up?" Danni didn't sound like she believed him. At this point, Marek didn't know what to believe.

Cherise walked out of the bedroom. "We did not break up. We're taking a break." Cherise took one look at Danni and ran to her. "Oh, thank God you're all right. I thought he was going to kill you."

"Which was why you ran off." Danni's narrowed eyes were a new level of pissed.

"There were guns, and they scared me," Cherise said.

"Guns?" If Jalen knew what was going on, he was one hell of an actor.

Cherise leaned against the wall, crocodile tears in her eyes. "My brother is a bad guy."

"I thought you weren't talking to your brother anymore." Jalen still looked confused, but there was a hint of anger. Join the club.

"He threatened me." A lone tear slid down her cheek as she twisted her hands.

Danni stepped toward her. "Cut the crap, Cherise."

"What crap? You saw him waving that gun. He's insane."

"So, this was all him?" Danni asked.

"Of course, it was him. Who else would it be?"

"You." Danni winced. It was subtle, but Marek caught it. Almost like she didn't want to believe it.

"Me? You saw how much they scared me. You know I'd never hurt you or Marek."

"Then why did you open the file?"

"I didn't." Cherise fidgeted even more erratically than when she'd first walked in the room. She was lying.

"Then who did?" Marek asked.

"I tossed my laptop in a garbage pail outside the building and ran here. I didn't want anything to do with him and his projects anymore." She rested a hand on Jalen's arm. "I'm so sorry he tried to hurt you. I won't have contact anymore. I promise. I just hate us being apart. We can go away. Just you and me."

"I told you before, I'm not leaving." Jalen ripped his arm away from her. He was a smart guy; he was probably starting to piece together the crazy going on around him. "I like it here. Why would I leave Chicago?"

"Is this about your job?" Cherise said *job* with such venom. "After everything that happened, do you think Dave and Marek will keep you? Even if he does, it won't be the same. We can go away." She moved closer, reaching for him, but he stepped back. "We can go live in

Berlin or Los Angeles. Anywhere but here. It will be like it was before. Remember? We can start somewhere else and just be us again. Somewhere away from my family."

"Then go. I told you to go if you need to leave. But I'm staying. My family is here. My friends. It's not just the job, it's everything."

"That's it, isn't it." Cherise curled her lip. Maybe Jalen wasn't as brilliant as he seemed. It was never smart to piss off the crazy in the room. "You have everything, and I have nothing. You never did love me the way I loved you. If you asked me to leave, I would."

"Cherise." Sadness and pity washed away the anger on his face. His voice was low. "See. That proves you're wrong. I would never ask you to leave what mattered to you."

Marek turned his attention to Danni. She'd said something similar. *I'd never ask you to turn your back on your company.* With bullets flying and all the drama, she hadn't turned away.

And maybe in the beginning it had been some weird guilt making sure she fixed her mistake, but it wasn't anymore. He could tell. Somewhere along the way, they'd found what they had way back then. Right here. Right now.

Hell, she was still here, and she didn't have to be. His chest swelled. If she could stand by him through all of this and forgive him for pulling her in, he could forgive anything she might have done. Who hadn't taken a freelance gig that went awry?

He just needed to get that damn laptop, and they could do their own version of starting over.

SOBS RACKED CHERISE'S BODY. There was a time Danni would have comforted her. Done anything to help her. Now all Danni did was stand back and wait.

Cherise wiped her eyes and faced Danni. "Why are you still here?"

"Cherise, where's the laptop?"

"The garbage. My brother—"

"He never left the building." Danni left out the part where he was covered in a white sheet. It wasn't her place to tell her. Not anymore. "So, where is the laptop?"

Cherise sighed, then bent down and drew the silver notebook out of her bag. "I didn't mean for any of this."

Danni was out of pity. "What did you mean, then?"

"I thought if I had the money, Jalen would come with me. He wouldn't have to work. We could be together. My brother and Jason made it into this crazy thing. I just wanted to go away." She sagged against the wall and slid down.

Irony was, she was going to go away. For a long time.

Danni pulled out her phone and texted Maggie. *Call Chase. We have the computer. Apt 2302.*

A few seconds later, her phone chimed. *They'll be there in five.*

Jalen's dark skin was about as pale as it could get. He looked confused. Sad. "You did all of this?" His eyes were on Cherise. Maybe he wasn't as confused as he looked. "You stole my data? To what? Get back at me?"

"It wasn't my idea. My brother made me do it, and then he promised money. I wanted us to go away, but you wouldn't go. Then I thought, since I had to do it anyway, maybe you'd come with me if you didn't have to work."

The longest five minutes ever later, the door to Jalen's

condo flew open and cops rushed in. Danni threw her arms in the air. Everyone did. Except Cherise. She was still balled up against the wall.

Marek nodded at the ball. "She stole the data. We have the laptop."

The cops pulled Jalen and Cherise aside, and Danni watched as they disappeared out the door. Maggie came in for a hug. "Oh my god, we heard your call come through on the police radio and hurried over." Two females bounced around Maggie and enveloped Danni in a mass of arms and hair.

"Oh my goodness, I thought we lost you." Jessi's face was covered in tears.

"Are you okay?" Leti pulled back and looked at Danni. Who knew what she was looking for. But with Jessi and Maggie pulling her close and Leti holding her at arm's length, Danni was practically nailed to the ground.

Was she okay? Danni didn't feel any different, but after the past week, she supposed she was different. She lost her friend, her potential boyfriend, and the ability to make extra money doing freelance work. But still. She was here with her girls' arms around her. And somehow, she felt it would all be okay.

"I'll get there." And she would. She had the best friends and coworkers a woman could ever want.

"Maggie." That was Chase's voice, but the tone wasn't something Danni was used to hearing when he talked to Maggie. It was the tone he saved for perps.

"Chase." Maggie could do cop voice too. Danni had heard that one aimed at her one too many times.

"I thought you went to get air." There might have been steam coming from his ears. If not, there should've been.

Maggie raised her eyebrows. "We went for a walk. There was air."

Danni didn't want to come between them. "Don't be mad at her. This is my fault." She was a horrible friend. "I told her not to tell you."

"I have words for you too." Chase pointed at Danni and used that cop voice. Then he turned his cop wrath on Maggie. "Why wouldn't you tell me what you were doing? You could've been hurt, and I wouldn't know where you were."

"You're right. But I was downstairs. I assessed the situation, and I made a judgment call."

"Well, your judgment—"

"If you want to keep your balls intact, do not finish that sentence." Maggie moved closer to him, and he might have flinched. "You need to trust me."

Chase sighed and moved closer, taking his balls into his own hands, figuratively speaking. "Look, I trust you. It's others I don't trust. If something had happened to you, no one would have known where you were. You need to trust me too. If this was something you all needed to do on your own. I would have given you space and backup."

"You're right." Maggie wrapped her arms around him as he nuzzled her neck. It started with a kiss and then the hands...

"Get a room." Leti finally voiced what they were all thinking.

Maggie smiled and pulled her mouth away. "You should get back to work," she told Chase.

"I should." He backed away and pointed at Danni. "And you. You need to trust me too. If we're going to work together, you need to realize I'm not the bad guy."

It was Danni's turn to sigh because he was right. He'd

proven over and over again that she could count on him. And Maggie loved him. "You're right. I'm sorry."

"Wow. Two women telling me I'm right and not fighting me. I should play the lottery."

"Don't get used to it." Leti tilted her head and smiled a sweet smile, although it had an evil glint to it. They thought Danni was scary. Hell no. Leti had her beat.

Chase left, and Maggie followed him to the door. "Ready?" she asked Danni.

"For?"

Maggie's face scrunched in sympathy. "We have to go to the precinct."

"Again?"

"Yeah, there are dead bodies and shit." Maggie came over and put an arm around her shoulders.

And it felt good. Something inside of Danni unfurled. The stress just seeped out with every squeeze.

"I talked them into letting me drive you," Maggie said.

"Thanks."

"Of course, I'm not going to let them drive you in the back of a squad car. You're not a criminal."

"I mean thanks for everything. The car. The ride. Believing in me."

"I always believe you." Maggie laughed. "I just have a bad way of showing it."

"Look at you two, working it out." Jessi opened her arms and enveloped them. Then Leti joined in. "Everything is okay."

Okay? Maybe not today.

But in a friend cocoon, soaking up her stress and pain, Danni could almost feel herself getting back to okay. They'd figure it out. They'd drink to her heartbreak.

They'd work jobs. And someday she'd would truly be okay.

TWENTY-FOUR

MAREK SAT at the desk in a spare office because his office was still off limits. Not that he was in a big hurry to get in there. The cleaning crew they'd hired would arrive later today, but then what? He'd sit there working while trying not to relive what happened? No thanks.

This temporary office might turn into the permanent office. So what if the view was of a back alley. At least it didn't remind him of dead bodies.

A knock on the door, and Dave walked in. He looked like nothing happened. If it weren't for the grimace when he sat down, Marek would think the man hadn't been shot—what?—three days ago. The days were still a blur.

"Shouldn't you be resting?"

Dave rolled his eyes. "Resting is for the weak."

"Or for the recently shot."

"Yeah. Yeah. I'm going to work whether I'm here or home, so might as well be here."

"There's logic there somewhere. I don't see it."

"You usually don't." Dave held up his phone. "I'm

scheduling a meeting with MetalWolke next week. I want you to meet with them."

"Okay."

"I'm not arguing with you on this..." Dave stopped and looked at Marek.

Marek smiled. "I'm not arguing with you, either. You were right. They stopped the breach. If they hadn't set up the encryption, we would have been unable to continue. As it is now, we're saying a few mea culpas to the government and presenting our plan to ensure it doesn't happen again. We'd be in a hell of a lot more trouble if that data had been compromised."

"Yeah, well, you did figure out who stole the data."

"Danni did." Marek almost felt pain in his chest saying her name. They hadn't talked since that night at Jalen's condo. By the time the cops let him go, she'd been long gone. And he wasn't sure if she'd want to see him.

He glanced down at his phone to see if maybe she'd called. Of course not.

Dave shifted in the chair. "We owe Danni. She's not so bad."

"Not so bad?" That was high praise coming from Dave. "Does that mean you approve of her now?"

"Don't go overboard. She just hasn't annoyed me in a few days. Next time you bring her here, I'm sure she will." Dave grinned at his phone. Something had changed in him. It could be the result of the shooting or almost losing the company. Something was different.

"I don't think I'll be bringing her here. I don't think she wants to be anywhere near me."

"I don't believe that, and neither do you." Dave looked up when Marek said nothing. "That woman loves you."

"Then why hasn't she called?"

"Why haven't you?" Dave huffed.

"Who said I didn't?"

"Did you?"

Dammit, he hated when Dave was right. "No."

Another knock. This time Jalen stood in the doorway. The man had seen better days. He'd also left the police station way before Marek. They'd kept Marek extra-long, probably because they were afraid he'd somehow disappear again.

Although they did apologize for his abduction. Off the record, of course. Not that Marek had any plans on suing them. They'd been doing their job. And just knowing that because of what happened to him they were changing their policies on relinquishing inmates in custody made him smile. The next person might not be as lucky as he was.

"Here's my letter of resignation." Jalen placed an envelope on the desk. "I'm really sorry."

Marek fingered the envelope and pushed it back. "You're leaving?"

"I figured it's the least I can do. That way you don't have to fire me."

Dave picked up the envelope and opened it. "Why are we firing you?"

"My ex did all of this. She stole company data, and you were shot."

"You spelled psychotic ex-girlfriend wrong," Dave said.

Marek grabbed the letter and read through. There was nothing misspelled and nothing about psychosis or girlfriends. "Dave, was that joke?" He probably didn't hide the pure shock in his voice. But really. How couldn't he be shocked? Dave never joked.

Dave huffed. "Screw you. I joke all the time."

Marek sighed as he put the letter back in the envelope. "Jalen, I can't stop you from leaving if you want to. We can buy out your shares, and you don't ever have to come back. But that's not what we want. Right, Dave?"

"No. You think we can run this place without you?"

Truth was, they might be able to if Danni came on the payroll. But she liked her job with Maggie. She wouldn't want to work here. Problem was, he didn't want someone else. He wanted Jalen. His friend.

"It's up to you, Jalen," Marek said. "This company is just as much you as it is us. We all failed. I should have gone outside to help secure our servers. You should have noticed your ex was slightly off balance." That was a nice way to say it, right? "And Dave—"

"Dave nothing. I did nothing wrong."

"Dave shouldn't have been so easy to shoot."

"Is that a boring joke, or are we starting to add fat jokes to the repertoire?" Dave rubbed his side. The gunshot wound obviously still hurt.

"Neither. I needed to come up with *something*." Marek leaned back and faced Jalen. "So, what will it be? You with us?"

"Always." Jalen attempted to smile, but it was forced. "I will make this up to you both."

"No need," Marek said at the same time Dave said, "Pick better women."

Dave pulled out his phone and flinched as he stood up. "I think we all have work to do."

"Maybe you should take the day off," Marek suggested. "You were shot."

"Well aware, but we need to rebuild." Dave smirked. "And I can't trust you two fuckups to do it on your own."

Marek scowled at him. "I liked it better when you didn't joke."

Dave laughed. It didn't happen often, but when it did, it was a sight. He grabbed his side. "Maybe I will leave at lunch. I'm still sore."

"We'll hold down the fort, and we won't fuck up."

"Go, man. We got this," Jalen added.

Dave looked up from his phone and smiled. "I know." And with that, he was gone.

"Thanks, Marek."

"You too, Jalen."

Jalen walked out the door and quiet descended on the room. Obrona might be limping, but they'd built it from scratch before and they'd do it again. It was what they did. And as long as they did it together.

He just needed to figure out how to get Danni into the equation. Maybe Dave was right. Again. He needed to call her. Or maybe Dave was wrong. He needed to do more. He needed to see her.

DANNI SAT on Maggie's desk and stared at the shot glass in her hand.

"Just drink it." Maggie tossed back her shot of honey bourbon. "It's the pre-party."

"I don't want to party." Danni was pouting. She didn't care. Her friends were dicks. They wouldn't let her enjoy her pity-party. Yes. It was a party, but when pity was involved, it was way less fun and way less annoying.

Leti tossed back the glass and coughed. "Tell me again how this isn't battery acid."

"This is smooth." Jessi turned over her now-empty glass and smiled.

"How are we friends with you? You don't drink. You don't swear," Maggie pointed out.

"I class up the joint." Leti downed a bottle of Yoo-hoo.

"With Yoo-hoo." Maggie poured shots of honey bourbon for herself, Jessi and Danni.

Jessi held up her shot glass. "I hear your yoo-hoo is very classy. Bedazzled and everything."

"My none-of-your-business-hoo is not bedazzled, bejeweled, or besparkled." Leti shook her head. "And I know you didn't hear that from anyone. Because no one has seen my hoo in a long time."

"How long?" Danni was curious. No one was going to see her hoo for a while. Since Marek hadn't called or texted, she knew it was over. He'd never forgive her. It sucked. But that was why the girls were here. To help her get over him by getting under copious amounts of alcohol.

"Finish your drink." Maggie held the bottle over Danni's still-full shot glass.

Did Danni mention she just wanted to wallow in her pity pool? She downed the shot. The sweet of the honey offset the burnt-caramel bite. The burn slid down her throat and warmed her chest.

Maggie raised her shot glass. "Let's get back to Leti's yoo-hoo."

Leti shook her head. "Let's not."

"Let's talk about the shooting lesson next week. Do we need to bring anything?" Jessi was practically bouncing at the idea of learning how to shoot.

"Just the guns you all bought."

"What if I don't have mine within the waiting period?" Leti tipped her empty glass side to side. Something seemed up with her. Whether it had to do with her yoo-hoo or the gun thing, Danni wasn't sure.

Maggie narrowed her eyes. "You better have your guns. That's why we're waiting till next week—for the waiting period. Which means do it now. But if you don't have your own or don't want your own, you still are coming, and you can borrow one of mine. It's important to know how to handle one, whether you plan on owning one or not."

The front door smacked against the frame.

"I got it." Maggie jumped up and walked around to the front of the office.

"You okay, Leti? If you don't want to learn how to shoot, you don't have to." Danni had been putting this off for over a year, so she understood how Leti felt. If it weren't for last week, she wouldn't be considering it either.

"Danni. You have company." Maggie came through the door with Marek at her back. "We'll head over to Sonny's. Meet us there."

The three women walked out the front door, and a key jingled in the lock as Marek just stared. Danni had barely registered him when her friends hightailed out of the building. She wasn't ready for this. She wasn't ready to talk to him. She needed at least two more shots of bourbon.

Danni couldn't take the silence. "Hi."

"Hi." Marek slid his hands in the front pocket of his jeans. They looked good. He looked good.

She wanted to jump him and beg for forgiveness. Kiss

every piece of his body and talk about the first thing that came up. She was pervy.

But really, she just wanted him to forgive her. She missed her friend. "I'm so sorry. I never—"

"I'm sorry I got you involved—" He laughed, an uncomfortable humorless laugh as they both talked over each other. "Look. There's nothing for you to be sorry about. I get with consultant work you don't always know the full project. That wasn't your fault."

Danni gripped the edge of the desk. "But I should have told you when I figured it out."

"You should have. I would have understood. But I get why you were afraid. I wouldn't want to lose you."

"You could never lose me." No amount of girl time or alcohol was going to make her forget him. Maybe dull the ache, but it would always be there. It had always been there.

"Haven't I lost you?"

She was so afraid to admit it, but at this point who cared. She had nothing to lose. "No. I'm yours. I've always been yours." Marek didn't respond. Her heart laid bare, and he just stared.

"That's funny." Nothing about this was funny. Or maybe it was funny to him.

The hope in her body burst. Her heart ground to a halt, like pepper in a mill. Shards broke off and bent. Each piece a new ache in her chest. The new pain was terribly familiar. She'd been close to having him. She'd been so close to having that happiness.

"Because I've always been yours."

And now to find her way back to him, get her hopes up and lose it again—it managed to hurt worse than before. Even her jaw ached as she attempted to smile without tears. He'd made his choice. She wasn't going to beg. No matter how much she wanted to. Wait.

He'd said something.

"What?"

He stepped closer, his finger sliding along the side of her cheek. "I've always been yours. I always will be. If you want me."

If? Why was that even a question? Of course, that didn't stop her from asking, "What if I don't?"

"Then I'll be yours, but alone. Miserably pining for you. Maybe I'll get a cat or seven."

"Wow, seven cats. I'm surprised my love isn't worthy of at least ten cats." She couldn't help the smile that spread across her face. He was hers.

The pain in her chest lifted, and even her insides smiled. It was like happiness wrapped in a rainbow wrapped in an Ewok. She was so sappy when she was happy. Oy.

He lifted an eyebrow. "Ten cats? That's crazy."

"But seven is normal."

"No one ever accused me of being normal." Marek's hand found its way back to her cheek. "But I have been accused of being in love."

Love. He was in love. She couldn't help but lean into the touch. She'd missed it so much. "Hopefully it's with me. Because I love you too."

"Of course, it's you. It's always been you. I love you, Danielle Stein."

Her grinchy heart grew two sizes that day, and her chest all but cracked from the pressure. He loved her. His hands were on her. She sighed. It was all perfect.

She lifted her chin and saw everything he'd just said written in his eyes. They sparkled with love or lust or happiness. Who cared which. He loved her. "So. What do we do about it?"

"We go to my place, and we make this happen. You and me."

She smiled but then grimaced. "Do we have to get cats?"

And there it was. That laugh. A deep rumble low in his chest. So deep and sexy, she wanted to bottle that laugh and rub it all over her body. "We can get whatever you want."

"You." She pulled his lips to hers. Soft, pliant lips. Gentle. "I want you."

EPILOGUE

LETI

"ARE YOU OKAY?" Leti patted Danni's shoulder. It was three weeks after the shootout with the bad guys, and Danni's friend Cherise had seen the judge today. She watched as Danni took off her slippers and sat next to Leti's desk to put on gym shoes.

"I'm fine. She did this to herself. She should have turned Charlie in." Danni shook her head. "And Marek is officially off their bad list. The Chicago PD sent a letter apologizing and thanking him for his help."

"Wow." Leti sat down behind her desk and opened up a new document. The whole Obrona/Marek thing might have started as a Danni helping a friend, but Marek still insisted on paying for the agency's services.

"Yeah, wow." Danni stood up and slid her cell phone into her jeans back pocket. "We're going to Sonny's to celebrate."

"It's going to be fun." Jessi came from the front, her fingers flying over the face of her phone.

"Is your mom watching Matty tonight?" Leti loved Jessi's little kid. He was adorable. Almost as cute as her niece and nephew—maybe even cuter—but she'd never tell her sister that.

"Yep." Jessi smiled and put her phone away. "He just had his bath, and she's about to put him down for the night."

"That's good." Danni smirked. "I hear our favorite lawyer, Enzo, might be making an appearance. So you'll want to be there."

The color drained from Jessi's face. She hadn't been a fan of Enzo's since they were held at gunpoint over a year ago. Apparently she must still blame him for that. Which was a shame, because he seemed to have a thing for Jessi.

Danni waved a hand. "I'm kidding. I don't think Enzo even knows we're going out."

Jessi exhaled, like she was relieved. Interesting. "I'm leaving," Jessi said, and glared at Danni.

A bit of an overreaction to Enzo's appearance. Leti would have to think about what that might mean later.

"Don't walk alone. I'll go with you." Danni didn't seem to notice—or care about the icicles being shot her way. "You coming, Leti?"

"I have a few things to do here, then I'll meet up with you all."

"Don't take too long or we'll come back and drag you." Danni tapped her fingers together, evil supervillain fashion. "If I have to socialize, so do you."

"Make good choices." Leti shook her head as Danni laughed.

Leti did not. She got the report Danni had filed, opened a blank invoice, and started filling in the blanks.

The back door shut, and then there was silence. Glorious silence.

She loved her coworkers, but sometimes they were a

bit much. Especially after a successful case wrapped up and no one was shot. That last part was the highlight. Not all of their cases ended without personal bloodshed.

Although, technically, Danni had been shot, it was barely a flesh wound. It didn't really count. If you asked Danni, though, she was a gangster now.

Leti finished and printed the invoice and sent it a copy to the email Marek provided. She took her time finishing her section of the report and filed the paperwork. She managed to milk this whole work thing for forty-five minutes.

She sat in her chair and stared at the screen saver. She had nothing else to do. She didn't need to be here anymore. But the alternative was a loud bar with her partners and their men raising the roof. Not exactly a draw.

Of course, there was always home. A hot bath and lavender soap, the latest Kristan Higgins book and... bubbles. Yay, bubbles. A glass of wine. It sounded like heaven. She could practically feel her muscles melt just thinking about it.

She was so relaxed, she must have missed the front door opening. But she couldn't miss the deep baritone voice. "Hello?"

"We're closed." Leti's voice froze as her eyes lapped up the man standing in the doorway. Good granola, he was hot.

"Do you work here?" The voice matched the body. Even in the relaxed jeans and T-shirt that hugged his chest, she could tell he had a nice body. And he had short-cropped dark blond hair. The kind that begged to be touched.

She gulped down a ball of air before managing to

make a sound that almost seemed human. "Yes, but we're closed." Not one squeak. She hoped.

"Then why is your front door open? Should you be alone like this?"

What, was she a child? "Trust me, I'm not likely to start eating the laundry detergent pods. I can be here alone." Who was he to question why she was here alone?

"It's dangerous. You lack all situational awareness."

Insulting too. Anger pulsed, heating her skin. "Are you here for a reason?" That might have come out harsher than she wanted. But he wasn't exactly friendly.

"I'm looking for Maggie."

"Why?"

"Are you one of her partners?" Was he incapable of answering a question? His tone. His attitude. His body. Well, his body was the one thing that wasn't annoying her at this point. But he went down in hotness factor just by being a jerk.

"How do you know Maggie?" It was like *Jeopardy*— answer a question with a question. She refused to back down. She'd worked in corporate America with entitled men her whole life. She'd even married one for a hot second.

"How do *you* know Maggie?" He crossed his arms against his chest and holy *caliente*. The arms were beautiful and thick. She loved arms.

Too bad they were attached to the body with that mouth and all the questions. She was done with questions. If he couldn't answer one, then he could leave.

Leti stood up. There was no way she was playing this game anymore. "You're trespassing."

The jerk's eyes went wide as Leti came around in front of her desk and crossed her arms over her chest. He stared at her legs and visibly gulped as his eyes slid up her body.

She wanted to ask if he liked what he saw, but he obviously did. It made her almost like the guy for his good taste.

"Wait, you're a PI, right? My sister said you guys dress like prostitutes sometimes to blend in on the streets."

Leti's face burned. Her collared red silk shirt was unbuttoned at the throat and few buttons down. She wasn't showing her girls, or the bra holding her girls in place. Black pencil skirt. High heels. It was evening casual, not streetwalker. Her mouth opened to say just that, but nothing came out. Not one word, grunt, or squeak.

"Oh my god, you're here." Maggie busted through the back door and ran over to the man who'd just called Leti a hooker. She wrapped her arms around him. "I didn't think you'd be back from Afghanistan until Christmas."

Maggie hugging. Afghanistan. Son of a biscuit.

The man picked up Maggie as if she weighed as much as a kitten. "I decided not to reenlist."

"Really?" Maggie's smile was wide. And it should be. She'd mentioned her brother in the military a million times, and he'd finally come home. "I see you met my partner, Leti."

"We hadn't gotten to introductions yet." Shrek smirked.

Smirked. Leti wanted to smack the look right off his face.

"This is my brother, Kevin." Maggie all but jumped toward Leti.

Leti did what any good friend and normal human

being would do and offered her hand to shake. "Nice to meet you." Not. He was the one who'd called her a street-walker, yet she had enough respect for Maggie to follow proper protocol and shake the big uncouth giant's hand and be polite.

His large hand enveloped hers, and he grunted. Grunted.

Shrek grunted.

"I'm so glad you're here." Maggie grinned at him. "We're at Sonny's celebrating a huge case. Come with us."

Us. The rest of "us" was at Sonny's, which meant Maggie was there to collect Leti. Great. Not just a night of drinking and barroom antics, now she'd have to deal with Shrek all night.

"I should finish these reports." Leti walked back around her desk and prayed Maggie would let it go.

"The reports will be here tomorrow. Let's go." Leti should have known better. It was some sort of perpetual intervention to get Leti drunk and laid. Not high on Leti's list of things to do.

Maggie slammed the off button on Leti's computer. "See? You're done."

"Your front door is unlocked," Kevin said.

"Shit. I forgot to lock it before I left." Maggie walked away, her keys jingling in her hand.

"So, Leti." Kevin loomed over her desk with another of those smirks on his lips. If it weren't so darn annoying, she'd be thinking about how nice those lips looked. She'd be thinking about how soft and kissable they were. But this was Maggie's brother, so it was a good thing she was too annoyed to be thinking about that.

"So" —she wanted to call him Shrek so bad it nearly burned her tongue— "Kevin." See? Polite.

Before he could finish whatever ignorant comment he had in his tiny brain, Maggie ran back into the room. "You two ready?"

"All set." Kevin leaned in close, angling over Leti's desk. He smelled good—like man. "Can I carry anything for you?"

Are you sure you can lift anything with that massive ego you carry around? "I think I can handle it." She opened the bottom drawer and took out her purse and keys. "I'll meet you there."

"I look forward to it." Kevin smiled as his eyes followed her out the door.

She swore she felt the heat of his stare as she left the building. Why was she even thinking about going to the bar? She should go home where there was no rude man with pretty lips. Maggie was so enthralled with her brother showing up, she wouldn't even notice if Leti snuck off.

So why Leti found herself walking past her car and following down the block, she had no idea.

But she did know it had nothing to do with Maggie's brother. Not one thing.

EXTRAS

If you enjoyed reading this installment of the Busted series, check out the other books in this series.

Busted Series (in order)
  Busting In
  Busting Out
  Busting Through
  Busting Up (Coming Soon)

Thank you for supporting an independent author. It would be great if you could leave a review or a rating wherever you purchased this book, or on Goodreads.

  Would you like to know when my next book is available? You can sign up for my new release email list at http://www.vanessamknight.com or like my Facebook page at http://facebook.com/vanessamknightauthor.

ABOUT THE AUTHOR

Vanessa M. Knight has always enjoyed writing, and once she found romance and mystery, she was addicted. She props her laptop in the suburbs of Chicago with her husband, son and menagerie of four-pawed claw-babies (AKA cats and dogs.) That laptop has partnered-in-crime to write contemporary romances with a dash of humor and splash of snark.

When she has a few moments to spare, you can find her singing off-key (but she assures everyone it's still considered singing), reading, kickboxing or killing a few brain cells as she stares at the many sitcoms and dramas available through the Internet and TV.

For more information on Vanessa, including her Internet haunts, contest updates, and details on her upcoming novels, please visit her website at www. vanessamknight.com.

OTHER BOOKS BY VANESSA

Breaking the Fall

www.ingramcontent.com/pod-product-compliance
Lightning Source LLC
Chambersburg PA
CBHW071549110726
47908CB00007B/2045